John Stuart Blackie

The wise men of Greece, in a series of dramatic dialogues

John Stuart Blackie

The wise men of Greece, in a series of dramatic dialogues

ISBN/EAN: 9783337305451

Printed in Europe, USA, Canada, Australia, Japan

Cover: Foto ©Andreas Hilbeck / pixelio.de

More available books at **www.hansebooks.com**

THE
WISE MEN OF GREECE

IN A SERIES OF

DRAMATIC DIALOGUES

BY

JOHN STUART BLACKIE

PROFESSOR OF GREEK IN THE UNIVERSITY OF EDINBURGH

Sed docemus nullam sectam fuisse tam deviam, nec philoso-
phum tam inanem qui non aliquid viderit ex vero.

LACTANTIUS.

London

MACMILLAN AND COMPANY

1877

Printed by R. & R. CLARK, *Edinburgh.*

CONTENTS.

TO

TOM TAYLOR, Esquire.

—◆—

EPISTLE DEDICATORY.

My Dear Taylor.—I have requested the honour of dedicating this book to you, partly that I might signify, in a small way, the respect which I entertain for your character and efficiency as a literary man; partly because, if there is anything of a wise conception in the structure of these dialogues, and any degree of adequacy in their execution, I know no person in these islands at once more willing and more able than yourself to pronounce a judgment on their merits or demerits, which I shall think it my duty to respect.   The conception of the book was simply this : Take the first six names in the list, Pythagoras, Thales, Xenophanes, Heraclitus, Empedocles, Anaxagoras, and you will see in a moment that, though few persons in these times, who have received what is called a liberal education, can be ignorant of these names, as of certain sign-posts, land-marks, or mile-stones in the history of human thought, very few persons, even of the best educated, have anything but the most meagre notion of the philosophical significance, intellectual dignity, and moral power of the men whom these names represent. What I have attempted is to give the general reading public, so far as they may care for wisdom, a living concrete notion of what the thought of Thales was in his day to the society of Miletus; what Pythagoras, with his school of moral discipline, was to Crotona; Xenophanes to Colophon, and so with the rest. And, as what we know of the pre-Socratic philosophy in Greece exists only in the shape of scattered notices and a few fragments, it appeared to me that the natural way of making these imperfect remains interesting was to follow the example of the architects, who restore a ruined edifice in the original style by the clear indication of its ruins; and, in order to do this two things were necessary, an accurate study of the fragments, and a sympathetic appreciation of the soul by which the fragments were originally animated. How far I have succeeded in this delicate work, scholars and thinkers will judge. I can only tell them that they will get here no mere soap-bubbles, lightly blown for a summer's recreation, but the produce of hard work, and years of study. I had no ambition, even if I had had the ability, to make a Pythagoras or an Empedocles a mere mouth-piece to spout my sentiments. I strove everywhere to give a true picture of what was actually thought and said by those old worthies, or at least of what lay in their most distinctive maxims by plain implication; and, if the lines of the portraiture shall seem to agree in a very striking way, sometimes, with certain recent phases of modern thought, or the obvious opposite of those phases, this is not that I have interpolated anything which, to the best of my judgment, did not lie in the original, but because the fundamental principles of all wisdom have always been present in the spiritual world wherever human beings in a normal state of culture have lived and thought. Reason is the light of the soul; and, though, like the sun in the heavens, it may be largely overclouded, and shine only by glimpses for a space, yet it is always there; and the glimpse, where it appears, is a sure prophecy of the full radiance, which, under more favourable circumstances will surely be revealed.

I have mentioned the above six names because it was the fragmentary condition of the sources of our knowledge of their wisdom that naturally suggested the work of imaginative reconstruction which these pages contain. The other two names, Socrates and Plato, stand in a different position. In the case of these two, I could not possibly entertain the vanity of pretending to expound their views of the most important truths in other form than they had done themselves; at the same time, I thought that a historical gallery of the principal figures in Greek philosophy would be felt to be strangely imperfect without these two great names, which in fact are as naturally the issue of what went before as the blossom of a beautiful flower is of the bud and leafage out of which it grew. Besides, the little book of Xenophon, which is our best authority for the Socratic disputations in their original shape, just perhaps because it is so unpretending and so sensible, happens to be little read; and a free English rendering, or *rifaccimento*, as the Italians call it, of one or two of the conversations in that book, seemed to me not unlikely, if fairly managed, to introduce Socrates in a favourable way to a class of readers to whom the simple prose of Xenophon might not be sufficiently attractive. As for Plato, I should certainly have excluded him altogether from my collection, had it not been that, as the greatest poet among the philosophers, he had a peculiar right to a place in a poetical portrait-gallery of the wise men of Greece; and besides, on reviewing the nine previous dialogues, I found that the important subject of Love had been altogether omitted, and that, for a sort of completeness, I could do nothing better than give the philosophy of that noble passion in the words of its greatest expositor.

And the reader may rely upon it that in these four last dialogues I have invented only a few adjuncts; all the essential facts in the account of the death of Socrates, and the whole formal exposition of the doctrine of Socrates and his great disciple, being given almost literally from passages of the Greek texts familiar to every scholar.

There are two points on which a word or two may render the position of the old philosophers in Hellenic society more intelligible to the modern reader and more profitable. These are their relation to the popular religion and to the political government of the States to which they belonged. Now, with regard to the first of these matters, the relation of early Greek philosophy to the popular religion was in the main friendly, and naturally so, because, though Plato at a more advanced period readily found matter of offence in Homer as a theologian, there was a richness, a significance, and a flexibility in the mythology of Greece which attracted rather than repelled a philosophy more indebted to constructive imagination than to scientific analysis. If in recent times philosophy, or what, in an unphilosophising country, readily passes for such, has been associated with anything rather than with piety, we must remember that this divorce of science from religion is something altogether abnormal, and to be regarded generally as the product of a reaction from certain aspects of

anthropomorphic orthodoxy, combined with the feeble-
ness of the constructive faculty, and the starvation
of reverential emotion, which are the natural conse-
quences of the usurpation of the whole man by the
barren processes of analysis and induction. Not
that there is anything contrary to piety in a sound
induction, for Bacon was a good theist, and so was
Locke; but that induction, like everything else, is
liable to be exaggerated or misapplied; and so scientific persons, who deal only with what is tangible and
measurable in the external world, fall into an incapacity
of believing anything but what they can collect with
their hands and count with their fingers, and perversely
endeavour to explain the multiplicity of phenomena in
the reasoned universe, without reference to that formative plastic unity of an inherent λόγος, without which
neither a cogniser nor a cognised in any world is possible. The Greeks were not so. The same Thales who
taught that water was the first principle of all things,
taught likewise that "all things are full of gods;" and
the fire of Heraclitus was instinct with λόγος or reason,
as certainly as the ἀριθμός of the pious Pythagoras.
And, if any person thinks that the theology of these old
Hellenic speculators was more akin to the Pantheism
of the Brahmins and Buddhists than to the theistic
dualism of the Christian churches, I believe we may
pretty safely say he is right; even Plato, whose
language in the main certainly is not Pantheistic, talks

of the world in the *Timaeus* as a θεῖον ζῶον, or a divine animal; but Pantheism has nothing necessarily to do either with atheism or materialism; it only asserts a necessary bond between the outward and the inward of the universe; and this is quite consistent with a pious faith in the essential unity of the τὸ πᾶν and the necessary postulate of an indwelling reason or λόγος, to render that unity possible; and it will be readily seen how much more easy it was to reconcile any sort of Pantheistic or semi-Pantheistic philosophy with an imaginative polytheism, like the Hellenic, than for a purely analytic physical science, such as that which now makes broad its phylacteries, to keep on amicable relations with a religion which glows furnace-hot with moral emotion, and a theology bristling all round with stereotyped dogma and scholastic formulas. So much for the general relation of philosophy in ancient Greece to what, by a somewhat free transference of modern phraseology, we may call the Church. Perfect orthodoxy, of course, or conformity in all points to the popular conception of the gods, was not to be looked for in a class of men inspired by a dominant passion for truth; but the orthodoxy of the Greeks was not a stiff, rigid affair, defiant of all change, and challenging all reason, like the Athanasian creed or the Calvinistic Confessions, but a very rich garden of beautiful flowers, which a thoughtful man might glean according to his own taste and interpret according to his own fancy. I have accordingly represented only one of my philosophers in an attitude of positive polemical attack towards the popular creed; and Xenophanes, in fact, is the only one who at an early period came forward as a public impugner of the polytheistic theology. Latterly, no doubt, as culture advanced, scepticism became more common; and the vulgar irreverence with which some leaders of the sceptical school attacked not only the popular faith, but the principles of all social ethics, gave some colour of justice to the intolerant spirit which, in the name of religion, vented itself on the head of a philosopher so characteristically devout as Socrates. But even in the latest times the great teachers of the Greeks were neither atheists nor agnostics: Aristotle and Zeno were as good theists as Socrates and Plato, though, of course, somewhat less fervid in their temperament and more analytic in their habit. The real atheists or agnostics among the Greeks in the days before Epicurus, were the sophists, against whose slippery doctrine of fingering externalism in all departments, Socrates, Plato, and Aristotle, asserted triumphantly for all times the doctrine of a divine dominant λόγος as the cause of unity and the bond of intelligibility in the universe. Our modern sophists, Hume, Bentham, the Mills, Bain, Grote, and others, have declared their natural kinship to their Hellenic pre-figurements significantly enough, by pretentiously setting Epicurus on the throne of Plato, industriously confounding Socrates with the sophists (with whom he had only the logical method and the reasoned discourse in common), and in every form of scholastic exposition preaching a morality not rooted in reason, and a philosophy not centred in God.

The relation of the wise men of Greece to Greek political life took shape pretty much as the same relation between similar parties in modern times. As a rule, the search after ultimate causes and the most catholic truths tends to draw a man away from that adjustment of opposing forces and balance of contending interests, in which the government of human beings in a free society mainly consists; and therefore we find for the most part that the Greek philosopher took no prominent part in public affairs. The θεωρητικός βίος, or contemplative life, and the πράγματα, or public affairs, were marked in their habit of thinking and acting by a very distinct line of separation. Even when a philosopher, like Socrates, was of a predominantly practical turn of mind, there were weighty reasons in the democratic constitution of Athens which forced him, however unwillingly, to retire from a scene, where his noblest teaching could find no audience, and his best actions were sure to be misunderstood. In a society where power was legitimately exercised by a mere majority, a wise man, who measured polls by quality rather than by quantity, would naturally not feel in his element; and so the philosopher in a land of unreined liberty, from the retreat of his Academic bowers, contented himself with preaching the philosophy of order, as a divinely ordained counteracting power, which might indirectly infuse some sobering virtue into the wild fire of democratic individualism. Thus Plato. His great predecessor and prototype, Pythagoras, had ventured a step further, and took up an educational position in the old Greek aristocracies, meant to mould society directly, somewhat in the fashion that St. Columba, and his school of missionaries in Iona, acted upon the moral character of the age to which they belonged. On the other hand, though philosophers do not naturally assume the character of revolutionists, as the hatred of tyranny, or usurped authority, was one of the strongest feelings in every Greek breast, it could not be but that, as occasion offered, a wise man might now and then appear as an apostle of freedom, or what we call a liberal politician. This attitude of the Greek philosopher I have endeavoured to portray in the case of Empedocles.

So much for the point of view from which this book was conceived, and from which it may be most profitably read. In so far as I may either have misconceived any important doctrine, or misstated any significant fact, I shall be happy to receive correction from you, or any person who shares your good qualities ; and am,

My dear Taylor,

Ever yours,

With sincere esteem,

JOHN S. BLACKIE.

ALTNACRAIG, OBAN,
October 1877.

PYTHAGORAS

ὁ βίος ἀνθρώποις λογισμοῦ κἀριθμοῦ δεῖται πάνυ·
Ζῶμεν ἀριθμῷ καὶ λογισμῷ· ταῦτα γὰρ σῴζει βροτούς.

EPICHARMUS.

B

PYTHAGORAS.

PERSONS.

1. PYTHAGORAS.
2. DIAGORAS, High Priest of Jove in Metapontum.
3. MILO, an Athlete of Crotona, disciple of Pythagoras.
4. Chorus of Maidens.
5. Chorus of Young Men.

SCENE.—*Before the Temple of the Lacinian Hera, on the coast of the Hadriatic, a few miles north of Crotona. The body of the stage is occupied by groups of priests and their attendants, with sacrificial implements; and a band of matrons. In the foreground a chorus of maidens; behind, a chorus of young men.*

CHORUS OF MAIDENS.

[Advancing, and forming themselves into a square, rank and file, in the front of the stage.]

STROPHE.

Fell was the force of Titan times,
When Kronos swayed the world with awe;
Ere Jove lent to the spheral chimes
The sweet accords of ordered law.

Red Heaven on reeking Earth made war,
And hot fire strove with hissing water;
And life was discord, din, and jar,
Of monstrous births that throve on slaughter.

But when the lawless troop was bound
'Neath sulphurous Ætna's throne sublime,
A kindlier dam the Father found
To nurse the hopeful birth of Time.

The ancient rule of Force and Fraud
He scorned, and choosing for his mate
Wise-counselling Metis, overawed
The strife that rent Earth's crude estate.

ANTISTROPHE.

Then to make fair reform more fair,
A babe, with glory on its face,
The mighty mother Rhea bare,
Stamped by the Fates for queenly place.

And gave it to the shining Hours,
With fostering care to tend it well,
And to the primal watery Powers
Conveyed it, safe from harm to dwell,

In ancient Ocean's sparry dome,
Laved by the stream of sleepless waters,
Where hoary Tethys keeps her home
With troops of twinkling-footed daughters.

And there to maiden grace she grew,
And there the fount beheld with awe
Whence men, and all the Olympian crew,
Their sacred generation draw.

EPODE.

A woman now she stood, a wonder
For stately tread, and blooming pride,
And the strong launcher of the Thunder
Claimed great-eyed Hera for his bride.

Where Thornax on the Argive billow
Looks down, and soft the cuckoo calls,
There the Fates spread the bridal pillow
That thrilled with hope the Olympian halls.

And every god brought gifts of beauty,
To her that slept great Jove beside,
And ancient Earth did loyal duty
With golden apples for the bride.

And the soft couch was curtained grandly
With clouds distilling nectarous dew,
And child-eyed flowers looked forth more blandly,
And the green blade more greenly grew,

When Jove knew Hera's love ; and sweetly
The Muses sound blithe Hymen's hymn ;
While round the hill of cuckoos featly
In tuneful dance the Graces swim.

And thus new seeds of strength were sown
For Him that wields the flashing levin ;
Now firmly stablished stood his throne,
And a new law from Fate was given,

PYTHAGORAS.

With bliss in store,
That freed from bonds of force and fraud,
By planful wisdom overawed,
All men should crook the loyal knee,
Thou thunder-belted king, to thee,
And great-eyed Hera, Queen of heaven
For evermore.

[*Diagoras advances.*]

DIAGORAS.

'Twas well enacted.   I have seldom seen
A seemlier pomp, and worthier of the gods ;
And for the hymn, our Metapontine bard
At the last great Diasia, for an ode
As like to this as tin to silver, reaped
A golden talent.   Our light temple bards
Will string a medley of Pelasgian myths,
That have no more coherence than a heap
Of coloured pebbles, spread out by the storm
Upon a windward shore, and with big mouth
Baptize it poetry !   Poets should be wise,
Else with long arms they perch their gods on high
For every fool to scoff at.   These loose tales
Some day will eat the heart from all respect,
And leave our holiest shrines like painted toys
For girls to play with.   But who comes ?   Ho, Milo !

[*Enter Milo.*]

Hail king of wrestlers ! on well-omened day
Well-omened meeting ! 'tis some moons since last

We met at Pisa, when the people hailed thee
Live Hercules, for that your shoulders bore
The heifer through the ring, which then for dinner
You did digest entire !

MILO.

A god-like meal !
I am right glad to see thee.   Never yet
Have I beheld Lacinian Hera's feast
So well appointed.

DIAGORAS.

'Twas a four-square work :
All parts did aptly fit, as to a ship
Well-corded tackle when it takes the breeze.

MILO.

The praise is hers, the wise Theano, our
New priestess, a disciple of Pythagoras.

DIAGORAS.

Pythagoras? surely I have known that name,
But not in western seas.

MILO.

He sojourns here
Some twelve moons only.

DIAGORAS.

Travelled whence ?

MILO.

From Samos.

DIAGORAS.

I now remember; once I heard the name
At Heliopolis from a learned priest,
Who said he was a subtle-thoughted man,
And for all sleight of mathematic lore
Named with the first on Nile.

MILO.

            I marvel not;
He says that mathematic is the porch
Through which our sense-bound groping intellect
Into the temple of pure reason passes,
Where sun-bright gods are throned.   'Tis strange
    to see
How he will sit, and look, and brood, and think
His soul out of itself into a square,
Or circle, or triangle.   In my school
A young athlete once found him with fixed gaze
Bent o'er the dust, where he had traced a web
Of inter-crossing figures; there he sat,
Motionless as a sphynx in Memphian sands,
Or Niobe on Sipylus; when, behold!
Even as a flash from thunder-pregnant cloud,
Sudden he starts, and like an uncaged bird
That flaps free wings, and shrills with ecstasy,
He cried—εὕρηκα—I have found it!

DIAGORAS.

            Well,
What did he find?

MILO.

     I know not, nor have wit
For such strange ken.   Some quaint equality
Of squares with squares, built on contrarious sides
Of a right-angled triangle ; but he said
To me one day that by this measure he
Would gauge deep hell, and take the girth of
    heaven.

DIAGORAS.

These mathematic men have thoughts that march
From sphere to sphere, and measure out the blue
Of infinite space like roods of garden ground,
And talk of suns and stars, as they were lights
From reef to reef in some well-sounded sea ;
But say, how do Crotona's sons affect
The Samian sage ?

MILO.

    As tides affect the moon,
Gay flowers the sun, or fish the wavy pool ;
They hold him of their very blood, who changed—
For that he knew our nobler nature—soft
Silk-vested Lydia—we interpret thus—
For our plain Doric use and hardiment
Of manly breeding.   There be evil women
Who kill with glances ; but this godlike man
Bears blessing in his look, and all who see
Drink gladness.   Like the strength of some blue
    mount
Swathed in the smiles of bright-eyed spring, he
    stands,

Reaping both love and worship.   Old and young
By cheerful magic of wise words he draws,
As Orpheus drew the beasts : nay, even women
He rings about him, eloquent to preach
Philosophy from spindles : everywhere
Love, awed by wonder, like a faithful page,
Follows his favoured footing where he goes.

DIAGORAS.

Who were his parents?

MILO.

　　　　　Thereby hangs a doubt.
Some say his sire was of Tyrrhenian stock,
To Lemnos first, and thence to Samos driven ;
Some vaunt him fathered by Apollo ; some
Deem him Apollo's self ; and some declare
He is nor man nor god, but god and man,
Aptly confounded for our double need ;
God for the strength that our ambition claims,
Man for the pity that our frailty craves :
Howbeit the air is rife with buzzing bruits
Of marvel since he came, so vouched that he
Must smother hearing who would bar belief.
'Tis voiced abroad that when he passed the stream
That flows by Sybaris, the floods did lift
Their crests with—*Hail, Pythagoras!*   And some
Do swear that on the selfsame day and hour
At Metapontum and Crotona, he
Was seen, two selves, as men report twin suns
Sometimes to sail the welkin.   All believe

He hath a golden thigh; and many tales
Are told of his mysterious communings
With Abaris, an Hyperborean priest,
Who from the frosted Caucasus to Greece
Posted through air upon a golden arrow.
The wild barbarian and the savage beast
His mild word tames.   An unkempt Getan youth,
Zamolxis hight, born in a bearskin coat,
He took and taught, and sent with wisdom's claim
To smooth the rude rough-mannered shaggy kerns
That roam on Ister's banks.   Nay, even they tell,
A Daunian bear, caught in a hut, he tamed,
Fed it with cakes and acorns, and adjured
To lick sweet blood no more.   But most they praise
How, when he preached in the Trincacrian land,
Of righteousness and temperance and truth,
The blood-daubed tyrant of Centauripi,
Pricked in his heart, and plucking out his lusts,
Flung down his sceptre, and his broad domain
Gave free to public use.

DIAGORAS.

                'Tis wondrous strange!
Full surely he is wise above the mark
Of wisest men, and by some mystic bond
Holds subject Nature tutored to his will.
But how stands he affected to the gods?

MILO.

As sons to sires whom sires delight to own.
There is no Greek from Padus to Pachynus

More strict in all religious exercise
That sacred right or use of country claims.

DIAGORAS.

I'm very glad on't; for 'tis sad, but true,
These wise men are not always wise to know
The gods, true wisdom's root.   All Italy tells
How Pherecydes mocked the Olympian Powers,
Boasting, albeit no altar ever knew
Or cake from him, or savoury thigh, his life
Flowed in a stream of fair prosperity,
As smooth as theirs who vowed their hecatombs;
For which bold blasphemy the Delian god
Scourged him with loathsome foul disease, that all
His festering flesh with live corruption swarmed,
And crept into putrescence.

MILO.

     'Tis a tale
Far voiced through all the isles; but Pherecydes,
Pythagoras says, was a god-fearing man.

DIAGORAS.

Grant it be so! but where the rings are spread,
A stone fell in the water; rumour swells
In multiplied additions as it rolls,
In circles ever larger with more lies,
But not from nothing.

MILO.

     Rumour hath not yet dared
To fling a shade athwart the pious fame

Of pure Pythagoras, who from fount divine
All truth and goodness draws; whose virgin soul
Such breath of chastest reverence breathes, that not,
Like others, in light-thoughted talk he names
The names of gods; but with well pondered phrase,
In solemn protestation only, swears;
A word, he says, is short and quick, but works
A long result; therefore look well to words,
And ever swear with prayer upon your lips.

DIAGORAS.

'Tis a most holy man; hath he then many
Disciples in Crotona?

MILO.

They are counted
Now not by tens or hundreds; but not all
Are sworn in bonds of secret brotherhood.

DIAGORAS.

What? brotherhoods? and sworn? at Metapontum
Our archons with a wary eye will watch
Such secret gatherings, where, as in a nest,
Ill-will is fostered, discontent enhanced,
Wild plans of crude ambition hatched, and schemes
Of deep-designing counsel laid, that breed
A state within a state.

MILO.

Of this you need
Fear nothing from Pythagoras; our guilds

Are peaceful, loyal, reverent, and pure
From fretful taint of sour democracy.

DIAGORAS.

What is their scope, their rule, their discipline?

MILO.

'Tis simply said : He is the supreme head,
And chooses whom he tries, and tries by test
Of eye, that in the outward feature reads
The inner soul.   He hath a wondrous gift
To know a true man by the brotherhood
Of truth, which breathes in all who love the truth ;
And having proved their will, capacity,
Courage, and single aim, he leads them through
The fruitful silence of a five years' school
Of pondered preparation, for a life
Of reasoned usefulness, remote from strife
Of hot ambition, and the hunt for gold ;
And having trained their minds by thought, their
    wills
By wise subjection to superior will,
He makes them grow in course of kindly acts
Like very brothers, owning him the head
Of their large family.   With their common goods
They help each other ; and what human woe
May cry for help, needs but the name of man
To stir the eager promptings of their heart,
And arm their hand with liberal grace to reach
Each poor unfriended sufferer, who receives
Unhired the loyal service of their love.

DIAGORAS.

How many be there of this conclave sworn
Here in Crotona?

MILO.

Some three hundred; but
Four years of their probation still remain.

DIAGORAS.

Are women of them?

MILO.

Certes; for he says,
Use not a suppliant or a woman harshly,
Both come from Jove, and wisdom hath no sex.

DIAGORAS.

He speaketh well.   In Athens men do use
Women to breed their brats, and spread their
    boards,
The slaves, and not the fellows, of their lords.

MILO.

Our Samian hath a just and gentle soul
That hates all masterdom, usurped beyond
The use of nature and the need of life;
Not women only,—inarticulate brutes,
And the mute denizens of the brackish pools,
Have claimed his care.   I guess your worship
    knows
The famous marketing he made last week
With the fishermen at Sybaris?

DIAGORAS.

In faith not I.

I have been some weeks absent at the feast
Of Atabyrian Jove in Agrigentum ;
And as a waxen tablet, smooth, unscratched,
My mind lies blank to write your tale upon.

MILO.

Well, thus it was.   He sauntered on the beach
This side of Sybaris, where some fishermen
With sweatful strain were pulling in their nets,
And says to them,—" A goodly draught ye draw,
Brave fellows, here ; and in my mind I know
The exact tale that your stout net involves."
They laughed, and said,—" Ha ! if you are a wizard,
And prove your vaunt, we'll do what thing you bid
Within our human reach."   The net was drawn,
And all the fish were counted on the beach ;
Ten score and ten, precise, as he foretold.
Then as they marvelling stood, he bade them fling
The finny gaspers back into the brine
Wholesale ; which, when they did, each bright-scaled
     thing
Paddled alert into the wrinkled pool,
No whit the worse ; whereat the sage took forth
Two golden Darics from his belt, and said,
" Here's payment for your draught : I well have
     gained
My wager, and the fishes gain their lives."
Wherewith he left them ; and the story ran

Through all Crotona, as from glen to glen
The travelling thunder rolls.

DIAGORAS.

                                Does this tale
Deserve our sober credence?

MILO.

                                Who were there
Can answer that; myself can only say
He hath a marvellous gift of casting count,
That overleaps the function of our wit
By Nature's common grant; and, for his love
To fish and every breathing form that moves
It is a prime point in his discipline
To touch the life of things with holy fear,
Which some do hold so nicely that they brook
No flesh for food, and do repair their bloods
With innocent herbs, sweet milk, and barley cakes.

DIAGORAS.

In Egypt there are sacred beasts that live
More honoured than the king; and I have heard
On Ganga's banks the twice-born priests withdraw
Their lips from blood, for subtle reasons laid
In their theology.

MILO.

              I have heard it said
That in his youth he travelled far beyond
High-cedared Lebanon, and the pastoral bounds

Of the men-hating Hebrews, to the banks
Of Indus and Hydaspes, gathering there
Deep-thoughted dogmas, about march of souls
Through masks of changeful bodies.

DIAGORAS.

Even so ;
And 'tis most likely that he spares the brutes,
Fearing to harm some soul of kindred man
That walks in bestial tenement encased,
For castigation of some bestial sin
That shamed his human form.

MILO.

'Tis very like ;
And in the common parley of the town
Himself hath memory of precedent states
In which he walked the earth : some say he was
Euphorbus, son of Panthöus, whose sharp spear
Wounded Patroclus on red Ilium's plain ;
Since when through various shapes of men he
       passed
By steps of just ascension, till he scaled
The top of virtue, and now lives a sage.
But these are matters which his wisdom shuns
To fling upon the glass of common minds,
Prone still to mar the image they reflect ;
All things to all men only fools will tell,
Truth profits none but those who use it well ;
So I have heard him oft.

DIAGORAS.

What man is that
With long white robe, and white-dependent beard,
Who with serene and sober gravity
Winds round the rock?

MILO.

Where mean you?

DIAGORAS.

Here below.

MILO.

It is himself.

DIAGORAS.

What self?—Pythagoras?

MILO.

Most surely: up the swallow rock he climbs,
And will be here anon.

DIAGORAS.

He comes this way.

MILO.

Jove speed the chance! now bring your questioning
Before the oracle; henceforth I am dumb.

[*Enter Pythagoras from below.*]

PYTHAGORAS.

How art thou, Milo?   Would I were as strong
In all the strength that makes a man a man
As Milo is in muscle!

MILO.

Were I as strong

In all the strength that makes a wise man wise
As now to sinewy grasp and litheness bred,
I'd be more wise than wise Pythagoras.

PYTHAGORAS.

Jove give you grace for many years to live
The Hercules of Crotona, more to earth
Than he in heaven to heaven! but who's your
       friend?

MILO.

A worthy man, high honoured priest of Jove,
From Metapontum come to grace the feast
Of the Lacinian Hera, sister spouse
To the great god he serves.

PYTHAGORAS.

Hail, honoured sir!

DIAGORAS.

Mine eyes are blest to-day, beholding what,
From the vague witness of the ear, I knew
At priestly Memphis.

PYTHAGORAS.

Wert thou in Egypt?

DIAGORAS.

The strong desire of wisdom stayed me there
Two years in converse with the learned priests.

PYTHAGORAS.

Would that all Greeks were with your wisdom wise
To learn before they teach ! we are the growth
Of yesterday, and in our green conceit
Deem that, unfathered by an older race,
We from our native Argive glebe upshot
And blossomed into virtue from a seed,
Self-sown, self-watered ! but where sacred Nile
Pours his salubrious flood through fields that heave
With rich vivific slime, old Wisdom sits
On hoary throne, and peers serenely great
Above us pigmies, as a glittering-crowned
Star-neighbouring peak o'erlooks the undulant
    downs
That edge the coast with greenness.   To be wise
Greece first should know her ignorance.

DIAGORAS.

" *We Greeks*
Are always children ;" so the high priest said
To me at Heliopolis ; and the word
Came like a goad, and like a nail remains.

PYTHAGORAS.

No word is worth that not in goadwise comes
And pricks to action ; men there be that make
Parade of fluency, and deftly play
With points of speech as jugglers toss their balls ;
A tinkling crew, from whose light-squandered wit
No seed of virtue grows.

DIAGORAS.

                    When I was young
Such talkers tickled me ; then all my soul
Lodged in mine ear, and facile fancy fed
On twinkling tropes : now, wary-wise, I learn
From no man who makes market of his wit,
But from the tree that in ripe season drops
The fruit of long years of unvaunted growth
I gather wisdom ; and in chief from thee,
Whose school of virtue is Crotona's crown,
Would gladly glean what truth thy ken may deem
Meet for my learning.

PYTHAGORAS.

We have a sentence famous in our school—
" *Wear not the types of gods upon your ring.*"

DIAGORAS.

A pictured parable, and meaning ——?

PYTHAGORAS.

                    This,
Show not to all men always all the things
Most worth the showing.

DIAGORAS.

                    And the application ?

PYTHAGORAS.

This simply—to the vulgar class with whom
Raw sense usurps ripe reason's seat we teach

Nothing; but on the unfilmèd eye we pour
Intelligential light; and to Jove's priest,
Who from the supreme wisdom wisdom draws,
Unsworn, unpledged, Pythagoras may unveil
The golden best of all Pythagoras knows.

DIAGORAS.

Jove make me worthy of your trust! even now
I talked with Milo of your doctrine pure
And discipline severe, and inly long
From your own lips to imbibe the sage discourse,
As he who scents a fragrant fruit desires
To sip its sweetness.

PYTHAGORAS.

   What I can I will
Give to your questioning; but I make no boast
Of novel dogmas; I have never forged
Private conceits, nor hugged, for they were mine,
The pretty pets, the bantlings of my brain.
Old truth I preach, from sempiternal source
Of primal inspiration, owned by men
When men lived near the gods; if I am wise,
I know whence wisdom flows; the biggest stream
Is but the small fed by the small, and all
By Jove's pure wells were fathered in the sky.

DIAGORAS.

The wise man of Miletus thus declared
The FIRST OF THINGS IS WATER; I would know
If he spake well in this.

PYTHAGORAS.

    Well: but before
His first of causes a diviner first
Gave law to wet and dry, and hot and cold.

DIAGORAS.

What first was that?

PYTHAGORAS.

    NUMBER.

DIAGORAS.

   How mean you this?

PYTHAGORAS.

Hear, and digest: this single word unlocks
The riddle of the world.   The world is order;
Order is numbered multitude, marshalled well
In calculated spaces.   See this flower
That spreads its starry coronet to the sun,
Beautiful, golden, in the dainty trim
Of its bright circlet, and the delicate green
Embracement of the cup that bears the crown;
Each part is numbered, every leaflet cut
With living arithmetic, nice and true,
That shames all skill of craftsman.   Count the parts.

DIAGORAS.

Five golden segments in the crown, and ten
Green leaflets in the cup, five large, five small,
With cunning alternation finely set.

PYTHAGORAS.

Count now the stamens that like satellites
Keep circular guard around the central germ.

DIAGORAS.

I've told them twice: I think they number ten.

PYTHAGORAS.

So right; and thus the number of the plant
Is ten, what else were lawless huddlement,
Chaotic, rude, unknown, unknowable;
But by the sacred limit of the ten
Now from the waste infinitude redeemed
Into chaste order's ranks, and disciplined
Into the file of beauty.

MILO.

      I see this now
For the first time; what published fools we are,
Looking with open eyes on miracles
From day to day—beneath—above—around,
And seeing—nothing !

PYTHAGORAS.

      If but Athena's grace
Would salve our eyes, we'd see a host of gods
In every tumult working to a plan.

DIAGORAS.

I've heard it said that 'neath the stony ribs
Of inorganic rocks there dwells a power

That moulds the obdurate atoms of the flint
Into fine angles, measured most exact
By mathematic rule.

PYTHAGORAS.

                    And I have walked
In lands where hills in measured platforms rose
Tier upon tier, and every tier was built
Of jointed blocks that fitted each to each
With nice compagination, like the bars
Welded in Vulcan's stithy; thou canst find
Nowhere in Nature where not number reigns.

DIAGORAS.

When the birds sing in spring, and zephyrs shake
The leafy grove, the rush of warbled sounds
That thrills the bosom of the fragrant air
With the wild gladness of new procreant life,
Seems a most sweet confusion.

PYTHAGORAS.

                    Least of all
In sounds confusion reigns; and melody,
Without nice number fitting note to note,
Would shriek like tempest in the tortured ear,
And rend all hearing with discordant bray.

DIAGORAS.

How know you this? What man that measures fields
With chain and rod and mathematic law,
Can tell the inches of the cuckoo's note?

PYTHAGORAS.

The cuckoo's note is a most cunning lute,
And lutes have numbered strings, and oaten pipes
Have numbered stops. Come thou to me to-morrow
In the cool plane-tree walk behind the school,
And I will show thee how the self-same string
With nicely varied tension gently glides
From wave to wave concordant, though the whole
Sweet sequence of brave harmonies that wake
The chambered ear to rapture ; break the law
Of numbered intervals that links the chain
Of just vibrations, and the clashing sounds
With grating din will saw the shrinking ear
Of him that heard in rooted ecstasy,
Till he pray Jove for deafness !

DIAGORAS.

            'Tis most strange !
But certes some things be that scorn control
And wanton in confusion.   Who hath measured
The cloud, the storm-wind, and the waterfall?

PYTHAGORAS.

God measures all things ; is himself the measure
Of all that is, hath been, or yet may be.
The headlong waterfall that o'er the cliff
Flings its full-breasted force, and fiercely smites
The grey rocks with its sweeping scourge, and in
The deep brown granite cauldron boils below,
With sleepless whirling eddies, and white foam
Of bubbles bursting still, and still to burst—

This water hath a number, every drop
Atom to atom joined by certain law,
Nice as the notes of melody adjured
From strings by harper's magic.   Take that crust
Of curled black lichen creeping o'er the face
Of the red rock; thou see'st no order there;
But if some god might point thine eye more keen
To see what now its grosser view ignores,
And thou mightst dive into its heart, and probe
The pulsing alleys of its tissued life,
Then wouldst thou find with fine ecstatic ken
A mustered and a marshalled beauty there,
As perfect as the ordered strategy
Of that proud Memphian conqueror who mapped
The world with battle-fields, and played with lives
As children play with bowls, and made all lands
The chess-board of his vast imperial scheme.
His movements, as they hurried to and fro
Freighted with death, seemed lawless as the rush
Of savage beasts unkennelled; but full well
He knew the portioned number of his host;
And with one glance from him, they from afar
Gathered the sundered looseness of their ranks,
And with concentric curious-counted speed
Bore on the station marked for doom, and burst
In calculated thunder.   Dost thou see
This small brown hillock?

DIAGORAS.

Yes; it is an ant-hill.

MILO.

How deftly they drive on, and whirl about,
Some here, some there, o'er one another's heads!
And some creep into holes, and some creep out,
And some with straws are galloping, and some
With little sticks are hobbling, and some push
A small white roll upon their tiny snouts;
Incalculable maze! I marvel much
If evermore they make this motley stir;
Their reeling makes me dizzy, as the light
Far shimmering o'er the million-pointed wave
Palsies the eye.

PYTHAGORAS.

The palsied eye proclaims
His own defect; and weak nerves are confounded
Where no confusion is.

DIAGORAS.

Is there none here?

PYTHAGORAS.

More order than in your weak brain or mine,
Or any brain that harbours human thoughts.
Not less than Memphian pontiffs, nicely trained
To measure the long-centuried march of stars,
Instinct with mathematic skill from Jove,
These puny craftsmen know what number means.

DIAGORAS.

Have they a plan?

PYTHAGORAS.

>Doubt not; as much as he
Who piled the numbered legions of the bricks
Into the pyramids that sentinel
The seven-mouth'd Nile.

DIAGORAS.

>'Tis wondrous strange.

PYTHAGORAS.

>Far stranger, if thou knew
The hot heart of that sphered metropolis,
Whereof thou now but seest the outer ports,
And a few hundred peaceful citizens
By our ungracious intrusion frayed.
Not Babylon the mighty, nor the pomp
Of hundred-gated, many-templed Thebes,
Hath streets more orderly.   Every lane, I wot,
Is numbered here, and every crossway swept.
This busy people, as their skill may be,
Hath each his portioned task; some delve and
    burrow,
And carve huge tunnels where a passage fails,
And span the void with arches, and some scoop
A drain for water, whose untimely swell
Might flood the colony; some are sent abroad
To cater stores for winter; and some pile
The newly plundered grain.   Some run, some wait,
Some sweat and serve, some hold a high command,
But each a needful work fulfils, and all
By mystic number's harmony combine
The swarming units to a jointed whole.

MILO.

And in my garden I have marked the bees,
Most cunning engineers, and ordered well.

PYTHAGORAS.

All things are full of cunning ; even fools
Have wisdom for their need ; and multitude
By number grouped, and by discretion used
Is power.   Hold thou this faith with grappling-
    hooks,
All things in the vast world are done by law,
And law is number, and all numbers are
The thoughts of gods that from deep counsel take
Significant masks to play their pictured parts
Upon the stage of being.   Every grain
Of the ribb'd sand is numbered, every whiff
Of every breeze, all fleecy mists that fleck
The blue concave, all bubbles of the brine,
All flies that swarm from hot-fermenting beds
In sweltering summer, every seed that floats
On plumy vans into the bosomed earth ;
All sounds of earth and sky, the chirp of birds,
The roar of lions, and the lisp of babes,
The pealing thunder, and the tinkling rill,
The trumpet-tongued exploits of dinful war,
And the low syllabled breath of fearful prayer,
God speaks their mystic number, and they are.

DIAGORAS.

At Heliopolis an aged priest,
White with the ripe repose of well-spent years,

Oft times at set of sun discoursed to me
Of special virtue in the ordered tale
Of every number, and above the rest
With eloquent loving preference he praised
The sacred trine.

PYTHAGORAS.

Wisely the wise man spake.
There is no number of rare quality
Like THREE; it is the strong and plastic bond
That bridges two extremes, and nicely shapes
From three a unity, a whole that meets
The claim of reason and the plan of Jove.
For Jove is one; and, when two stand apart
Without a third to link them, unity
Is lost, and God divided from Himself.
Thus earth and fire, the heavy and the light,
Are bound together by the graded kinds
Of air and water; as to fire the air,
So to the air the water; and as air
To water, so is water to gross earth
By just degrees of apt proportion tuned;
And thus by process of well-blended threes,
And linked gradations cunningly combined,
The sundered many to their primal type
Slide kindly back, and the great world is one.

MILO.

And therefore three libations at a feast
Give perfect thanks; and in wise Homer's song
By three great deities each hero swears,
Dark-clouded Jove, Athena, and Apollo.

DIAGORAS.

Oft times in pictured Memphian fanes I saw
Three seated gods one common altar grace;
And the priest said an old thrice-sacred law
Forbade their sundering.

PYTHAGORAS.

              Something more than law,
Nature and the necessity of things
Demand the three.   On Ganga's sacred banks
The gymnosophists to a triform GOD
Pray wisely.   Three in one, and one in Three,
Strong to create, to save, and to destroy
Eternal Trine of functions that must be,
While the Unlimited and Absolute walks
Self-bounded into Finitude.   They are fools
Who deem that aught in holy creed revered
Stands by a law which he who made can mar;
Jove may not will to do what if he willed
He were not Jove; a trinity in God
Egypt and Greece, and Ganga's sons adore
By the essential virtue of the Trine;
Even as in man, in whom a god doth dwell,
Between the naked Thought and harnessed Deed,
To bridge the gap the spoken Word appears,
And through the word full-panoplied the Thought
Goes conquering forth in stable act complete;
And thought and deed by word are unified,
Being three into one energizing whole,
A trinity in unity of powers
That makes a man a man, the world a world.

DIAGORAS.

Thou hast unveiled my sight; and now I see
Where I saw nought, the office of the THREE;
And I remember Asclepiades
The wise old leech in Metapontum, skilled
In all the virtues of all herbs that grow,
Said that Demeter gives the nurturing wheat
Fruited from flowers whose number is the three.

PYTHAGORAS.

That any child may learn who in the spring
Looks in the bloom that shoots out from the sheath
By summer's heat unhardened.   There you count
Three threads erect, that stand with yellow caps
Like sentinels around the chambered cell,
Where swells the foodful grain.

DIAGORAS.

                 How wonderful!

PYTHAGORAS.

All things are wonderful; who wonders not,
Hath eyes and sees not; wonder is the key
Of knowledge and of worship to the wise;
And if there be who with unloving hands
Push the rich loveliness of things aside,
Nor bend the knee before the shaping Power
That works in blazing star, and breathing dust,
Poor frosty souls! if I could strain cold ice
To my warm bosom, I could live with them
In bonds of love; but let them live alone,

Knowing that nought is worthy to be known,
Nourished by heartless sneers and hollow jests
And worshipping—if worship be for them—
Their little selves!

DIAGORAS.

                              Would God that all
Our priests in Metapontum with like phrase,
Seasoned their chanted liturgies; but now
They turn the crazy mill-wheel of old rites
With plashing driblets, and rehearse their store
Of monstered legends to a gaping throng,
Which makes the prudent scoff; and much I fear,
Lest with the rank offence of sleepy prayers
And fables moulded when the baby-world
Lay cradled in light dreams, fair Greece be turned
From faith, and live divorced from holy fear
That links men with the gods.   Ourselves have
      taught
The babbling sophist to bemock the gods;
Ourselves, who shame divinity with tales
That make chaste maidens blush; and now our youth
Are trained to slight our worship, and to serve
The gods with sham lip-mumbled prayers, of which
The heart knows nothing.   Oft times I have wept
With tears that no man sees, and I make moans
With moans that no man hears, when I revolve,
How, if this rank-sown sceptic seed shall shoot
To natural topping, our fair host of gods
That makes a world a garden good for men,
Well watered and well sunned, shall, by the frost

Of pert-mouthed witlings blasted, shrink and droop,
And blacken into dust, trod under foot
Of aweless men, who in the sun delight
To spy black spots, and make most holy things
A theme for laughter, and a text for sneers.
Of powers they talk, and forces, vortices,
Figures, and spaces, fulness and a void,
Attractions and repulsions, atoms wed
Blindly to atoms, and all blindly borne
Through blank infinitude with fortuitous reel,
Till with a random bump they meet, and from
Their chaos strike out order; this they teach,
And this they vend for wisdom; but of Jove
They speak not, by whose counsel all things stand,
Dread thunder-launching lord; nor of his spouse,
The great-eyed Hera, matronly and proud;
Nor of Apollo with his blazing darts
Chasing god-hated darkness from the sky;
Nor of the flashing-eyed Athena, wise
To purchase peace by prompt display of war.
All this must perish, if dear Greece shall stint
Her lovely faith, and barrenly increase
Mere itch of knowledge, leaving to lean eyes,
For the bright smile that warms the face o' the
          world,
A bald, disgodded, lightless, loveless grey!

PYTHAGORAS.

Fear not; the faith that in the hearts of men
Lives now shall live for ever. The Jove that reigns
To-day, eternal as the stable skies

Whose power he wields, sits on unshaken throne.
All things are full of change ; but all the change
Is the new mask of him that changeth never ;
If Zeus might cease to reign, another name
Shall launch the thunderbolt and wheel the spheres ;
Greek or Barbarian, Jove shall still be Jove,
Voiced with Hellenic or Phœnician breath,
His fateful essence with impartial glance
Shoots through the shifting shibboleths of creeds
With multiform acknowledgment, yet one Power,
Who by the heart, not by the tongue, discerns
His worshippers ; names are but minted signs
For needful currency, the thing behind
By thousand symbols symbolled is but one.
Zeus recks not what we call him, how men may
With hoar traditional pomp of customed style,
Parade him for their reverence ; he is pleased
With the best form that suits each suppliant's need,
And owns alike the wise man's reasoned hymn,
And the rude savage with his mumbled charm
And neck-strung amulet.   And for the tales
That bards with fancy's airy tissue weave,
When men have ceased to hear them and believe,
Jove is well pleased that Time shall ring their knell.

DIAGORAS.

Grant it be so : yet must I fear the hand
That plucks a flower from a well-woven wreath ;
A drunken Hercules may pull down a house
That long shall wait the master-builder's craft
To set its shaken joints.   Jove sits secure

In heaven, you say; 'tis well; meanwhile below
We rock on seas of doubt, and see old thrones
Start from their roots, by sharp earth-shaking throes
Of fearful change.   And if the grey report
Of ancient piety shield our shrines from touch
Of shameless force, and awful reverence shun
To rend the sacred vest that robes a god,
Not shielded by such fear, our archons sit
On the high bench of state.   I long have marked
How in this land the bonds of old respect
Are snapt; and now a green unseasoned brood,
Blown with the bubbling yeast of yesterday,
And spreading broad their fans of mushroom wealth,
Spurn the conditions of their birth, and stretch
Unlicensed hands to snatch the ancestral mace
From ancient honour's gripe.   Fair order thus
Is marred in States; old dignity departs;
The due gradations of just rank and place
Are levelled; no man owes respect to man;
And each man seizes what he knows to hold
By right of might and sleight of juggling phrase;
For all are free they say, and equal all,
And one as good as t'other.

PYTHAGORAS.

                         I have known
Enough of men and their unreasoned ways
To deem your fears not causeless.   Liberty
Is a strong wine all men would gladly quaff,
But few quaff wisely; 'tis a gallant ship,
That with full-bellied sail spread to the breeze,

Needs weightier ballast and a wiser helm.
Men are like school-boys wishing to be free
From masters whom, to learn, they must obey;
The boys are stupid, foolish, what you will,
And still will wish the thing that hurts them still;
But this remember, if the master be
False to his function, and unlearned to spell,
No one will blame the boys if they rebel.
Take hence your lesson; you by old descent
The natural heads and helmsmen of the State
Are lawful masters of the school, and sit
On thrones of order; if you order well
Your States are happy, and your seats are sure;
Men hate control; but for the fear of worse
They live content when they are well controlled.
The reins are yours; and, if some colt shall kick,
Use well the lash, and Jove will help the strong;
But if you live self-pleasers, being perched
On thrones of honour for the general weal,
And use the people but as sheep to shear
That you may sit in woolly coats, while they
Stand shivering in the blast, then righteous Jove
Will send twin scourges to chastise your sins,
The democrat and despot, this of that
The lawful offspring, both of liberty
The natural growth, where pampered privilege
Rules for itself, and to its work untrue,
Neglects the many and corrupts the few.

DIAGORAS.

Wisely you speak: ourselves the vipers breed
That bite us; insolence in the few begets

Hate in the many; hatred breeds revolt;
Revolt, where all are free to rise and rule,
Breeds anarchy, whose wild chaotic reign
Calls in the despot with strong will to keep
Sharp knives from maddened hands; and thus we
    reel
From vassalage to vassalage, through fits
Of drunken freedom,—glorious for an hour!

PYTHAGORAS.

We are but children practising to walk,
Still, stumbling, still to tempt our feet again.
The gods are patient; time is long; and change
Treads on the steps of change, till men shall learn
From mighty heads discrowned and trampled
    thrones,
That Wisdom only reigns by right divine,
And where the wise rule, and the fools obey
Not force, but aptly-balanced forces sway;
And for this end in our sworn brotherhood
We work here in Crotona, training each,
By course of wise obedience disciplined,
To know his betters, and to own their rule;
Thus each for each, and all for all are trained,
As in the high-wrought quaintly builded ode
Note answers note, and verse to verse responds.

MILO.

Our Greekish ears, I fear, shall sooner hear
The spheral chimes than win this harmony
From the harsh bray of democratic brawls.

PYTHAGORAS.

Milo, all growth is slow; but Jove hath made
The blustering March to pledge the blooming May;
The seasons come; we cannot spur their coming.
And if the Greeks, in wisdom's work the first,
Should lag in polity behind the march
Of some barbarian tanling, cradled now
Behind the Oscan hills, 'tis but a page
In the great lesson-book of Time,—a word
The stammering school-boy cannot spell to-day,
But some day will, when moons that grow from
    moons
Bring sweet from sour, and ripeness from the
    crude.
The gods give leash enough for human fools
To follow fools, and loss to breed more loss,
Till men by blunder upon blunder piled
Shall choose to cease from faith in multitudes,
Who, weighing wisdom by their blustering breaths,
Fling in the air their smutty caps, and cry
Huzza, to every flatterer! The crude world
Takes centuries to learn one mellow truth.

DIAGORAS.

And I in this short hour have learned enough
To last me for a life. What sound was that?

MILO.

It is the chorus of young men which rounds
This festive day with melody. Stand we aside,

While they shall mass their files.　You will admire
Theano's skill, as you admired before ;
The youths were trained by her ; the verses drew
Their numbers from her fine harmonious soul.

*The chorus of Young Men advances on the platform before the
temple, and disposing themselves as in the opening chorus of
Maidens, sing as follows :—*

STROPHE.

When man first rose from teeming ground
A rude unfinished thing was he,
And looked with blank amaze around
On the strange sky, and land, and sea.

Whether from Egypt's genial mud
When earth was young he crawled to view,
Or Argive Inachus' sacred flood
The big untutored baby knew.

Naked he stood ; to veil his shame
No curious-tissued rag he wore ;
No edged tool he knew to frame,
Or sheltering roof, or barring door.

But in the self-built cavern rude
His lazy length on stony bed
He stretched supine, and all his food
Was mountain berries black and red.

The horn'd and talon'd brood he feared,
The nightly wolves that howl and roam ;

And when the snake his crest upreared,
He slunk into his craven home.

A helpless, shiftless, aimless thing,
With weak, unpractised, blundering brain ;
In woods he owned the lion king,
And the wild bull upon the plain.

ANTISTROPHE.

But when his brain to firmness grew,
And Thought his manly stature gained,
The wildered world its master knew,
Force bowed the neck, and Reason reigned.

The sturdy ox, the snorting steed,
The light-heeled, the slow-gaited brute
He caught, and trained to serve his need
With lustier loins or fleeter foot.

The pointed flint he made his tool,
His sceptre was the bleachèd bone ;
The splintered oak, the twisted wool,
The cleavèd slate his service own.

From sifted sand the twinkling ore
He drew ; with nicely sundering sleight
Black iron's adamantine store
He charmed from stone to arm his might.

And where he came with skilful plan
And reason's mild subduing law,

The dwindled forest fled from man,
The waste a blooming garden saw.

And tents with polished poles were reared,
And pillared domes, and vaulted aisles,
And porch and pictured wall appeared,
And towers, and proud palatial piles, .

EPODE.

And kings with sceptred honour ruled ;
And hostile clans in brawling bred,
By common dangers harshly schooled
Took law from one imperial head.

But most to help the noblest need
Of human thought, Religion grew,
With wingèd hymn, and awful creed,
And myth of various woven hue.

And prophets spake, and oracles
Gave fateful note of coming harm,
And sacred rites and holy spells
Smoothed the guilt-stricken soul's alarm.

And saintly sage and thoughtful seer
On meditation's brooding wings
Sublimely borne, with vision clear
Pierced through the sensuous veil of things.

And through creation's starry girth
With reverent joy and wonder saw

Of things in heaven, and things on earth
The mystic number and the Law.

And heard with raptured ear the chime
Of spheres on spheres that wheel for ever,
The swell and fall of shoreless Time,
The roll of Life's exhaustless river.

And taught man's creeping soul to rise
From stony glebe and dusty sod,
And track with ever new surprise
The flaming footsteps of a god.

Such strength by fate's far-stretching plan
To wise deep-thoughted man was given
By Jove, who rules the Olympian clan
And great-eyed Hera, queen of heaven.

PYTHAGORAS.

Good sirs, adieu ! these vesper notes shall ring
My lullaby to-night.   To-morrow morn
Jove give us happy meeting, when the great
Procession crowns the feast !

MILO.
                Farewell, good master !

DIAGORAS.
Jove rain great grace on wise Pythagoras !

THALES

Ὁ μὲν οὖν Θαλῆς ὕδωρ εἶναι τὴν ἀρχήν φησιν, λαβὼν ἴσως τὴν ὑπόληψιν ἐκ τοῦ πάντων ὁρᾶν τὴν τροφὴν ὑγρὰν οὖσαν, καὶ διὰ τὸ πάντων τὰ σπέρματα τὴν φύσιν ὑγρὰν ἔχειν, τὸ δὲ ὕδωρ ἀρχὴν τῆς φύσεως εἶναι τοῖς ὑγροῖς.　　　　　ARISTOTLE.

THALES.

PERSONS.

1. THALES, a Philosopher of Miletus.
2. CTESIBIAS, the Friend of Thales.
3. Chorus of Maidens and Youths.

SCENE.—*The villa of Thales, near the sea-shore; the philo-sopher discovered sitting on a low ledge of rock, tracing mathe-matical figures in the sand.*

THALES.

It must be so; the complete rounded form
Which, in the wide cærulean's flaming bound,
And in the briny droplet of the sea,
Asserts its beauty, and declares its power;
This perfect whole, with all equalities
Conditioned so that part to part responds
With native nice adaptness, like the notes
Which cunning harper lures from measured strings
Of a well-tempered lute—it cannot be
But in this circle's finely-featured round,
Born of its beauty, by its law controlled,
Lie other forms with fair-proportioned bounds,
Which whoso thinks may from their germ forth-draw,
As a keen-nosing hound from brake to brake

Scents out the game.   Well! let me see: I shape
This circle on the ribbèd sand, and make
Within its half a triangle, and find,
Change as I may the legs on either side,
Still on the base the bridging angle stands
A right angle.   And why?   It cannot be
Far hid.   Ha, now 'tis clear! I cut in twain
This topping angle by a line which meets
The centre, and my one triangle makes
Two equal-legged triangles, and each half
Of the top angle hath an equal fork
With that which fronts it at the adverse base,
With corresponding slant; and both the halves
Make up the whole; and right angle must be
That in a just three-cornered figure sums
The other two.   O foolish, foolish Thales!
That saw not this before, even with a glance,
But pondering went, and picked my painful way,
As some wayfarer stops with feeling foot
From tuft to tuft across a faithless quag!
Well, well! all men are dull of wit, and why
Should I out-top my fellows?   We have gained
A footing slow but sure: the cosmos stands
By numbered nice congruities; and, if
From stage to stage with wary move we march,
Threading the fine invisible links which bind
The distant, unapproachable, undreamt,
To things of close touch and familiar ken,
O then! with measured angles fine we'll tell
The travel of far-wheeling orbs, and be
Prophets of storm and sun's eclipse, and sign

The eccentric comet's pathway, ere he comes !
We'll swim the air with light-blown spheres, and
    sup
With Jove some day, like fabled Tantalus,
And reap—pray Heaven—more blissful fruit than
    he
From empyrean converse !

[*Enter Ctesibias.*]

CTESIBIAS.

          Thales, is this you ?

THALES.

Ctesibias !   All hail, good friend !   You are
The gladfullest sight that holds mine eyes since I
Returned from Libya.

CTESIBIAS.

          May the gods rain joy
On my best friend !   When came you to Miletus?

THALES.

But yesternight.

CTESIBIAS.

          Had you a favouring breeze ?

THALES.

Winged like a bird, and as an arrow straight
We shot from Pharos.

CTESIBIAS.

    Good luck dwells with you.

THALES.

Not always.

CTESIBIAS.

   When did any god behold
Thales askance?

THALES.

Once.

CTESIBIAS.

    When?

THALES.

       You will remember
When on a cold and crisp December night
I walked out in the fields to meditate,
And read the stars, and as I gazed, I strode
Unwitting of my steps, into a ditch,
And gored my knee, and scarred my skin, and from
Its just compactness well nigh wrenched awry
This jointed frame.

CTESIBIAS.

     And all Miletus then
Laughed at philosophers, and every dull,
Soft-witted, pudding-brain felt wiser then
On two sound legs than Thales, whom the god
Graced with the tripod to the wisest due,

And whom the tripod, by its proper lord
Unwisely wise disowned, refused to quit,
And still returned, as to its baffled bite
A greedy fish.   Do you still read the stars?

THALES.

I read the sand.

CTESIBIAS.

How so?

THALES.

Look here.

CTESIBIAS.

I see.
What mean these circles?   Do these lines contain
Some wisdom of the Egyptians from the banks
Of the sweet-watered Nile?

THALES.

They understand
Triangles there and squares, and every bound
That limits land; else when the flood o'erswept
Their fields with fertile mud, no man were wise
To claim his father's roods.

CTESIBIAS.

I oft have heard
Our sailors say the strangest of all lands
Is Egypt: what say you?

THALES.

　　　　　　　　　　O ! passing strange.
The world contains one Egypt, and one Nile,
Which floods like ocean, when our streams retreat,
And creep in threads beneath the blanchèd stones;
Think all things there to all things here reverse,
And thus know Egypt.　Women walk abroad,
While men sit weaving carpets in the shade
Of their own eaves; all burdens on their heads
The bearded bear, the beardless on their backs;
No shrine of Memphian god or goddess holds
A priestess, but all where the male enacts
The sacred rite; and every priest doth show
A shaven crown, as who esteems profane
The honour of his hair, and with their feet
Serviced for hands they knead the foodful dough.
From right to left they write, and circumcise
Their flesh from Nature's fulness; but what most
Out-steps all march of reason is their bond
To brutes, which other men do hotly hunt
Out of all breathing room.

CTESIBIAS.

　　　　　　　　　　I've heard it said
They worship leeks.

THALES.

　　　　　　　　　　That I never knew;
But I have seen them crook most loyal knees
To crocodiles and cats.

CTESIBIAS.
> To crocodiles!

THALES.

Ay!   And for crawling cruel crocodiles
They build high-pillared fanes, more stately domes
Than Pisa piles to Jove.   A crocodile
They keep in chambered circumstance apart,
And trick his arms and legs with jewelled gauds,
And spread soft cushions for his flanks,—the flanks
Which shake with scaly terror when he floats
The troubled floods, that every troutling flies;
And cushioned thus in purple pomp he lies
With most devoted service from a guild
Of linen-vested and bald-pated priests,
Like some light leman whom a brainish youth,
Fevered with frothy spume of puberty,
Mis-names a goddess.

CTESIBIAS.
> I do thank the gods
That I was born a Greek, and no barbarian.

THALES.

In this, believe, my pebble follows yours.
They have some sacred legends about cats,
And crocodiles, and hooded snakes, and hawks,
That may excuse their oddness.   But for us
The wisdom of the thunder-rolling Jove,
And the strong maid that from the Father's head
Unmothered leapt in full-grown armature;

The glory of unshorn Apollo's locks,
Refulgent with the golden gloss of youth ;
And His broad-breasted might who holds the seas
In harness, and from out their pregnant beds
Sends finny myriads forth to thrill the floods
With glancing life ; these are the 'gods whom Greeks
May wisely worship, by such worship raised
To high communion with a nobler kind,
And by their reverent contemplation changed
Into some taste of likeness.

CTESIBIAS.

You are moved
Most timeously to pious thoughts.   To-day
Is the great feast of whom your lips have named
The strong Poseidon ; here his temple stands,
Where halts the festal pomp to hymn the god
With many-winding sweep of numerous verse
From craft of praiseful band.   Lo, where they come !
Sit we apart a moment.

[*Thales and Ctesibias go aside to leave room for the procession
to advance.   Enter in rank and file distinguished citizens of
Miletus, the priests of Poseidon, the marine Aphrodite, the Didymean Apollo, and other local gods.   Then a chorus of boys and
girls, who sing the following hymn in front of the temple.*]

I.

GENERAL CHORUS.

God of the waters, Poseidon the mighty,
Lording the brine with thy queen Amphitrite,
Brother of Kronos Supreme,

Zoning the globe with thy slumberless current,
Scourging the rock with thy sharp-hissing torrent,
      Ruling in flood and in stream,
Hear from the hall where the blue wave rides o'er thee,
Hear from the cave where the sea-nymphs adore thee,
      Brother of Kronos Supreme !

II.

CHORUS OF MAIDENS.

Holiest water's
Beautiful sheen,
First of thy daughters
In glory was seen
The fair Aphrodite,
The golden, the mighty,
Of beauty the Queen !
Holiest island's
Sea-girdled frame
Of far and of nigh lands
The fairest in fame,
Fronting the high lands
Cythera we name !
For there from the bosom
Of billows benign
The foam bore a blossom
Of wonder divine :
The waters were stirred
With musical swell,
Like the voice of sweet birds
In a deep woody dell ;

With roseate blushes
Like breath of the morn
The blue billow flushes,
And lo ! she is born,
The fair Aphrodite,
From watery sheen,
The golden, the mighty
Soul-conquering queen.
Moulded from essence
Of undulant shows,
In bright iridescence
To glory she rose.
Through the breadth of the waters
Sweet tremor was spread,
And the Nereid daughters
From white coral bed
Came trooping uncounted.
The gambolling crew
Of Tritons came mounted
On dolphins to view ;
But their riotous chorus
Was bound by the spell,
And the challenge sonorous
Was dumb in their shell.
Young Amorets round her
Did sportively play,
And the Zephyrs that found her
Stole fragrance away,
As clothed on with beauty
Sublimely she soars,
Where the Hours, in their duty,

Unbarred the bright doors
Of the welkin to meet her;
And each god from his throne
Rose raptured to greet her,
First star of the zone;
And the strongest above
Was a child in that hour,
And Jove was no Jove
When she smiled in her power;
And Poseidon the mighty
Rejoiced when he saw
The sea-Aphrodite
Thrill heaven with awe,
His fairest of daughters,
More dear than his eye,
A gem from the waters
To brighten the sky!

III.

Chorus of Boys.

In the old heroic time,
From the cloudless Attic clime,
The son of Cadmus voyaged with a people strong
    and free;
From the good Milesian land
He drave out the Carian band,
And bade the Greeks be captains of the island-studded
    sea!

On the courses of the deep
With a fearless rein we sweep,
And East and West in bonds of golden amity we bind;
Like fleet birds on the wing,
From land to land we bring
The reward that lightens labour to the toilsome human
kind.

By Helle's sounding shore,
Where the swirling currents roar,
And Priapus loves at Lampsacus the fiery flushing vine;
And in the Thracian hold
Of Abydos, rich in gold,
We reared Apollo's golden head to flash across the
brine !

Where the Euxine's gusty flail
Smites the tightly-reefèd sail,
Beyond the blue Symplegades we ploughed the horrid
main ;
Where Sinope flouts the storm,
And the glancing tunnies swarm,
The willing Paphlagonian received our golden chain.

In the Amazonian land,
Where Lycastes rolls his sand,
We bade the frosty Pontus glow with sparks of Attic
fire ;
With the fruits our labour bore
We sowed the barren shore,
And fattened with our merchandise the plains of
Themiscyre.

To Poseidon be the praise,
Who across the liquid maze
Cut a highway broad and open to a people strong
and free,
To Poseidon, and the Queen
Born of water's foamy sheen,
Who bade Miletus lord it o'er the island-studded sea!

IV.

General Chorus.

God of the waters, Poseidon the mighty,
Lording the brine with thy queen Amphitrite,
Brother of Kronos supreme,
Zoning the globe with thy slumberless current,
Scourging the rock with thy sharp-hissing torrent,
Ruling in flood and in stream.
God, to whom rises the worshipful pæan
From the myriad isles of the laughing Ægean,
Quick with the summery beam :
Mighty with vans of the whirlwind tremendous,
To lash into fury the billow stupendous,
Brindled with gloom and with gleam,
Mighty to snaffle the hurricane's wildness,
Smoothing the rough with a spirit of mildness
Softer than infancy's dream :
Lord of the waters, Poseidon, broad-breasted,
Riding the billows, blue-necked, many-crested,
Rolling with limitless stream ;
Hear from the hall where the big wave rides o'er thee,

Hear from the cave where the sea-nymphs adore thee,
Hear where the men of Miletus implore thee,
   Regent of ocean supreme !

CTESIBIAS.

Now they are done.

THALES.

   And will make sacrifice ?

CTESIBIAS.

Anon ; but first they wend them round the bay,
And at the other temple of the god
That visages Meander's mouth they chaunt
The hymn again, then to the king of storms
They fell the swarthy bull.

THALES.

       My heart goes with them.
All gods compel our worship ; but each man
Within his soul's particular shrine reveres
Some partial power ; and from my heart there
   mounts
A hymn with largest sweep of song to praise
The Regent of the waves.

CTESIBIAS.

       Even so with me
It hath been alway.

THALES.

     And for most rightful cause,

Not only that the sea-queen beautiful,
Our loved Miletus, draws her wealthy store
From favour of the trident-wielding god,
But subtle reasons with wise Homer's verse,
Make league to vouch our preference.

CTESIBIAS.

How so?

THALES.

How so?   None in this land should better know
Than my Ctesibias, who not with gold
And silver only prinks his princely hall,
But with rare garniture of learnèd scrolls
Makes every wall to preach.

CTESIBIAS.

Would that my books
Were measure of my wits, and I could count
My high-summed knowledge as I tell my tomes!
In Homer's song Poseidon lifts for Greeks
A mighty mace, but from superior Jove
Reaps sharp rebuff.

THALES.

Not this I mean; for all
Must duck to Jove, and follow to what end
His marshalling finger points, else blindly borne
To whirling chaos, spoiled of unity
And fair coherence: but of water's power
In the first mingling of prime elements

To mass the world, before the Fate assigned
The cosmic helm to Jove, the poet sings
As ever, wisely.

CTESIBIAS.

Homer doth not grub
Into the dark roots of the world, nor flings
His song, like sea-bird's cry, in gustful air;
But o'er the lightsome flower's sun-tinted bloom
Flits like a bee, and sucks the nectared sweet.

THALES.

'Tis the most proper bliss of bards to sip
The top-cream of enjoyment: yet sometimes
The darksome root more than the lightsome crown
Brews healthful food and medicinal juice;
And I about the roots am fond to grope,
And find that poets, when I ask for facts,
Oft tickle me with fancies finely spun,
And fob me off with phrases.   But good Homer
What could be known and was known in his day,
Knew all; and, sometimes wise beyond himself,
Redeemed some waif of wisdom from an age
Of simpler faith, and broader lines of truth,
Some shell of thought from an old ocean spume
That in the hurtle of his deedful verse,
Hot with the chariot wheels of reeking war,
Shows like a gaping stranger in a town
That streams with market; or, as sometimes we see,
A separate crystal gleaming, all compact,
From close embracement of the stiff old clay.

CTESIBIAS.

Most likely so ; but where does Homer praise
The power of Water ?   I would hear the line.

THALES.

" *Ocean, the Father of gods immortal, and Tethys the
    Mother.*"

CTESIBIAS.

Now I remember ; 'tis where wily Hera
Borrows the amorous cest of Aphrodite
And girds her charms, and in its virtue strong,
Cozens the Thunderer's might, and proudly lays
His bolt asleep.

THALES.

        So to the point exact ;
And Ocean means the water, and the power
Of that fine flowing permeant element,
Whose subtle essence, like a viewless breath,
Pervades all space, and latent lurks in all
The frame of things.

CTESIBIAS.

        The frame of things is firm,
Compact, and solid.

THALES.

        Not of things that live.
All vital power in soft and succulent bed
Lies cradled, and in moist enswathement grows,

F

But frosted in concretion's gripe, becomes
Another name for death.

CTESIBIAS.

But seeds are hard;
And from the groovèd stone the blushful peach
Swells into downy sweetness.

THALES.

But the stone
Holds a soft kernel; what you call the seeds
Are but the shells that shield the seeds from harm;
There is no life but where the liquid reigns.
Cast round thy gaze, and see with feeling eyes
The living tide and pulse of fluent things;
Where the young sap climbs up the vernal twig,
Where the hot blood careers through throbbing
    veins,
Where the hard womb of barren-gaping earth
Drinks in the genial drenching from the sky,
Or where the stars in sempiternal round
Are fed by steams that blossom from the sea,
All where old Ocean works, by Homer praised,
Father of gods and men.

CTESIBIAS.

But the Ascræan,
If I remember, tells a diverse tale;
Father of gods, he says, was Uranus,
Black Earth their dam.

THALES.

      In that he surely erred,
Swerving from Homer. Earth from Ocean comes,
Not Ocean from the Earth ; the liquid holds
The solid in its womb ; the firm hard bones
Grow from the yielding flesh ; the flesh from flow
Of the more yielding water. Age to youth
May sooner pass than from unwatery crust
Be birth of water. Yet Hesiod hath some snatch
Of the great power of liquid, when he sings
The progeny of Pontus.

CTESIBIAS.

       I remember
The passage well. My first schoolmaster was
A grave Bœotian, a poor fisherman
Who lived by dredging sponges at Anthedon,
And went a-voyaging and was wrecked, and found
A lodgment at Meander's slimy mouth,
And—for he could not beg and would not starve—
Became schoolmaster ; and from him I learned
To con the whole theogony, and all
The works and days to boot. He said that none
Knew the true doctrine of the gods but those
Bred neath the slopes of Helicon, who quaffed
The lymph of Hippocrene.

THALES.

      Well, every bird
Does well to praise its nest ; Bœotia's bard
May teach Bœotians, and where wheaten loaves

Are few, men will esteem the barley cake.
But let me hear the lines.

CTESIBIAS.

Pontus begot the seer of the sea, the truth-speaking
    Nereus,
Eldest born of his brood, yclept the infallible old man,
Kind and gentle and good, and wearing in faithful
    remembrance
Sanctions of law, and counsels of right, and maxims
    of wisdom.
Then with the Earth he mingled in love, and mag-
    nanimous Phorcys
Leapt to the light, and great-limbed Thaumas, and
    beautiful Ceto,
Likewise Eurybia, wearing an adamant heart in her
    bosom.
Nereus mingled in love with Doris of beautiful tresses,
Daughter of Ocean the perfect stream ; and the vast
    unfertile
Deep soon swarmed with a brood of desireful maidens
    immortal,
Proto and Sao came forth, Eucrante and Amphitrite,
Glaucè, Eudora, Thetis, Eïonè, and Galenè,
Spio, Cymothoè, Halia lovely, and Thoë the rushing,
Meletè's grace, Eulimenè's pride, and the shining
    Agavè,
Doto, Pasithaè fair, and rosy-armed Euneicè ;
And with Dynamenè Erato came, and the tripping
    Pherousa,
Sistered with Protomedea, Actæa, and lovely Nisæa,

Doris, and Panopè fair, and beautiful Galatea.
  Shall I say more?

THALES.

                      O yes, tell out the roll!
The names do ring most sweetly in mine ear,
And march into the audience of my thought
With apt suggestion.   Names are pictures : he
Who stamped these sea-maids with their signatures
Was wise to paint with words.

CTESIBIAS.

Then was Hippothöè named, and Hipponoè rosy-
    armed, and
Fair Cymodocè, with fair Cymotolegè her sister,
And Amphitrite the delicate-ankled, in wake of
    the storm, who
Sails with a charm in her touch, and smooths the
    fret of the billow ;
Cymo likewise, and fair Halymedè, with beautiful
    crownlet,
Pontoporeia, and wreathed in smiles Glauconomè
    fair, and
Laomedeia, Leiagora, and Evagora ; likewise
Lysianassa, Polynomè, and Autonoè ; fairest
Then of the fair Euarnè appeared, all blameless in
    beauty,
Psamathè, twinkling with light, and beaming with
    godhead Menippe ;
Pronoè then, Eupompè, Themisto, Neso, Nemertes,

Youngest, but gifted the most with the wit of her
    father prophetic ;
These to Nereus were born, the blameless seer of
    the billow,
Fifty daughters well skilled in works of maidenly
    cunning !

THALES.

Bravo ! and fifty fifty times, and that
Increased by myriad fifties, were too small
To count the issue of that primal fount
Of pregnant virtue !   Tell me this, good friend,
How many children have you known from one
Milesian mother at a birth ?

CTESIBIAS.

                I knew
Porphyronymphe, Apollonius' wife,
The high priest of the Didymean god,
Who brought a threefold burden to the light ;
But they, I wis, were slight and flimsy brats,
Like plants that grow in pits where light is scant
And breezes come not : and at Colophon
Spermatothalpe, spouse of Polygen, shook
Four chickens from her lap : but they, alas !
Fell all, like green buds, by untimely frost
Nipped in the May.

THALES.

            And you may well perceive
The why of this mischance.   Man doth contain

Too little of the fluent fruitful force
In his strong-jointed frame, built up of earth
Firmly, for earthly uses; but the sea
Breeds monsters like itself, immense, with swinge
Of huge vitality, marvellous to send forth
An issue countless as the waves that flash
Their multitudinous twinkle to the orb
That rides the noon.   I knew a fisherman
Who vouched me once a single cod contains
Some hundred myriad codlings in its roe.

CTESIBIAS.

I well believe; but deem you Hesiod dreamt
Of mullet's spawn or sturgeon's, when he sang
Of Nereus' daughters?

THALES.

               Poets are inspired,
Like her who raves at Delphi, to cast forth
From the hot crater of their god-stirred thought
Types that outride the compass of their ken,
And hold far fates in germ.   Science doth limp
After, with sober count, and slow remark,
And nice inspective glance, to understand
What it might not create.   The birds whose flight
Gives wise forewarning of the mustered storm,
The snails that from their holes creep forth to catch
Far-scented rains, tell what they know not, stirred
By Nature's prophet power.   All prophecy
Comes without knowledge, being truth direct
Shot from the heart of the informing God,

Like rays from Helios, far before, and far
Beyond our bounded sense.   The typeful dream
Zeus to the poets gave to frame and paint,
For us to spell its lesson ; they of gods
And goddesses, in air, and earth, and sea,
Tritons and Nereids, a gamesome group,
Sing with sweet sport and reverential joy ;
We, whom you call the wise, though wise in this
Chiefly to know the limits of our ken,
We, in our sober reason's current phrase
The home-grown vesture of quotidian thought,
Teach from their text, with less of pictured lore,
But with a serious awe that inly chants
One hymn with them.   Our science doth not scant
Our piety.   O ! if Homer's self were here,
I could discourse to him of water's power,
Of Ocean, father of immortal gods,
And Tethys, primal mother, in a strain
That hearing even Homer might commend.

CTESIBIAS.

Are you a poet ?

THALES.

        No ; but poetry
Is writ in Nature's face, which any man
With open sense may read.   Great Homer's eye
Looked on the lives of men, I on the life
Of nature : and the perfect river, Ocean,
Whose broad untainted stream engirds the globe,
Speaks to my thought a truth, which, had he known,

He would have hymned in strains that dwarfed the
    praise
Of Ajax and Achilles.

CTESIBIAS.

         Does the belt
Of Ocean gird the globe in other sense
With you than with the poet?

THALES.

             He but spake
Of this broad briny humour, which our ships
Tread as a common pathway : I intend
The cosmic water's subtle-streaming force,
Interfluent, circumfluent, without
End or beginning, all in all complete.

CTESIBIAS.

I pray thee, dearest friend, let thy friend know
More of this doctrine.

THALES.

        Marvellous is the power
That binds the fluent floating stores within
The dewy-curtained chambers of the sky
To the broad expanse of the crisped flood
Which men call ocean, sea, and fiord, and mere,
A mystic cycle ; in whose start we see
Only the end of that which went before,
And from whose end a fresh young birth wells forth
In plenitude exhaustless.   From the sea
The breathèd vapour mounts ; no eye discerns

The floating bells of the transmuted wave
Which yet impregn each wandering wind that blows
With juicy potency, engreen the hills,
And from the harsh face of the wrinkled rock
Make the exuberant creeping pulp fling forth
A fringe of shining tongues.   Soaring through air
(Which is itself a sea of wider wave
More light and tenuous), the vaporous breath
Of the vast ocean masses into clouds,
And sails abroad, and kisses every peak
Snow-capped, and sleeps on every verdurous slope,
And through the green and long-withdrawing glen
Creeps, footed like a dream.   Then in the cool
Of dim grey-vested eve it weepeth down
In gracious drops its fine vivific dew,
And, pearling from high craggy cornice slips
Into the mossy cradle of a stream,
Around whose birth each star-eyed flowret peeps
With modest grace benign.   The baby flood
Unheard beneath the oozy greenness flows,
Then trickles with a tremulous pace through low
Invisible crannies, and in rivulets winds,
Till at some favouring turn it breach the brae
And bursts, a brook !   Then down the steep it trots
With fretful purl, then leaps and rushes on,
Impetuous, and in boisterous league made one
With sister floods, it swirls, and boils, and roars
In mighty cauldrons, and with sleepless din
Deafens the eagle's clamour.   Then at once,
Charmed into mildness, through long glades it glides
Where shepherds fence their folds to fend their flocks   .

From wintry drift; then rolls into the plain
Where stout-thewed farmers from its fertile slime
Reap fatness; and the frequent hamlet grows
That on its fulness feeds, and lives by draughts
Of its unfading freshness.   Then, to crown
The triumphs of the life-dispensing wave,
The city rises on its banks, with walls
And towers, and temples of the gods, and long,
High-tiered, palatial dwellings of proud man,
A wonder to behold; and great ships sail
Into the bosom of its queenly flood,
And mighty bays their broadened wings outstretch
To greet its coming.   Thus the blissful flow
Ends where it started, and when ended starts,
Unfainting, deathless, potent to perform
Perpetual harmonies.

CTESIBIAS.

       Now, I need not ask
Are you a poet?   Only take these words
And march them out in the majestic roll
Of—
*Sing, O goddess, the worth of Achilles, the god-like
    Pelides !*
And all Ionia will declare there are
Three most religious poets worthy found
To praise the gods, as gods are duly praised;
Homer, and Hesiod, and Milesian Thales !

THALES.

Did I not tell thee that all men are poets,
When they may yield their heart-strings as a lyre

Freely to Nature's touch? if we are blind
'Tis for with open eyes we blink; if fools
'Tis that we stand apart, and plant ourselves
In our most crude and impotent conceit
Too high for Nature's teaching.   We would teach
Before we know to learn, and thus we die
Mere fools as we were born.   But who comes here?

CTESIBIAS.

I think it is the page of the high priest
Who serves the gods, whose praise we hymned
     to-day,
Good Posidonius.

[Enter a page from Posidonius.]
PAGE.

Wise Thales and Ctesibias hear my hest;
The high priest greets your worthiness, and bids
You both partake the sacred feast to-night
In honour of the god.

THALES.

       Tell him, we come.
[Exit Page.]
Farewell, Ctesibias; the day declines;
I must be gone.   We with the worthy priest
Shall bravely sup.   Who sups with pontiffs lines
With gold his stomach.   This Posidonius fails
In nought of priestly duty; keeps a cask
Of special Samian for this pious tide.
All liquid things are best, and of this best
The best is wine well used, ill used the worst.

XENOPHANES.

Ξενοφάνης ἔλεγεν ὅτι ὁμοίως ἀσεβοῦσιν οἱ γενέσθαι φάσκοντες τοὺς θεοὺς τοῖς ἀποθανεῖν λέγουσιν· ἀμφοτέρως γὰρ συμβαίνει μὴ εἶναι τοὺς θεούς ποτε.   ARISTOTLE.

Ἓν τοῦτο καὶ πᾶν τὸν θεὸν ἔλεγεν ὁ Ξενοφάνης, καὶ ἀγένητον εἶναι.   SIMPLICIUS.

XENOPHANES.

PERSONS.

1. XENOPHANES, a Philosopher of Colophon.
2. DAMON, a Schoolmaster.
3. APOLLODORUS, a Priest of Apollo in Claros, near Colophon.

SCENE.—*A garden behind the schoolmaster's house in Colophon.*

[*Enter Damon and Xenophanes in conversation.*]

DAMON.

'Tis very strange !

XENOPHANES.

        All things are full of strangeness
To seeing eyes.   Say, where got you this stone ?

DAMON.

From a sailor boy, who being in Syracuse,
At the stone quarries, near the famous shrine
Of Temenite Apollo, picked it up.

XENOPHANES.

Have you other such ?

DAMON.

Yes, I have one from Paros,
And one from Melita.

XENOPHANES.

Pray show me them.

[*Damon goes back into the schoolhouse, and returns with
some minerals in his hand.*]

DAMON.

Here they are.

XENOPHANES.

[*After looking at them minutely.*]

These are the types of fishes.

DAMON.

This other has no type, but it is dotted
All through with pinkish pebbles, round as peas,
And little hollows like the airy bells
That rise through stagnant pools in heat of noon.

XENOPHANES.

Whence came this stone?

DAMON.

From Thera.

XENOPHANES.

I have seen
Such like from many quarters. They are all
Children of fire, and in huge cauldron born
Beneath the seething sea.

DAMON.
> Fire 'neath the sea !

XENOPHANES.

Nay marvel not ! that vine-enwreathèd rock,
Stout Doric root, whence fair Cyrene sprang,
Was once a molten slag, a glowing crust,
Shot from the fervent tumult of the deep
By central fire, then by corrosive tooth
Of wasting weather pounded.   In this wise
Big worlds were brewed, and genial beds were
    spread
For verdurous wealth to grow.   These stony types
Of finny creatures mailed with glancing scales
Sprang from the primal fire.

DAMON.
> How mean you that ?

XENOPHANES.

These fishes in the fish-abounding sea
Were bred, which now upon the topmost ridge
Of long-stretched hills the wondering quarryman
With clinking hammer from dark bed redeems
Into the stare of day.   When a strong blast
Flung them by thousands huddled on a beach,
They gasped and died, and in much mud enswathed
For myriad years their bony framework lay,
Paving the unplumbed deep, whence suddenly
The insurrection of long-prisoned flame
Heaved them in giant sport, and made them thrones
For gods to sit on.

G

DAMON.

       This is wondrous strange !

XENOPHANES.

The story of the world, as in a book,
Lies scriptured in the rocks.   If men had eyes,
In a poor pebble scraped from shelvy shore
They might read more than now they dare to guess
With all their dreamings.

DAMON.

                I must teach my scholars
To read this book.

XENOPHANES.

            Much better so than what
You teach them now : lewd tales of shameless gods,
That mutilate their sires, and eat their sons,
Cozen and cog, and lie, and falsely swear,
And fill the lucid azure halls serene
With brawls and bickering, ribaldry, and lust :
I marvel that on earth we live no worse,
Having such faulty patterns in the sky.

DAMON.

You judge not evenly.   Homer names the gods
Givers of good, friends of the friendless poor,
Stay of the feeble, refuge of the stray,
Of right the arbiters, the foes of wrong,
And stern avengers of a perjured tongue.

XENOPHANES.

Homer is bad and good, bitter and sweet,
But his vice harms more than his virtue heals.
When on one tree both fruit and poison grow
He's a wise child who knows to eat and live.
Hold forth to men in your right hand the truth,
And in your left a flattering lie, they'll take
The left unasked, and leave the right to beg.

DAMON.

I once did praise your wisdom, scarcely now,
Hearing you thus blaspheme the wisest bard.
If there are spots in Helios' face, and flecks
In the clear round of the night-wandering moon,
These are but specks which wiser who ignores
Than who observes.   The gods are shining types
Each of his own perfection, all together
Lords of a perfect Universe.   Complete
In golden beauty Aphrodite stands,
Here in queenly state, in manly grace
Apollo, Hermes in bright bloom of youth ;
But wisdom, sovran virtue, chiefly dwells
With Zeus, the ægis-bearer, and the maid
Who only of the Olympian's high compeers
Launches his thunder, and his counsel knows,
Flashing-eyed Pallas, by whose thought inspired
Each Jove-born hero, first in peace and war
Controls the council, rides the battle-field,
Fights with the gods, and conquers all but fate.
'Tis but this morn when to my eager imps
I read the first song of the tale of Troy ;

You know it well, where Agamemnon, wroth
With the Greek host for taking back the maid,
Meed of his prowess, gave his men command
To reave, for reparation of his wrong,
The fair Brisëis of the blooming cheeks,
Achilles' rightful prize ; whereat the chief,
His big heart boiling 'neath his shaggy breast,
Blazed up in wrath, and flung in bitter spite
Sharp stinging words against the Jove-born king.
Then on the moment's inconsiderate spur
He grasped his sword to draw; when lo! from Heaven
The daughter of high-counselling Jove shot down
And stood behind, and seized his yellow hair,
And with the power flashed from her flaming eyes
Charmed down the hot sedition of his blood
Into most loyal meekness.　Even so
In every song the wisest bard sets forth
Bright types of wisdom pictured to the eye
Through changeful gloom and gleam of war, which gain
A firmer hold of sense-bound men than all
The laws of Solon, or the awful lore
Of Orphic mystagogues.

XENOPHANES.

　　　　　　I have listened well ;
Have you aught else to say?

DAMON.

　　　　　　Ay, if I chose
To ape the rhapsodists, who in solemn feasts

From hour to hour in choicest sequence chaunt
The tale of Troy divine.   It is a song
Which doth unroll the counsel of high Jove,
In one grand show of rapid shifting scenes,
As when a fleet strong-winded racer runs,
Nor bates his pace from starting point to goal,
And, if he stumbles once, replants his foot
More firmly for the fall

XENOPHANES.

                    Some men get drunk
With wine, and say they worship Dionysus;
You're drunk with Homer, and not fit to hear
Sober reply from me.

DAMON.

Speak on.

XENOPHANES.

                              I too
Will sketch a picture from the bard.   You know
The song where Paris and king Menelaus
Do battle, making each his life a gauge
For the issue of the war.   A truce was sworn,
And hoary Priam came from Pergamus
With lambs for sacrifice, and blood was poured,
And Agamemnon lifted holy hands
Before the host, and looked to heaven, and prayed,
And on his head who broke the oath invoked
A fearful curse; and thus the paction ran;
If Alexander, son of Priam, slay

The fair-haired Menelaus in the fight,
The lovely Helen, and all her costly stores
Shall he possess, and in the dark-hulled ships
The Greeks steer home.   But if the righteous Jove
Give glory to the fair-haired Menelaus,
Then Helen, by her rightful lord resumed,
Shall sail to Greece, and the Greek men shall pay
A fine to Troy, that in the years to come
Each wanton guest may fear to break the laws
Of hospitable Jove.   You know the rest.

DAMON.

Go on.

XENOPHANES.

    The king was conqueror, and the prince
Slunk from the mortal peril of the fight
Wrapt in a mist of refuge, by device
Of golden Aphrodite.   Helen now
Was forfeit to the Greeks, and Peace held forth
Her liberal arms to greet returning love,
When lo ! in heaven the full-eyed spouse of Zeus,
Grudgeful that Troy no bloodier bane should brook
Than the pricked skin of princely tenderling,
With Jove's assenting nod sent Pallas down
Into the breast of Pandarus to breathe
The perjured purpose.   He, by her inspired,
Shot from his Lycian bow the lawless bolt
That drew the righteous judgment of the Fates
On traitor Troy.   Is this a picture fair
For men to see, and learn to hate a lie ?

And with such primer in his hand, will you
Dare birch a boy who weaves a cunning tale
To cheat the master or befriend a chum?
Small wonder the barbarian oft-times rates
The Greek for falsehood; he may falsely swear
With Pallas for his voucher.   How came this,
That the wise singer makes his gods do deeds
That many a human knave would blush to own?

DAMON.

I know not; there are learned men who know
To smooth the blur; but for my needful use
I am content to think not Homer's self,
But some unskilful wandering spouter wove
This patch into the purple.

XENOPHANES.

            You are honest;
At least you choose not, with far-laboured shifts
Of forged conceit, to prove that black is white,
And rough is smooth, and every crooked straight,
As I have known some deft expounders do,
Who make the bard a peg on which to hang
Their own pet fancies.   But this suits not me,
Nor with my nail to scratch a scale or two,
And say I've healed the leprosy.   So you
Stick to your text, and I will stand by mine;
While you admire the paint, I cannot choose
But fear the poison.   I must still believe
Homer has gods that cheat poor trustful men,
As Hesiod men that cheat all-knowing gods.

If idiots maunder wisdom, Homer sings
Sublime theology; if asses bray
Divinest melody, the Smyrnean bard
Shall teach my children what a pious Greek
Should think of Zeus.   But who comes here?

DAMON.
                      I think
It is the priest from Clarus, our good friend
Apollodorus.

XENOPHANES.
            He's no friend of mine.

DAMON.
How so?   Whose fault is that?   He is a man
That hath more craft in making friends than foes:
Men score him high in Asia.

XENOPHANES.
                For a priest
He hath all priestly virtues.

DAMON.
                What are these?

XENOPHANES.
He hath a solemn look, a stately air,
And a grave face to welcome mummery,
And for the need a gracious smile put on,
Which wins weak women and women-hearted men.

In all traditions of the holy shrine
He is a walking record, and in all
The doctrines of its hoar theology
Infallible.   He is an honest hater,
And when he wounds a foe delights to leave
A sting behind ; and, when he loves a man,
Prays Jove to bless him for the coat he wears
More than the heart that beats beneath the coat.
He is a shepherd, all whose sheep must bear
His brand ; and who displays it not must stand
Disowned outside the shelter of his fold,
And rot i' the rain.   But soft !—he comes !

[Enter Apollodorus.]

APOLLODORUS.

         All hail !

DAMON.

Long live the high priest of the radiant god !
What cast of luck hath brought thee here to-day?

APOLLODORUS.

There is a festal sacrifice to-morrow
At Clarus to the god.   We crave your presence,
Dear Damon, at the rite ; and, for your friend,
This son of Dexias, whom I partly know,
If he will share our worship, we with him
Will share the friendly board.

XENOPHANES.

        I'd rather not.

APOLLODORUS.

For why?

XENOPHANES.

My reasons love their home,—my breast.

APOLLODORUS.

If they are reasons kin to holy light,
They'll peep out from the windows of the soul
Gladly, to greet the day.

XENOPHANES.

    Nay, do not deem
I court the darkness; but my words are not
A coin to serve all needs, a seed to spread
On every soil; I would not give sharp tools
To children; nor with noon-day light invade
The night-bird's nest.

APOLLODORUS.

    The god I serve doth love
The sharp-eyed hawk.

XENOPHANES.

    Hear me; if you have eyes
That love the light, and will not blink at truth
Like the great mob of men, nor overbear
With saucy spleen the nay that meets your yea,
I'll make you freeman of my thought, and you
May use it to your humour. If your faith
Were mine, my faith would follow where you lead;

But having kindled mine own torch from fire
Not stolen from thee or any man, I walk
Where I find ways, and where I find a shrine
Of reasonable worship, worship there.

APOLLODORUS.

The gods I worship are the gods of Greece.

XENOPHANES.

The gods you worship are no gods at all.

APOLLODORUS.

Ha! say'st thou so?   I've long suspected this;
And more—the general voice impeaches you
Of most unseasoned speech; but now mine ears
Avouch a worse offence; you are declared
An atheist, and you glory in your shame.

XENOPHANES.

I am no atheist; I did deny
Your gods; the one true God I humbly own.

APOLLODORUS.

What God? what one? there is no one but Zeus,
Father of gods and men, Apollo's father.

XENOPHENES.

God nor begets nor is begotten.   You
What tender seedlings show and bursting buds
In chain of generation, link from link,
To that great Cause transfer, which to all growth

Is seed and soil in one.   You should be wiser.
Some show the birthplace of your gods, and some
The sepulchre of Zeus, and both make clear
They are no gods whose nature not transcends
The limits which all finite life confine,
Growth and decay.   A cause may not be born.
Your Homer's golden chain hath many links,
But the last link from supreme Jove depends,
To his firm footstool bound.   This Jove I own;
Sole source of all, causer and caused in one,
Not him in Ida born and sepulchred.

APOLLODORUS.

Thou doest well to own the supreme Zeus;
And with wise reverence too dost well withhold
A gaping ear from every pious tale
Of poet's fancy bred, or peasant's dream.
But their true shapes, their names and titles, all
By hoar tradition's signet vouched, command
Our willing credence.   What wise Homer sings
We own; but, for the Cretan, he doth bear
Repute of lies; with Crete let lies remain.
Art thou more wise than Homer?

XENOPHANES.

                   In some things
A carpenter is wiser.   Homer sings
The wain he could not make.

APOLLODORUS.

                  What things know you
That Homer knew not?

XENOPHANES.

      I have thought and proved
The nature of the gods.

APOLLODORUS.

       That Homer knew
And Hesiod. Every pious Greek receives
The names and natures of the gods from them.

XENOPHANES.

I blame not Homer. What he knew he sung
With blossomy phrase and with full-breasted glee
To laud his heroes. Of the gods he knew
Just what he heard, the common talk of men,
Which he had gleaned, as lightly as a girl
Wandering at thoughtless ease in leafy spring
Plucks from the grassy knoll a yellow flower,
And sets it in her bosom. Homer knew
That Zeus was strong above all strength of men,
And nothing more.

APOLLODORUS.

    Strong, and in counsel wise.

XENOPHANES.

So be it ; but his gods are men, and think
With human thoughts, and work with human hands,
And fret, and fume, and fuss, and make a pother
Like brabbling hucksters. Man is ever noisy.
Small labour makes him sweat, and then he struts

In grand procession for his paltry deed,
And compensates by breadth of flaunting show
For lack of substance.   When he cracks a shell,
He blows a trumpet; and no end of drums
Into a mimic thunder swells his praise.
But Zeus is quiet as a sleeping child,
Then when he most achieves, as frailest stalk
With noiseless increase shoots from hour to hour
Into the stature of high-tufted trees;
And all this vasty globose Universe
From the unmoved all-moving Mind depends,
As lightly as a bell-flower in the breeze
Hangs from the stalk.   Men to the gods are like
As workman's work is to the workman's wit,
Not otherwise.   And yet all types must limp
Long leagues behind the truth, when of the gods
We lisp with baby lips.   The demiurge
Who sphered the world is to the world much more
Than wisest workman to his work.   All eye,
All ear, and all intelligence, not so
As men know knoweth he, but knowing makes,
And all his thoughts are deeds.   The sculptor shapes
The marble to his wish, a thing extern;
Jove is both shaping power and shapen thing,
Sculptor and marble, thought and deed in one.

APOLLODORUS.

This is most dreamy talk—a god who is
Himself, and something else, and everything!
You take the human body from the god,
And leave behind what no man comprehends,—

A name, a sound, unknown, unknowable,
One and yet many, a something and a nothing.
This thing you worship; and for such grey mist
Greece must resign her fairest heritage—
Gods whose familiar face she knows and fears
As children fear a father whom they love!

XENOPHANES.

You worship your own selves, and make your gods
A monstered self.   As one who stands sublime
Sometime on mist-wreathed mountain-top beholds
His shadowed self colossal in the clouds,
And deems that phantom form a Titan, so
Great Zeus must take his shape and quality
From man's reflection.   If your nose be flat,
Woolly your hair, and big your hanging lip,
Roasted your skin, and by the tyrannous sun
Burnt black as blasted Typhon, Jove, forsooth,
Must gloom like you, and only Ethiop men
Be limners to the Thunderer!   In the North
The roving Scythian, with his carrot curls
And flaring cattish eyes, must lend his mould
To heaven's high lord; and so we make our gods
In our own likeness, and we cringe the knee
Before the magnified deformity
Of our poor human selves!   'Tis well that sheep,
Oxen, and asses, and the grunting kind,
The slow earth-crawling toad, the slimy worm,
And all the vermin of the festering pool,
Have got no hands to mould the clay withal,
Else would they knead out gods, and people heaven

With crawling, shambling, braying, bellowing Joves,
A sight to blot the stars out !   So 't must be
When man will make his creeping thought the
        measure
Of what as far outwings our proudest flight
As Homer's song a gnat's.   The lichen crust
That with its juiceless patches spots the crag
Is, to yon reach of rosy oleander
That flames the watered glade with pride of bloom,
More like than we to Jove.

APOLLODORUS.

                    He blames the gods
Who cheapens their most godlike creature, Man.

XENOPHANES.

The gods do laugh to see their creature man
Ween that he knows what passes men to know.

APOLLODORUS.

We know the sun, being warmed by his heat ; the
        gods
By their good gifts to men : the foodful corn
Comes from Demeter, and the gladdening grape
From Dionysus ; wisdom from wise Jove.

XENOPHANES.

The gods, you say, taught men to cleave the clod,
And strew the genial seed ; and Semelè's son
Trod Earth in triumph, making rocks to blaze,
With the vine's purple grace—mere idle tales !

For thus you make the gods bad schoolmasters,
As knowing not that scholars are best taught,
When taught to teach themselves.   Who learns to
          swim,
Unschooled in wavy water?   Who to think
Except by use of thinking?   What a man
With shaping thought and hand may for himself
No god will for him.   Human wit is slow,
Stumbling nine times for one firm footing gained,
But still made strong by striving, and sharp-eyed
To find the light through darkness and distress
By time and toil, and Reason's happy guess.

Apollodorus.

This is the fruit your atheist wisdom bears!
The gods do nothing; and what man achieves
He does by stumbling, blundering into light
Out of mere blindness; if this text be true
Something may come from nothing, and all things
From anything; our sires were moles; and we
May wake some day and find a monkey's whelp
Give laws from Solon's chair!

Xenophanes.

                    You talk of gods
Much too familiar for my reach, as if
Yourself had been arch-chancellor to Zeus
When first the stars peeped forth.   I rather choose
To spare my words, than by unlicensed guess
To fool the truth.   To father Jove I bend
The reverent knee; with brother man I talk;

With him I weep, with him I toil, with him
I breast the storm of life, to sink or swim.
The glory of Olympus makes me blind;
Earth is my home, and earthly is my task,
To live a man with men, and nobly strive
To make bad good, and crown the good with
       best;
A task more glorious than with fervid wheel
To whirl the Elean dust, outstrip the wind
With emulous-flying feet, or make the cheeks
Of stout antagonists crackle 'neath the hail
Of blows from iron fist.   My wisdom loves
Within their human bounds to lead mankind
To reason, and, to reason's pointing true,
To shun the evil, and the good pursue.

APOLLODORUS.

You are fair preachers; but without the gods
And the pure faith breathed into human breasts
In primal times when gods did walk with men,
Your wisdom is a tree that hangs i' the air
Rootless.   Our true Hellenic Zeus, you say
You cannot own; Olympus strikes you blind.
Where will you end? and in what mighty void
Of Nothingness shall storm-tost mortals cast
Their anchor?   Have you any creed at all?
If not in Jove, say then do you believe
In Pluto and in Hades, the dim home
Of souls disbodied, in Elysian fields,
The blissful islands, and black Tartarus,
Den of the damned?

XENOPHANES.

These things I'll know when I
Return to earth and water, whence I came.
Or here or there, by God's high gauge my soul
Is safe, if by the one appointed path
I seek salvation.

APOLLODORUS.

What path is that?

XENOPHANES.

A priest
Should know this better than the wisest man.
What boots your worship, and your sacrifice,
Your sprinkled bloods, lustrations, ceremonies,
Well-parted livers, fitly spiring flames,
Omens and oracles, amulets and charms,
Your fumigations, festal pomps, and all
The drowsy tale of mumbled litanies,
If how to please the gods the one sure path
Your wit miscounts.

APOLLODORUS.

Not so ; we please them well,
Even by that service which your words bemock.

XENOPHANES.

Alas, poor priest ! if this be all you know,
Greece must owe thanks to Thales and myself,
And wise Pythagoras, who with modest doubt
Fill up the gaps with which your doctrines gape.

And for your service, which with gay festoons
Ye decorate to hide its hollowness,
As men do strew the dead man's bed with flowers
To mask death's ugliness, it never raised
From ground the stumbling foot of one that groped
For truth, or chased the dark from clouded brain.
Your prayers do vex the gates of heaven for what
Jove gave you eyes to see and hands to find.
You plant false trophies where no fight was won,
And wail where wailing proves that grief is mad;
For, if the god you serve immortal be
Why weep for him? if mortal, why adore?

APOLLODORUS.

I've born the unchastened onslaught of your tongue
Too long; a fool is he who treats with fools.
'T is time that Colophon should know what snake
She nurses in her bosom. To blaspheme
The public gods, and by unsanctioned will
Set forth strange gods, confounding sacred wont
Is capital by law. Farewell, good Damon!
The glorious god shall greet my pious friend,
A welcome guest to-morrow.

DAMON.

                 Ay! without fail.

[Exit Apollodorus.]

He's gone. And you, Xenophanes, have walked
Into a nest of wasps with open eyes.
Straightway he'll go and mightily infect

The city with himself, till every breast
Bristle with bans against your impious head ;
And then, if one can rest in peace beside
A buzzy army of mosquitoes, you
May brook sweet sleep in Colophon.

XENOPHANES.
                                      You are right.
I was too hasty; 'tis an evil humour
Sown in my blood; a boyish bold delight
To pluck full-robed pretension by the beard,
And tear the mask from reputable lies.

DAMON.
Grant they be lies, they sit enthroned in hearts
Of thousands, and may reck no breath from thee ;
Not wise is he who wisely talks to fools,
And lends to foes a spear to pierce his skin.
For me, I own the gods, nor seem to find
Your new religion wiser than the creed
That Homer sings, and general Greece receives ;
But I respect your doubts, and from your tongue
Crave honour for my faith.   But for this priest
He's like a dog, to whom he loves most fond,
But whom he hates he bites.   Yourself have drawn
The lightning from the cloud that smites your head.
What's marred may not be mended; you must leave
This country for a time.

XENOPHANES.
                                      I'd liefer live
Upon the rim of Aetna's burning bowl

Than herd with men, with whom to draw free breath
Is sin, who hold free thought in freeman's breast
For treason and rebellion.

DAMON.

      All approve
That he is zealous for the gods.   A priest
Is by his office sworn to gag the mouths
That fling defiance on his country's creed.

XENOPHANES.

If I could fancy, as some sages teach,
That souls of men once walked in brutish case,
I'd say this fellow lived an owl, a bat,
Blindworm, or mole, or any lightless thing.
As when you lift an old grey stone, the grubs
Run troubled from the broad-invading beam
And healthful breeze, so from the sun of truth
And sifting ventilation of discourse
These bigots flee.

DAMON.

     It grieves me sore to think
You are not safe in Colophon.   I lose
A wise instructor, and a dear-loved friend.

XENOPHANES.

'Tis no new purpose in me, dearest Damon,
To leave the Lydian land, tho' this hot priest,
Or my hot stomach, spurs my will to take
The jump of action.   I am scarcely more

With this loose people pleased than with their priest.
If Homer's gods are scant so good as men,
At least his men are men; but now the Greek
Here in the East hath caught the Eastern taint,
And crisps his hair with gold, and sweeps the street
With purple, spreading, like a lady's kerchief,
Sweet perfumes round, and all the day they creak
Their shoes upon the well-paved agora,
And ask what news; and all the night they drink.
I'll wend me Westward.   What the pomp of wealth
And the far-reaching arm of power commands
Let Asia boast; what the adventurous thought
May scheme, and the slow-gathering hand can store
With careful harvest of long sweatful years
Is the West's heritage; and, if the gods are kind,
I'll have my part in't.

DAMON.

Would you might remain!

XENOPHANES.

It cannot be; yourself have spoke my doom.
Though every pine on high Galesus' brow,
And every ripple in cool Halè's brook,
Cried out, *Xenophanes, stay here and love us!*
I must be gone.

DAMON.

When a few years have run,
And smoothed the memory of this crude offence,
You will return.   Your wisdom being known
With proof of years will make them seek the wise.

XENOPHANES.

It needs the wise to seek the wise ; they'll call
Xenophanes back when schoolboys sigh for books,
Slaves carry crowns, priests sit at Wisdom's feet,
And women languish for philosophy.
But when I'm dead and lost to human quest,
With my name blazed for some not worthless deed
In the far West, as with the gods may chance,
Belike they'll fetch my dust, and gild my bones,
And show my monument for an obolus
To gaping loungers.

DAMON.

    You are sharp of speech.

XENOPHANES.

I'll take a vow of silence for a year!
Meanwhile farewell ; meet me at Notium,
Where Plution, my friend, with freighted keel,
Waits bound for Syracuse.   If the wind hold fair,
We'll sail to-morrow.   Let me see you there
Once more before I go.

DAMON.

    The gods be with you !

[Exeunt.]

HERACLITUS

Ἐκ πυρὸς τὰ πάντα συνεστάναι, καὶ εἰς τοῦτο ἀναλύεσθαι· πάντα δὲ γίγνεσθαι κατ' εἰμαρμένην, καὶ διὰ τῆς ἐναντιοτροπῆς ἡρμόσθαι τὰ πάντα.   DIOGENES LAERTIUS.

εἰμαρμένην λόγον ἐκ τῆς ἐναντιοδρομίας δημιουργὸν τῶν ὄντων.   STOBAEUS.

HERACLITUS.

PERSONS.

1. HERACLITUS, Son of BLYSON, an Ephesian.
2. AENESIDEMUS, a Priest of Diana of the Ephesians, in
   Ephesus.

SCENE.—*The country near Ephesus.   In the back-ground the
Temple of Diana of the Ephesians.   In the middle distance a
winding road.   In the foreground Heraclitus is discovered sitting
on the banks of a brook, playing at astragals with a boy.*

BOY.

I'm tired with playing.

HERACLITUS.

     So am I, but you
Should not be so.

BOY.

    I'm tired; 'tis very hot.
I wish I had a broad-brimmed hat like yours.

HERACLITUS.

You're hot with victory; five times you have caught
All the five pebbles on the back o' your hand.

BOY.

My mother taught me in the rainy weather
Last Maimacterion.

HERACLITUS.

You beat me hollow.

BOY.

'Tis a girl's game, and little praise for me.
When skies are foul and meads are moist, it can
Beguile an hour; but when the Titan sun
Rides forth in strength, and freshening breezes blow,
I seek a sport that draws the muscles tight,
And leave this to my sisters.

HERACLITUS.

You're a brave boy;
You'll be an admiral some day, no doubt,
And sweep the seas with triumph.

BOY.

You are wise;
Do answer me a question.

HERACLITUS.

If I can.

BOY.

They say that you know all things.

HERACLITUS.

> Who are *they?*

BOY.

The people; everybody; the high priest.

HERACLITUS.

Well, well, a silver drachm or two, no doubt,
Of virgin knowledge, native from my mine,
Will stamp me rich in their conceit, whose soil
Is packed with rubbish.   What I know I know,
And what I guess I guess, and where I find
Place for my foot I plant it firmly there.

BOY.

Why does the sun not burn all night?

HERACLITUS.

> A lamp

Can burn no longer than the wick supplies
The needful oil.   The sun is blazing mist
Fed by the vaporous issues of the sea,
Which, while the vapours last, burns on, then dies.

BOY.

Then every day a new sun shines on Earth.   

HERACLITUS.

Of course; as every spring new Oleanders
Flush the grey gorge.   All things are full of change,
Yet changing in a changeless round, the same.

BOY.

Why does the Moon not give both heat and light,
Like her strong brother?

HERACLITUS.

                She is nearer placed
To this gross Earth, and being grossly fed
With earthly humours, gives less heavenly light.
The hottest virtue loftiest mounts, and thence
In streams of quivering radiation shoots
Life through the vast of things.

BOY.

                'Tis passing strange.

[A sound of flutes and tambours is heard. A procession of singing boys and girls, with a long accompaniment of peasants and citizens, passes along the road in the middle distance. They are followed by the image of Diana of the Ephesians, drawn in a sacred car, preceded by the high priest. As the procession moves on, the following hymn is sung:]

Hail to the Queen of the vasty creation,
Hail to the fountain of joy and of life,
The goddess that loves the Ionian nation,
The maker of peace, and the soother of strife!
    Hail to the virtue with various names,
    Whom country from country in rivalry claims!
    We worship Thee, worshipful Virgin and Mother.
    Thou art the Queen, and we know of none other;
    Jove is thy sire, and the Sun is thy brother,
        Holy Artemis, mighty mother!

Hail to the mother of life many breasted;
Its food from the mother each creature receives,
The eagle that soars o'er the peaks snowy-crested,
The swallow that flits 'neath the lowliest eaves.
Hail to the virtue, etc.

Hail to the goddess that rideth the lion,
The tamer of tigers, the bridler of bears!
The leopard kneels down when her chariot is nighing,
The hind hath no fear when in triumph she fares.
Hail to the virtue, etc.

She maketh the stream of the sacred Cayster
With fruitfullest slime to impregnate the mould;
Jove rains, and Apollo smiles down on his sister,
And flushes the meadow with vegetive gold.
Hail to the virtue, etc.

Her's is the glory the summer is heir to,
The green-mantled glen, and the fresh-tufted tree;
She touches the herbs, and with magical virtue
They brew the sweet juice for the flower-working bee!
Hail to the virtue, etc.

Her's is the strength of the proud rising palace,
She wears on her head a tiara of towers;
Who live by her rivers, and drink from her chalice,
Grow rich by the bounty that Artemis showers.
Hail to the virtue, etc.

Praise ye the queen of the vasty creation
Praise her with tabor, with fife, and with flute!

Praise her with pæans of high inspiration,
And for ever be dumb who to-day shall be mute !

[The music passes.]

BOY.

I can no longer stay : I must be off
And join the troop.

HERACLITUS.

Zeus bless thee, gallant boy !

[The boy runs off after the procession.]

HERACLITUS.

[Putting his feet into the brook, and looking on the water.]
The same, and not the same ; how wonderful !
Here and not here ; a YES, and yet a No ;
An ever-changing play of contradiction ;
A thing that is, and by that being still
Ceases to be ; such thing am I, and all
The things I see.   This thread of wimpling water,
In which I bathe my feet, is fled and lost
To me for ever, even while I touch it.
    Nor man, nor god, into the self-same flood
Can enter twice.   There is no thing that stands
Self-based, self-strung, self-cased, that in the face
Of the still-changing universe can say
I am myself, and to myself belong,
With proper lordship separate and apart.
The stoutest things are but the fleeting foot-marks
Of the great, hidden, silent-marching Power,

Whose steps are being, and whose walk is life.
As in the garden creeping herbs put forth
Long sprawling arms far from their parent root,
Which arms strike out new roots, from which new plants
    plants
Seek separate nurture, bearing many now
Which late were one, and still are one by grace
Of common pedigree, and common sap,
And common soil, from which they draw their
    life ;
So all things in the all are one and many ;
Many, like germs upon a sprawling stem,
One in the stem to which the germs belong ;
All living, and of one great life the parts,
Parts which from infinite to Infinite
Exist by growing, and by growing die.
Yet Death is but new start of life, and life
New food for death.   There is nor death nor life,
In separate quality and in act ; but both
Are nicely mingled, flowing each through each,
Threads of one web.   No single thing exists : +
As when we mix a bowl of Kykëon,
The draught well stirred doth make a wambling
    whole,
Which is nor wine nor honey, and yet both.
There is no individual drop can stand ✗
And say, I am myself, or wine or honey ;
But every drop by others interflowed
Makes all a something which no part can be ; ✗
So is the world a complex web, where thread
Still crosses thread, an interthreaded maze,

Where every thread with shifting virtue thrills
Now up, now down; the same, and not the same.

[*He continues for some time looking into the water,
muttering to himself*]

The same, and not the same, how wonderful !
All things roll in the mighty whole,
Like the flow of a sleepless river,
Ever the same, and never the same,
Swirling on for ever !

[*Enter Aenesidemus from behind.*]

AENESIDEMUS.

Ho, my good friend !

[*Patting Heraclitus on the shoulder.*]

HERACLITUS.

What ass is here that brays through heavenly hymns ?

AENESIDEMUS.

The hymns are ended ; the procession closed.

HERACLITUS.

Ha ! is it you, all-reverend friend ? I meant
The hymn a god was harping in my soul ;
But may the many-breasted Queen forgive
My harsh address ; your coming found me rapt
In meditation.

AENESIDEMUS.

You are wont to brood ;
But on this festive day amid the throng

Of worshippers by holy fervour fired,
The friends of Heraclitus sought in vain
The wisest man in Ephesus.

HERACLITUS.

        That matters not ;
Here too are gods no less than in the temple ;
The pomp of worship fills the gaping eye,
The gaping ear luxuriates in the swell
Of rival choirs ; but these feed not the soul,
Which rather, by the rush of dinsome shows
Dumfounded and distraught, retreats and finds
Converse with gods in awful solitude.

AENESIDEMUS.

The living world is full of sounds and shows.
But tell me ; well thou know'st I love thee, much
Desire that all should love thee, even as I ;
Therefore thine honest fame in Ephesus
I would build up. There goes a common bruit
That Heraclitus doth deny the gods
Whom general Asia worships. I have heard
Thee called an atheist, and have wept for thee.

HERACLITUS.

Weep rather for the fools that call me so ;
All things are full of gods, whom who not sees
Is blind at noonday.

AENESIDEMUS.

      I knew thou wert too wise
To think with those who, living in a palace

Fair and well-builded, with ungracious lips
Disown the builder.   But there are many gods,
Even as thou say'st, and not from all men all
Claim equal reverence.   In Ephesus
We worship Artemis.

HERACLITUS.

                The first of gods,
The fount of Godhead to all gods is Zeus.

AENESIDEMUS.

In this all Ephesus doth chime with thee.

HERACLITUS.

If so, I with myself would disagree.

AENESIDEMUS.

How? is thy Jove not ours? who then is Zeus?

HERACLITUS.

Zeus is what many dream and few discern.

AENESIDEMUS.

Speak plainly.   If thou knowest more than others,
I would be taught.

HERACLITUS.

                To my thought Jove is FIRE.

AENESIDEMUS.

Nay; 'tis Hephaestus lords the plastic Flame.

HERACLITUS.

He's but the hand that works; the head is Jove;
Even as Apollo from the Father's fount
Wells oracles to men.   There is no god
Owns force or function, or wields shaping power
Divorced from Jove.

AENESIDEMUS.

    Here also I avouch
Thee orthodox in what all Greeks believe;
Yet to make Zeus the all-devouring might
Of Fire hath strangeness to Ionian ears.

HERACLITUS.

Strangeness, of course; for Truth is ever strange
To fools; and the unreasoning multitude
Clamours at Reason as a monstrous thing
Like beggars' curs that bay with vicious bark
At each well-vested traveller, as who own
Only their master's rags.   But, my good friend,
Be wiser thou, not numbered with the mob
Who dream fond dreams, and dream their dream-
  ing true.
Fire is in Nature the divinest Power
All-permeant, all-plastic, all-instinct
With vitalising force.

AENESIDEMUS.

    Somewhat I catch
Thy meaning, but would gladly hear thee more.

HERACLITUS.

Know then this earth on which we stoutly tread
Is but a thin crust and a hardened slag,
Beneath the which strong fiery currents flow
Through realms of smoky vent and caverned flues ;
And with this nether fire the fire sublime
Holds converse in the strong far-travelling sun,
Essence of light and heat, begotten high
In the pure ether, which with flaming belt
Enspheres the world, mother of countless stars ;
These fires——

AENESIDEMUS.

All men the Empyrean know,
Prankt with the pomp of ever-twinkling lamps,
Which light the gods upon their path sublime,
Thick as with isle and islet quaintly sown
Blossoms the broad Aegean ; but the stream
Of subterranean fire whereof thou speakest
I know not, nor have heard.

HERACLITUS.

Thou knowest more
Than thou dost deem.   Thy knowledge is a babe
Conceived in darkness, born to find the light.
Hast heard of the Chimaera ?

AENESIDEMUS.

Who has not ?

HERACLITUS.

Well, in Cilicia even now the soil
Spirts jets of flame from that dire monster's throat.

AENESIDEMUS.

Say'st thou so, truly?

HERACLITUS.

      What I say I saw
Even with these eyes; and furthermore, have seen
In divers parts hot fountains, bubbling wells,
And hills that steamed with sulphur, all avouching
The hidden working of the travelling fire
That underscoops the earth.

AENESIDEMUS.

      I do bethink me,
Once in my youth with wondering eyes I saw
A mountain spitting fire.

HERACLITUS.

     Fair hap was yours;
Where saw you this?

AENESIDEMUS.

     I was a little boy,
Some fifty years are flown, when from the East
A fair Phœnician galley bravely rode
Into our harbour, westward bound, in quest
Of tin in far Britannia, where it grows

Native with copper.　My father, as you know,
Was no home-bird bog-trotter of the shop,
That loved to weigh the obols safely won,
And count them in the tiller day by day,
With grateful tinkle to a thrifty ear,
But rather chose, as hunters track their game,
By the bold venture and the perilous chance
To gather gold.　So with these trading men
He made a common purse; and—for my mother,
Dear soul, was gone to the dim shades below—
He took me with him, and in Trinacria, where
We anchored for sweet water, I beheld
A flaming mountain.

HERACLITUS.

Aetna was its name?

AENESIDEMUS.

Even so.

HERACLITUS.

'Tis bruited over all the East;
But tell me how it showed?

AENESIDEMUS.

The time I well remember.　It was June;
The day was hot, and all the hills around
Were swathed in sickly white, and ominous clouds,
Massive and gross, like mighty battlements
Of Titans when they warred against the gods,
Towered in the air, and awful silence held

The expectant earth, a stillness like the pause
Before the clash of battle.   At set of sun
An earthquake came and shook men from their
        homes ;
The solid ground did rock, and swoll, and sobbed,
And rose and sank like to a thing diseased
That pants in agony.   From house to house
Of the near town, the giant tremor ran,
Which straightway toppled down, and lay in rows
Like a mowed phalanx in a battlefield.
Rocks left their seats ; the lowly valleys heaved ;
And trees did with their branches flog the ground.
Nor was the sea long unparticipant
Of the land's fever, but with swift retreat
Fled from the rattling beach, and back anon,
Like a mad racer, leapt upon the land,
And from its foamy mane and hissing crest
Tossed huge destruction.   All was blank dismay,
And all stood trembling who not bit the sod,
Deeming that Zeus for sins of men had doomed
This frame of things to ruin.   But now came
The fiery horror to which this ague fit
Was but the prelude.   Who looked up beheld
A pitchy pillar of thick-volumed smoke
Shoot bolt to heaven, and then disparted spread,
Even as the flat top of a mighty pine
Blinding the day ; then with explosive roar
The huge side of the mountain gaped, and belched
Red rivers, which in surges rose, and smote
The threshold of the gods.   The troubled sky
Rained cinders down, and rocks, which hurtling fell.

A sulphurous mist o'ercanopied the earth,
Through which the blue-red lightnings flaring shot
Their forky tongues ; from their long-centuried beds
The rivers fled, which straightway were usurped
By streams of molten granite that o'erflowed
Their narrow banks, and with a fiery deluge
O'erswept whole cities.   If I spent a day
In Tartarus, where blasted Typhon lies,
And all the blasphemous serpent-footed crew
Of Jove-denying monsters, I might not
Behold more terror than invaded then
My scared regard.

HERACLITUS.

    Would I had shared with thee
So grand a terror ! but consider now
Whither this tends.   Not Sicily alone,
Such subterranean fiery vents contains,
But the whole earth is tunnelled with them ; and
Huge cindered mountains once ablaze with fire,
As you may see by scratching, which reveals
The hollow bubbles' mould, and glassy slag,
And the light white-blown pumice, now are cropped
By woolly sheep, and to the careful hoe
Yield the heart-gladdening vine ; and thus we live
Engirdled by a fiery belt above,
And by a fiery furnace scooped below ;
And by the power of this fine element
All things are what they are, and may not freeze
Into the hard and wasteful barrenness
Of a dead chaos.

AENESIDEMUS.

But the Fire I saw
Made chaos rather.

HERACLITUS.

As the woodman's axe
Makes chaos in a wood ; but the wood grows
The better being thinned.   The thing you saw
Was but a part ; as when a worm is crushed
Beneath some conqueror's chariot wheels, one breath
Hath ceased, but the wide sentient earth no less
Echoes with pæans.   From the yeasty wave
Ye can no more interpret the benign
And genial essence of the pregnant deep,
Than from a sudden spurt of reinless flame
Tell the fine power of heat.   The reinless flame
Hath its own work ; it only can subdue
The stubborn adamant ; but the subtle fire
Which doth ensoul the flow of crimson blood
Burns, but not blazes, to the measured march
Which men call life.   All life is heat, and heat
Is fire well tempered and by reason reined.
Deem not the essence of creative fire
A wild, untempered, reckless-rending power,
To waste a city or consume a straw.
Instinct with reason and inventive force
It moulds the world, and, magical, transmutes
This thing to that, and that to this again ;
In all and of all, as the flowing sap
In the green tree, or in the living bone

The vital blood.   'Tis the incarnate reason
That is the world and makes it.   What we call
Making is but the being of the world,
Which is by ever being something new;
And what it makes must still unmake, that nothing
May stand apart, and by its being bar
The prime necessity of ceaseless change,
Which is a law to Jove.

                AENESIDEMUS.

                    But Jove, thou said'st
But now, was Fire.

                HERACLITUS.

                    And even so I say
Again.   Nought is in heaven or earth but Fire
Of things that live, if any death there be;
The virtue of all being centres here:
Fate and the Furies, Justice, Reason, Law,
Necessity, and Jove, and Fire, are names
For one thing many.   Names are marks which bring
Food to the foolish, to the feeble fear,
Sport to the wise, mere jugglers' tricks which strike
The gaping throngs with wonder, while the man
Who is the fellow in the fine deceit
Stands and admires the trickster, not the trick.

                AENESIDEMUS.

Is Jove a juggler, and is life a cheat?

HERACLITUS.

Spell not my words too gingerly.   I say
What men call many things are one, transformed
By Fire's all-fusing virtue.

AENESIDEMUS.

                              How can Fire
Become its adverse ?   Water quenches flame.

HERACLITUS.

I thank thee for that instance.   Tell me first
How ice becometh water?

AENESIDEMUS.

                              By added heat.

HERACLITUS.

Then solid things to fluid change by power
Of plastic heat, a rock becomes a river ;
And that which murders red-faced Fire, itself
Was born of very Fire.   See here the type
Of the vast universe.   Fire in the watery form,
Masked in its contrary, moulds all things to life.
Heat makes the humid ; heat to reason joined
Subduing hardest things to liquid laws,
With procreative virtue pulsing flows,
A mighty sea, whose waves are vital seeds.
Down through the fluid every soul descends
That with incarnate separate entity
Stands manifest to sense.   This vital sea
Ye call OCEANUS, ancientest of gods,

And with his foamy-footed daughters wisely
Make populous the brine.   Their name is legion;
And kin to them is Dionysus, born
Of rainful Jove, himself the sapful life
Of smooth-leaved ivy, and the needled fir,
And fervid-blooded vine.

AENESIDEMUS.

You use the words
Of wise old Homer; but your sense, I deem,
He little dreamt of.   You interpret him
To grace your fancies with his honoured name.

HERACLITUS.

Whip Homer from the schools, and with him send
Archilochus!

AENESIDEMUS.

What! shall all our learning go
For nothing? did the old theologer
Of Ascra teach in vain?   Are we all fools?

HERACLITUS.

Learning more cumbers than informs the soul;
Strong thinkers, like alert athletes, wear not
Their limbs in bandages.   What I know, I know
Direct from Jove, who not more surely spake
To Homer than to me.

AENESIDEMUS.

Methinks you nurse a huge conceit.

HERACLITUS.

　　　　　　　　　　　　　　I nurse
What thought a man, being complete man, may nurse.

AENESIDEMUS.

What boast is this? mortal of mortal born.

HERACLITUS.

Not so; all mortal from immortal flows;
Gods are immortal men, men mortal gods.

AENESIDEMUS.

You deal in riddles.

HERACLITUS.

　　　　　So does the god who sits
Upon the navel of the earth at Delphi.

AENESIDEMUS.

You say that Jove is Fire; what is Apollo?

HERACLITUS.

The flaming right hand of his father Jove.

AENESIDEMUS.

And she, the mighty mother, many-breasted,
Whom general Asia worships and all Greece,
If thou be doctor in old Hesiod's room,
Say who is she, and what her virtue?

HERACLITUS.

                       Plainly
Her form declares her nature.   From her breasts
The milky juice, the food of delicate life,
Flows copious ; and with quaint display all round
Cinctured with figured zones, she proudly shews
Her shaggy children whom she feeds and rears ;
She is the Earth by genial heat informed,
With pregnant humours gushing into life.

AENESIDEMUS.

Thy words are fair : but, should the people ask
If Heraclitus holds one creed with all
That worship Dian, I were loath to swear
The rightness of thy creed.

HERACLITUS.

                       Swear not at all,
As what implies that thou dost lightly speak,
Apart from swearing.   Ever speak the truth,
Nor with one crude unpondered word divorce
Thy small particular from the general fact
That links the world ; only true words prevail ;
And light opinions, lightly squandered, are,
To thwart the truth, not stronger than a fly
To baffle Boreas.

AENESIDEMUS.

                  I would my tongue
Were Orpheus' lyre to move thee.   Why dost thou
Still sit apart as one possessed, who loves

The lonely places where the bittern booms,
And fenny vipers creep, and spotted newts
Crawl 'neath the crumbled granite.   In this land
Thales was wise, and with his wisdom knew
To rule the olive market.   But you sit
Self-banished here, with perverse waste of wit,
Spinning a strong entanglement of thought,
That but enmeshes thee and profits none.
Keep not thy wisdom to thyself, but rise
And spread it as the lavish sun his light.
It suits the rich to squander ; with their wealth
To serve the public.   All who live must serve.

HERACLITUS.

I serve the public?   If I did so, they
Would serve me as they did good Hermodorus,
And banished him, for that with too much love
He would advance their good.   " Let none presume
To do us good, except as we shall please,
And with such partners as we choose to name ;
Who does us good against our will usurps
Our liberty."   And so, to prove them free,
They cast out the best man in Ephesus.
Who serves a kicking horse may look to earn
Kicks for his kindness.   I am wiser grown.

AENESIDEMUS.

But a good rider rules a restive steed.

HERACLITUS.

Ay ; but the People, many-headed brute,

Tiger and ass, viper and bear in one,
Was never tamed ; and who such brute would lead
Must be his slave.   My humour keeps me free.
Talk we no more to-day : Farewell, good friend !

AENESIDEMUS.

I do commend thee to the mighty Mother,
That free from error she may keep thy soul
In the true faith and worship of herself.

HERACLITUS.

As I do thee.   The mighty Mother bless thee !

[Exeunt.]

EMPEDOCLES

Insula quem triquetris terrarum gessit in oris,
Quae, cum magna modis multis miranda videtur,
Nil tamen hoc habuisse viro praeclarius in se
Nec sanctum magis et mirum carumque videtur,
Ut vix humana videatur stirpe creatus.

LUCRETIUS.

EMPEDOCLES.

PERSONS.

1. EMPEDOCLES, a Philosopher of Agrigentum.
2. EMBADIUS, a Citizen of Agrigentum.
3. ˙Other Citizens.
4. PAUSANIAS, a Physician, Friend of Empedocles.
5. SENATORS of Selinus.

SCENE.—*In the city of Agrigentum, or in the neighbouring district.*

SCENE I.

The market-place of Agrigentum. Enter Embadius and other tradesmen and citizens of Agrigentum.

EMBADIUS.

Well, my masters, your talk of yesterday wore a serious face, and must be looked to. I have now been vamping neat's leather for thirty years in Agrigentum, and I ought to know where the shoe pinches. I have made all sorts of shoes : sandals and slippers of most multiform variation, and shoes properly so called. I have made Spartan shoes for men, as red as boiled lobsters, to look warlike ; I have made felt shoes for fine ladies, with cork heels to make them look lofty ; I have made hunting shoes, after the fashion of short-kirtled Dian, for Numidian hunters; and heavy shoes, with hobnails, for swine-herds, stone-breakers, and muleteers in the Nebrodian mountains. If any man in Agrigentum ought to know where the shoe pinches, that man is old Embadius, whose head hath snowed itself into a precocious winter by ministering comfort to the soles of all Sicily.

FIRST CITIZEN.

Well, sir, your occupation, though a lowly one, is of high service. But what hath this to do with our discourse of yesterday? Our talk, I guess, was not of shoes.

EMBADIUS.

Timotheus, thou art a most literal-witted knave; hast thou no comprehension of similitudes? I spake of shoes, true; but the shoes were an allegory. I meant, of course ——

SECOND CITIZEN.

Of course he meant the oligarchy.

FIRST CITIZEN.

O, I see now!

SECOND CITIZEN.

Ay, Timotheus you can see, when you are told to see, and sometimes not even then.

FIRST CITIZEN.

Peace, yellow beak! what Embadius would enforce is, that we, the people, are the feet; that the laws of

Agrigentum are the shoes; that the oligarchy, the Ten Hundred who make the laws, are our shoemakers; and, being shoemakers, they make shoes which, being shoes, ought to solace our soles, but do in fact torture our great toes most outrageously.

EMBADIUS.

Thou hast applied the similitude justly. Gorgias could not have expounded it more aptly according to the just laws of the art rhetorical.

FIRST CITIZEN.

And does it not hold most properly that, as the feet were not made for the comfort of the shoes, but the shoes for the comfort of the feet, the Ten Hundred hold their places and brook their power not for their private pleasure and profit, but for the service and satisfaction of the people.

EMBADIUS.

Athenian Solon, whose ashes have slept in an urn for ten times ten years and more, were he to leap into flesh again, could not have spoken more wisely. Thou art the very man for our need. 'Tis plain we must have a revolution.

SECOND CITIZEN.

Certainly a revolution. Why should we stuff sausages to feed the beast that devours us? Why from our proper sweat lend strength to their sinews to tramp our lives out? Why should we, who count by thousands, sit out all night in the cold with our nets in the sea, fetching ourselves rheumatism and ague, that these who poll by the hundred may sit by the fireside and fatten on the fry?

FIRST CITIZEN.

There thou sayest well. Whoso belongs not to the Ten Hundred hath no place in Agrigentum. We belong to the city, but are not citizens; slaves rather, nay, worse than slaves; for any liberty we may boast of seemeth to consist in this—we are free from the bother of keeping the reins in our own hands, only that we may feel the bitterness of a strong rider's goad in our ribs. Worse than slaves, I say again, to every intent; for slaves indeed find who care for them, and live not scurvily from the superfluity of sugared crumbs that drops to them from their master's table. We are nobodies in Agrigentum; we must make ourselves somebodies.

SECOND CITIZEN.

Well, then, how shall we proceed? Let us elect Embadius for our captain; rouse the people; storm the council-chamber; drive out the few; and install the many, that is, ourselves, in their seats.

EMBADIUS.

Softly, softly, my masters! Embadius is an honourable man; but the people will not be led by an honourable man who trades in neat's leather. They will have a gentleman to lead them. We may not confront the polished and blazoned worshipfulness of the Ten Hundred, with our blank smocks and un-curried roughness. We shall show like an army of crows marching against eagles. We must have an eagle to flap for us.

SECOND CITIZEN.

Are we not men? are we not brave? have we not brains? do we lack brawn?

EMBADIUS.

Young man, thou understandest these things not. The world is governed by show, by custom, and by authority. I tell thee a revolution never was made, never can be made, to any prosperous issue without the help of that very oligarchy whom the revolution shall overthrow. The burglar bribes the servants of the strong man's house, and thus enters. Excuse the similitude. We are not burglars, neither you nor I ; but we are about to proceed violently against the house of a strong man. Therefore, I say to thee, young man, we must proceed with discretion.

FIRST CITIZEN.

Well, then, let us tell the tale of them. Who are the men drawing their blood from the founts of the old families, whom we might invite to be head of this tumour?

SECOND CITIZEN.

Tumour! you old blunderer! don't degrade us by calling a revolution a tumour; no doubt, you meant to say *tumult;* but this word no less hath a bad odour; say rather, an eruption, an eruption of Aetna, or an irruption into the houses of the oligarchs.

FIRST CITIZEN.

Peace, pedant! What say you, Embadius, to Hipposthenes, the son of the rich merchant, Chrysogonus, who married the Carthaginian captain's daughter?

EMBADIUS.

He is like all other sons of rich merchants, the first article of whose creed is that their fathers gathered gold with much thinking that they may scatter it with none. There is nothing very bad about the youth, but neither is there anything very good. He hath no measure in his doings, but either loafs about the streets like a dainty girl, perusing a jeweller's window, or drives about the country like Orestes hounded by the Furies. But the worst is, he is utterly destitute of counsel. He hath science only in dogs and horses, cocks and quails, dicing, drinking, dancing-girls and flute-players; and his special dexterity is in spirting water upon tinkling scales, to hit the heads of gilded mannikins. There is no cottabist in Sicily to match him. Nevertheless, he is infinitely better than a school-boy who goes unwillingly to school, or a crab that goes backwards, or a mule that will not go at all. Put him on a horse's back and he will ride gallantly whither a god may drive him. But, as aforesaid, he lacks counsel. We must sauce our enterprise with brains, my masters; otherwise, the hot crudity of our start may engender wind, and we shall explode.

FIRST CITIZEN.

What say you to Polus?

EMBADIUS.

Polus is a right supple sophist. He hath a tongue lithe as a lizard's tail, and loud as the flap of a goose-wing. He is a hero of most catholic championship, who will plead for any cause, and fight for none. He is no oligarch; that is one virtue, though scarcely a virtue in him; for, having no quality of reverence in the inventory of his brain-pan, how should he affect to crook the knee to pedigree, or bow the head to authority? He carries himself with a most regardless lightness to all things, and hanging the world on his little finger, says, it is my jewel. He cares not for the people; in fact, he cares not much for anything but Polus. He is a good fencer; he fences with his tongue; but he hath neither cause nor country, nor conscience; and, conclusively, is no patriot. Dismiss him.

FIRST CITIZEN.

Then there is Polyphantes.

EMBADIUS.

Dream not of him. He is a rank oligarch. Once he gave the people a banquet; for why? Not for that he loves the people, but that the people might love him. He hath a most royal pride in dispensing. If the people are contented to be beggars, he will delight to show his liberality by feasting them; if they style themselves brothers, it will be the office of his dignity to spurn them.

FIRST CITIZEN.

What hold you of the worthy physicians, Acron and Pausanias?

EMBADIUS.

What all Agrigentum holds. There are no better men in Sicily, friends of the people, true to the back-bone. Nevertheless they are of that quality which is more quick to spy what is bad in the conduct of affairs than apt to strike for what is good. Pausanias, certainly, will go with us; but he will be more pro-fitable in teaching another to move than in moving himself.

SECOND CITIZEN.

What other? Empedocles?

EMBADIUS.

Whom else? There is no man in Agrigentum will serve our purpose like the son of Meton. He carries a weight and authority with all classes that belongs to no man else. He is clothed with a certain majesty that sits upon him as naturally as a helmet on the head of Mars, and as lightly as a plume on an eagle's wing. There is not a senator in the whole hall of Audience can do a base thing and look Empedocles in the face. The splendid purple of their fair pretences pales at his breath, and shrinks to tatters at his touch. He is a man from top to toe; cataphract behind and before; plated with golden proof against all knavery.

First Citizen.

He is in sooth right noble both in blood and bearing; there is no house in Agrigentum of more unstained precedents. I remember his father's father, a right lordly man, coming home victor from the games, his high-blood steeds tossing their saffron manes, rich and soft, as the cream which my Xanthippe skims from the milk of the dun cow, snorting a challenge to all riders, and out-pacing all runners, like Hermes pitted in the stadium against the lame Hephæstus.

Embadius.

Our city was ever famed for horses. I remember when good Exaenetus, being victor at the games, rode through the streets with a group of ten times thirty chariots, drawn by white horses.

Second Citizen.

But for Empedocles himself, it is rumoured that he is tainted with strange fancies, shaping his life more to the whim of private conceit than to the known rule of general consent. They say he eats no flesh; and on one occasion, having to make sacrifice to Olympian Jove, that he might spill no blood—for the which he hath an emphatic horror—he bolstered up an ox with a wooden frame and painted canvas, and stowing it full of all sorts of spiceries, thus enacted the sacred rite.   Now this is both a folly and a sham.

FIRST CITIZEN.

And an impiety to boot, if true.

EMBADIUS.

A wise addition—if true.   But 'tis an idle tale, believe me, that squares with Empedocles' wit as nicely as a beggar's cloak does with a king's back; a patch, doubtless, taken from the wardrobe of that meek and milky-blooded brotherhood, who, being banished from the Oscan land for their impertinent oligarchic pedantries, crossed the strait at Zancle to fill with their dreamy stuff any empty polls that might be found here waiting for such furnishing.   But Empedocles—trust me, for I know him, and have weighed him every grain, and surveyed him all round —Empedocles is not the man to feed on dreams; and, if he hath an imagination, his fancies have pith in them very different from that Pythagorean juggle about triangles that contain nothing, and figures whose sums are less substantial than soap-bubbles.

SECOND CITIZEN.

Yet was he seen only two nights ago, upon a bare ridge, beneath the cold moon, gazing at the stars, and muttering to the breeze, and holding parle with him-

self like a madman.   Certainly he hath melancholic
lunes, and affects solitude.   Some say he gives himself out for a god.

EMBADIUS.

Peace, young pea-blossom !   You know no more
what such a man as Empedocles cogitates beneath the
moon, than a mite does about a cheesemonger.

FIRST CITIZEN.

Or a worm about a war-horse !

EMBADIUS.

Pythagoras, as I said, was a dreamer ; but one wise
rule his maundering fraternity had, *videlicet*, that every
young man should keep silence for seven years after
the first sprouting of his beard, before he unbarred the
fence of his teeth in open council to counter thwart
long years and large experience.   Let us, therefore,
my brave masters, put this business, so forth, into
shape.   We will speak to Pausanias, that he speak to
Empedocles, that he head the conjuration ; and our
complotting shall not be in vain.   Follow me ! have
your finger on your lips ; keep your tinder dry ; and
your knives sharp ; and Empedocles shall help you to
help the Ten Hundred lightly out of their chairs.

[*Exeunt.*]

SCENE II.

*A villa in the high country, on the banks of the Acragas, north
of Agrigentum.   Empedocles comes forth from an arbour and
appears on a platform from which there is a view of the city.*

Pythagoras was a marvellous man; if he
Had not a golden thigh, as story tells,
His words are ore more precious than the grace
Of golden Aphrodite.   But what gold?
What would this foulest fair addition, still
Tagged to the good?   O vain, sense-juggled world,
To symbolise the best things by the worst,
And seek divine significance in what
Of earth is earthiest, and bears no more
Kinship to man, and what in man is best,
Than this dull clod to life.   What thing is gold?
It is a stage piled high for dwarfs to stand on,
And deem them giants: 'tis a venal whore,
That sells her womanhood for short lease of life
More loathly than the grave; a painted hag
That cooks her stale unseasoned cheek to mock
The bloom of Hebe; or, if I must deal
In mild comparisons—(though my boiling blood
Ill brooks them, when I see how men are fobbed
Out of all manhood by this swindler gold)—
Then let me say this gold is a long ladder,
With steps that soar to heaven or sink to hell.
Ay! there's the rub! the blessing or the bane
Lies with the climber, as he plants the steps
Upwards or downwards; to his feet they are

But arrant slaves, blind hands that wait his will,
For good or evil.   Blind things cannot lead ;
And if strong Briareus had an hundred arms,
Lacking the wit to wield them, he would boast
From fate a bitter boon, a hundred whips
To flog himself.   O, foolish, foolish world !
One thing is needful, for one thing I pray ;
Zeus, grant me wisdom !   Daughter of great Jove,
Immortal, flashing-eyed, divinely chaste,
Give me a glimpse of that most glorious truth
Thou sharest with thy father ; touch mine eyes,
As thou didst salve the sight of Diomede,
With heavenly virtue, that, dull films removed,
I may behind this mortal strife behold
The gods that weave the broidery of the web
Which men call life.   For this one thing I pray,
And consecrate to thee this day my soul,
Making my wish thy slave ; and for such boon
The juggling gold, and all the glistering pomp
That struts upon the painted stage of man,
The blazon and the boast of fools, I fling
For swine to tramp on !

Pythagoras was a marvellous man, and yet
His numbers tell not all the mystery
That moves the wheel of life.   All things must share
Redemption from old chaos ; shapeless things
Were no things ; shape from numbered sequence grows,
And bounded number.   This the Samian saw ;
And sooner shall a blind man flood the world
With light, and asses bray soul-soothing hymns,

And screaming vultures thrill the groves with song,
Than worlds be worlds where marshalling number fails.
But we must number something ; there is dust
Of gold, and dust of earth, and briny spray,
And dust of mealy flowers.   We cannot coin
Gold into cowslips, cowslips into gold,
By counting two or three, or perfect ten,
Or the high-honoured function of the four.
All quality, all substantial virtue, lies
In the great elemental roots of things,
And these are four ; a child may tell their types,
Earth, Water, Air, and all-ensphering Fire ;
Earth makes the solid framework, the strong base
Of firm resistance, and the peg on which
All lighter being hangs, the soil whence springs
The delicate-petalled flower, and sturdy tree,
And with broad-breasted native strength upbears
The starry architecture, home of gods.
Then comes the pure and all-interfluent power
Of billowy Water, peopling every creek
And gaping hollow of wide-bosomed earth,
With lake and sea, and richly-rolling stream,
Clear-bubbling well, and roaring cataract ;
Here dwells the softening quality that subdues
All hardness, so made docile to receive
Fair shape, and rounds each sharp invasive line
To graceful sweep of softly-falling curve,
And oozing subtly through each viewless pore
Lives latent in the stone, and slowly breaks
The flinty heart of most obdurate rock
To serviceable grain ; here teems with power

The fecund finny tribe; no living thing
Lives without liquid, and the stony seed
Feels the insinuant dew, and the green blade
Bursts forth miraculous.   Third mighty root of things
The soft-breathed Air, mother of life, appears,
With music on its wings, and floats sublime
With tenuous substance through its sphery flow,
Finely dispersed, and bears from life to life
Far-waving pulse of odorous messengers,
With soothing wafture.   Then divinest root
Of things that be, all-moulding Fire is named,
Soul of all soul, and very life of life;
Most pure, most quick, most unconfined, most keen
To stir all vital rapture, or to burst
All bonds of corporate jointure, and create
What men call death.   Of this the mighty gods
Are framed compact, robed in essential flame,
Undying forms, like mortal men, but free
From mortal taint; great far-careering spheres
Of fiery virtue, scattering radiant force,
Through all the sentient world that undulates
In subtle transport to the touch divine :
These are the roots of things, the cosmic strings
Which mighty Number tunes to harmony,
And plays the hymn called Life.
                              But I am borne
Too hotly to my goal.   These primal seeds
Were weak to shape a world without thy force,
Primeval Aphrodite, Queen of Charms,
Thou and that rival Might, whom to subdue
Was still thy boast, Discord, and Jar, and Din,

Contention and Debate.   Strong Love and Hate
Divide the world; but with diviner sway
Love wields, and welds, and unifies what else
Were a long bicker and a deathless strife
Of unharmonious opposites.   All things
Would start centrifugal, and fill wide space
With strange distraction; but thy virtue came,
Sweet reconciler of harsh contraries,
Zoned with all blandishment; and at thy touch
The strong bowed to the weak, the rough received
The soft in sisterhood, and blissful bonds
Made male and female one, and thus arose
That balanced mean of sundered opposites,
Which men call health and beauty, reason, right,
And every praiseful name.   But not stern Fate
And strong Necessity, and the hoar decree
Of deathless gods, by sempiternal oath
Sanctioned and sealed, allowed the Cyprian's reign
For ever; else sweet sameness had grown tame,
Fond iteration wearisome, and all
The hostile hues that make a varied world
Been merged in blank identity.   Discord lives,
A snake still scotched by Love, but never killed,
Which, when the world would slide into repose,
And hug itself in unadventurous ease,
Knocks at the door, whips off the rosy dream,
Drags forth the sleeper, shakes the tenement,
And all the soldered opposites rebound
Into their primal hates.

                              Thus might I sketch
Rough-handed outline of a doctrine fit

To fill the gaps which wise Pythagoras left ;
And by the favour of the prophet-god
Whose laurelled rod I bear, I will enquire,
And with persistent-searching ken unravel
The tangled tissue of this shifting web
Which men call life, still weaving, still unwoven ;
And what I find with faithful voice declare.
    And yet how little can a mortal man
Know worth the knowing ! narrow is our view,
Feeble our grasp, and many an adverse fate
Buffets our sense, and blunts its keenest edge,
Defies our conjuring, from our torture slips,
And with seven-bolted mystery bemocks
Our crude surmises.   In the dark we sweat,
Feeding on glimpses, through our little span
Of life much like to death ; and, when our lamp
Sinks with a puff, we pass away like smoke,
And are not ; knowing what each chanced to know
In drift of circumstance, but of the whole
Incognisant, nor functioned to cognise
By sense that peers without or pries within.
So it must be ; we cannot burst the cage
Whose bonds are bounds that shape us what we are ;
For limit is the very law that makes
All Finites possible ; and, to be at all,
We must be marked off from the boundless whole
With divers functions, aptitudes, and powers,
Each in his own encasement, which to pass
Is to break down our being.   Therefore I,
Within the limits of my little life
Will chastely live, and piously depend

On the great source of life, even as a babe
Hangs from its mother's breast.   But who comes here?

[*Enter Pausanias.*]

The good gods love thee, my Pausanias!
Would I were sick, that so the drugful leech
Might profit me the more!

PAUSANIAS.

                    Are you quite sure
That you are not sick?

EMPEDOCLES.

                    Sick of mine own self
I am sometimes, and of the thoughts that strain
My faculty to think, more than they glut
My greed to know.

PAUSANIAS.

                    Empedocles is wise,
And should not strain the cord till it may crack.

EMPEDOCLES.

I have been musing, like a keen-nosed hound
Close on the game once started.

PAUSANIAS.
                    You are lost
Too much in thought. What are those scrolls that lie
There on the table?

EMPEDOCLES.

'Tis a book.

PAUSANIAS.

                    More books!
And verses too, by Jove!   In sooth you spin
Your soul too hotly out; you will not live
Half your just time.   Is this a tragedy
Like those you flapped out, when you imped your wings,
Or have you piled another Xerxiad,
Like that your sister burned?

EMPEDOCLES.

                    Not so, good friend;
These were light essays of the fledgling then
When but to fly was pleasure.   I have now
Wise purpose in my verse; and with thy science
My song is sistered.

PAUSANIAS.

Troll a little stave.

EMPEDOCLES.

Hear me, friends, who dwell where Acragas mingles
    his golden
Flow with the sea, who cherish wise thoughts, a bless-
    ing to mortals,
Friends all guiltless of harm, and a haven of love to
    the stranger.
Hail! a mortal no more, but like to immortals in
    honour

Wreathed I walk through your street, and crown'd
    with worshipful badges ;
Cities fling open their gates, and old and young to
    receive me
Stream in reverent throngs, and woo my ear with
    petitions ;
Some the secrets of fate, and some the hope of their
    labour
Eager to know, and some with limb-distorting diseases
Bent to the ground, or pierced with pangs that harry
    the vitals
Take the word from my lips, like drops of balm to
    the wounded.

PAUSANIAS.

Well promised !   May the cake you eat be white
As that you knead !

EMPEDOCLES.

    Little he still receives
Who little hopes ; weak is our ken to grasp
The far swing of the vasty world, but strong
A wise man's arm to save who will be saved.

PAUSANIAS.

Read on.

EMPEDOCLES.

Come and learn from my lay what drugs the drugful
    physician
Brooks to strangle disease, and lighten life's burden
    to sapless

Sorrowful eld.   The secret I know to fetter the cold
    wind's
Bluster that blackens the tree and blights the blade
    to the farmer;
I can banish the breeze, and swell its current at
    pleasure.
Listen to me, and from black-browed storms thou
    shalt bring in its season
Warmth to yellow the grain, and, when green leaves
    droop in the summer,
Up from its wells thou shalt conjure the freshening
    might of the river
Over the gasping land; the dead that wander in
    darkness
Hearing thy call shall revisit life's lightsome dwellings
    to praise thee !

PAUSANIAS.

'Tis well to praise our skill, and helping hand;
But science hath its bounds, and we must hope
Within our human reach.

EMPEDOCLES.

           I am content
To be a man.   I would not fight with gods;
But how far wing of mortal wit may strain
We know not till we try.   The bird that sits
In wiry cage, well pleased, will never find
Proof of its pinion.   Man may bridge the seas,
Back turn the rivers, underbore the hills,
Yea rein the reinless fire and puffing steam,

If but in Nature's track, devoutly traced,
Careful he walks, and what he aptly schemes
With caution dares.

PAUSANIAS.

Beloved Empedocles,
All men admire thy daring, and allow
Thy skill supreme ; and I much more than all
Cling to thy strength, as to the elm the vine ;
But in the crowd I live, and glean what men
Say of my friend—mostly a mass of dreams—
But sometimes seasoned with a dash of truth
That gives my love to ponder.

EMPEDOCLES.

Art thou come
To preach to me to-day ?   I love the man
Who shows my sins.   How shall the surgeon's knife
Bring saving lancet to a wound untold ?
The sickly soul that hugs his sickness dies ;
Make me clean bare, and probe me to the bone,
And with no butter on thy knife, Pausanias.

PAUSANIAS.

Well, let me play the surgeon.   Sooth to say
Thou art too much alone ; thou dost remove
Thy life from the great life of Agrigentum ;
Cranes herd with cranes, with oxen, oxen.   Men
Should troop with men.

EMPEDOCLES.

Blame me not, friend, in this,
Here in the solitude I hold discourse
With gods, who in the forum's wrangling din
Are overbawled.   When gods would speak to men,
They choose not markets, where contentious crowds
Make mighty chaffering for a paltry gain;
Nor theatres, where sounding plaudits swell
To strut of buskined revellers; nor shrines
With swarms of wondering worshippers enringed,
And seas of praise; but in the soft-winged breeze,
In the green stillness of a pastured wold,
By brooks that whisper 'neath a fringe of ferns,
Or wimple through a cowslip-broidered mead
In woods at noon, when not a leaf is stirred;
On grassy slopes mantled in mellow gold,
When summer suns are soft and evenings sweet,
And in the fall of gentle night, when drifts
The frequent fire-fly through the breezeless grove,
They speak to the heart, alone with man alone,
That he with whole will to their awful charge
Lend no divided ear.

PAUSANIAS.

There you are right;
We learn to think in solitude, to live
In stream of men.   But you—you plant yourself,
Self-moulded and self-tutored, in their front,
And in a high regardless humour cuff
The crest of their opinion, without need

In things indifferent.　They are children—well,
Not wise is he who children treats as men ;
The potter makes the dish, but not the clay ;
The angler trims his bait to suit the trout ;
And even so you, if you would fish for men,
Must note their likings.　People see your dress,
But not your soul, and they are much offended.

EMPEDOCLES.

My dress !　O ! peacocks claim their plumes, but not
Empedocles his coat !—What more? . Sweep clean ;
Mince not your mission.

PAUSANIAS.

　　　　　　Dear Empedocles,
I have no mission, but in love I speak.
If your red cloak offends a furious bull,
You should not wear it.　Dress makes not the man,
But helps the popular verdict on the man,
And, if a king walks forth in beggar's weeds,
He passes for a beggar.　For your dress,
They say ——

EMPEDOCLES.

　　　　That is the foolish part of men
In Agrigentum.

PAUSANIAS.

　　　　Well, well ! most men are fools ;
They say that you are blown with huge conceit ;
And blame that, like the unshorn god, you nurse
Strange length of locks ; that like a king you wear

A purple mantle, and invest your feet
With Amyclean boots, whose brazen ring
Proclaims your coming.   Some say you put forth
Your words like oracles, and in all your port
Affect the god.

EMPEDOCLES.

Pausanias, you know
Empedocles better ; know I not affect,
But am, the voice of God to all whose faith
Accepts the truth I preach.   There is no truth
That God not teaches ; and the thing we know
We hold as surely from inspiring Jove
As when we breathe the fluent air instinct
With vital force.   And, for my body's clothing,
By Hera, all my blood fumes up to think
I should be so belorded by the whim
Of the unreasoned many, that my cloak
Is not mine own to choose.   There's young Gorgias
Wears golden shoes, making his feet to chime
With his golden mouth.   Nature's a gaudy dame ;
With golden cups she studs the mead, with bells
Of purple every steep sun-facing crag
She richly hangs, with flash of purple stars
Fringes her streams ; why should a man be grey ?
I'll not wear duffel when all nature flaunts
In flaming garniture.   I will wear purple.

PAUSANIAS.

Purple beseems your kingly state of thought :
But for the people who should own your state

To bate some jot of your most kingly due
Were kingliest policy. You stand too high
Above their judgment. Gods must stoop to help
Their creeping worshippers.

EMPEDOCLES.

What they understand
The rabble will despise.   If the gods walked
The streets like common men, the common man
Would hold them common.   If I walk apart,
'Tis that I fear in fellowship with them
To share their baseness.   Sooner than be used
For their base ends, a pliant clay to take
Their mould of low instructions, I would leap
Into hot Ætna's boiling bowl, and die
A cindered death.

PAUSANIAS.

Thus would you die in flame
Like Heracles, and be a god like him !

EMPEDOCLES.

Just so ; a bonfire draws the dullest eye,
Where men, like moths, do feed the flame and die.
The people worship what doth make them stare,
And know not what they stare at.   But who comes ?

PAUSANIAS.

I know not ; 'tis a goodly company
Of reverend seniors ; strangers, by their look.

EMPEDOCLES.

Right; and by the shining parsley in their caps
I read them from Selinus.

[*Enter a body of senators, and other citizens from
Selinus.*]
                                        Gentlemen,
You are right welcome: in your palmy groves
Oft times I walked, and loved your city well;
What business in this hot and reeking time
Brings you to Agrigentum?

SENATOR.

                        A grievous hest
Compels us to disturb your sapient ease,
A business full of weeping and of wail,
And rueful moaning, and black-mantled woe;
Our hope in you, as night-lost wanderers seek
The guiding light.

EMPEDOCLES.

                        Would I were wise in what
Men need my wisdom! what I can I will.

SENATOR.

A sore disease hath come upon our people.

EMPEDOCLES.

Disease! home bred, or brought from yont the sea?

SENATOR.

The cause is dark: some say the air is sown
With seeds of death; some that the sun's eclipse
Hath tainted nature; some that summer's heat,
Beyond all seasonable wont, hath fired
The currents of the blood; some that the serfs,
The old Sicanian malcontents, have drugged
The wells with poison; some that stinted prayer
And offering niggardised have turned the smile
Of gods to frowning; but we rather deem
A ship from Carthage, stranded on our coast,
Did with his other out-cast stores disgorge
An Aethiop, hated of the gods, who brought
This evil from his country, where the sun
Breeds monstrous maladies; from whose lethal touch
The mortal terror through the land was spread,
And, marching like a scythe behind the grass,
Mowed down all lustihood, and heaped the ways
With death.

EMPEDOCLES.

      Alack! alack! but this thing let me know,
What tokens had the harm?

SENATOR.

                        Its ugly face
Was worse than its black core; its way to death
More dire than very death. As lightnings strike
The tallest towers, and winds the topmost trees,
So first the head and citadel of man

This plague usurped.   The fever of the brain
Shot flame into the eyes; and throat and tongue
Like fresh paint blistered in the sun, did show
The hot infection; and revolted Nature
Belched forth her bile, till she had pumped her well
Clean dry; but still she strained, and struggling lay
In gasping hiccup, empty of all birth
But sheer prostration.   The disnatured skin
Showed livid, flecked with crimson, blossomed o'er
With loathsome sores.   Nor rest nor soothing sleep
The victim knew.   Anon the feverous fire
Like a strong wrestler grasped the heart : the bowels
Did rage like furnace; and like brize-stung ox
Beneath the sultry star, the tortured wretch
Intolerant of vesture, naked lies,
To hug the oozing moss, or dripping rock,
And still the more he drinks the more he cries
For the cool draught that heals to enforce the harm.
Eight days or nine this living death they drag
(So tough is Nature), till life finds its sole
Relief in death.   Or, if their strength defies
A nine days' torture, more like death than life,
With maimed and blasted forms they scare the day,
Having eyes that see not, feet and hands curtailed
Of toes and fingers, like the blackened stumps
Of branchless trees when some outrageous heat
Hath fired the forest; and—fresh food for tears—
Some from the burning anguish save their frames,
To maunder with their joints of reason cracked,
And with a blank and idiot stare look round,
As one who, started from a hideous dream,

Rubs undiscerning eyes.　But worse than death,
Or the long deathly torture, or the life
That's booked half way to death, is the despair
Of help from god or man that goads the soul
Into a reckless unconcern of all
That gods or men call right.　All prayer is dumb
I' the sacred shrines ; all aid from man but brings
Double distress, death to the helpless, death
To him who hoped to help ; to use the hour,
While hours are counted, is the one strong law
That rules ; from death to death the prowler roves,
To seize what all may lose, and few can claim.
The dead unburied lie about the walls,
Like stranded fish, when strong-winged blasts for weeks
Battered the beach, or with their loathly wreck
Bestrew the temples and pollute the gods.

EMPEDOCLES.

O Jove ! ye snap my heart-strings ; was no help
From cunning leech ?—no drug ?—no charm ?

SENATOR.

　　　　　　　　　This plague
Holds such hostility to the thought of life
That even the vultures who on carrion feast,
Tasting the ruin of our tainted frames,
Drop dead.

PAUSANIAS.

　　　　　Ye see how he is moved ; our art
He knows much better than ourselves ; and if,
In all the range of his far-reaching ken,

Hope lives for you, he will nor sleep nor eat,
Till you are helped.   Mark where he meditates !
I know his wont when any sudden force
Of sorrow grips him ; he will go apart,
Ponder and pray, and from the god who heals
Body and soul implore the wise device
That lames disease, and baffles death, and turns
Sharp pangs to pleasure.   Mark ! now he will speak.

EMPEDOCLES.

I thank the gracious god whose laurel bough
I bear prophetic, I have probed the harm
Even to the core !   Right worthy seniors
Of a most worthy city dear to me
By ties of grateful memory, if the god
Deceives me not, and gods may not deceive,
Both root and remedy of your dire disease
I see in vision.   Every mortal plague
Is doubly gendered, as, to make a growth
Both seed and soil combine.   That leprous son
Of swart-faced Aethiopia in your blood
Distilled a venom, harmless else, but that
Yourselves the soil and atmosphere do breed
Which in their motherly womb receive the germ
That bears a bloody blossom and black fruit.
'Tis not the flood that drowns the leaking boat ;
The leak invites the flood.   Yourselves have bred
The snake that bites you.

SENATOR.

                How so, my lord ?
How could we know ?

EMPEDOCLES.

               Men could know much,
And more than much, if, having eyes to see,
They saw, and, having thoughtful organs, thought.
You have a river that flows by your town?

SENATOR.

Ay, the Selinus, creeping through a marsh,
Smothered in mud, and coated with a web
Of lazy bubbles, happy paradise
Of newts and adders, and the Museful frogs !

EMPEDOCLES.

Ay ! lazy bubbles ; but most quick to breed
The subtle poison that with viewless teeth
Tears the fine tissue of the tenuous thread
Which mortals call their life.   This lucid air,
Which shows so pure, and fair, and innocent,
Is a wide sea, where oft-times there may swim
To mortal eye invisible, thick swarms
Of harmful things, whose hostile essence holds
No parley with the fleshly frame of man,
But through the avenues of our breath will walk
Into the temple of stout breasts, and steal
The god from out the shrine.   On your green pools
The bubble bursts, and winged death flies round
Thick as the thistle down o'er stubby fields,
Before the autumnal breeze.   Listen to me !
Above the town, some thirteen stadia,
The river forks in two, and losing halt

Its current hath no power to plough its way,
But in the reedy mesh entangled rots.
Bank up the fork, and with projecting mound
Compel the water's undivided stream
To sweep the valley : thus you dry the marsh ;
The healthy flood flows on ; and hottest suns
Can brew no ferment to impregn the air
With floating foulness.   This the god reveals
To me : and in Apollo's holy name
Empedocles commands you to make clean
The river's path ; else shall the glorious Sun,
Giver of life, bring death to you and yours,
And your dear homes, where babes drink mother's
          milk,
Be fields, manured and sown by your own hands,
To grow rich crops for Charon.

SENATOR.

                        We will obey ;
But does the god demand no sacrifice,
No holocaust, no precious thing, which we
Torn from our heart roots, would right gladly bring
To soothe his wrath ?

EMPEDOCLES.

                    The most wise gods demand
That you should use your reason, being made
Not like the brutes, but planful like themselves.
Farewell ! Apollo keep you ! waste no words !
When the great Healer shows the healing plan,
Each squandered minute is a murdered man.

SENATOR.

We go, my lord.   The city thanks the god.

[*Exeunt Senators.*]

PAUSANIAS.

How blest the function of my god-taught friend,
To scatter healing as the fragrant flower
Exhales delight, and with a breath to melt
The frost that numbs a nation !   Would that here
Thou wert less chary of what thy shrewd wit
Could work for Agrigentum.

EMPEDOCLES.

                    The sower works
When he sows seeds; the reaper when he reaps;
But oft-times, when the reaper piles the sheaf,
The unthinking many praise him, how he toils
For the public good ; but no man notes what sweat
Fell from the sower's brow.

PAUSANIAS.

                    'Tis very like ;
The people see the flower and eat the fruit,
But think not of the root.   But one may be
Reaper and sower both, root, flower, and fruit,
In one heaped excellence, and win due praise
From thinker and from thoughtless.   Such an one
Is my Empedocles.

EMPEDOCLES.

Pausanias, I see

Plainly your scope.   You would entice me back
Into the battle and the babblement
Of those contentious factions in the town,
Which I have left, as you, my friend, should know,
That I may grow in studious solitude,
And consecrate my soul to search of truth
In service of Apollo.

PAUSANIAS.

Very good;

But, if your mother or your brother cried
To you, in mid the service of the god,
You would not let them starve?

EMPEDOCLES.

No, but if I

Were measuring the stars, and in the ditch
A drunkard fell, I'd let the drunkard lie!

PAUSANIAS.

Drunkards and brawlers are like nettles; he
Who touches harms himself, and helps not them;
But if your brother fell into a ditch
Not drunk, but wandering in a starless night,
Or pushed into it by an insolent sot,
What would you then?

EMPEDOCLES.

Why, then, I'd leave the stars

And flog the sot, and pull my brother out.

PAUSANIAS.

Like a true man, and like a sage who loves
His fine thought much, but his poor brother more !

EMPEDOCLES.

Now your conclusion ?

PAUSANIAS.

                If the ship o' the state
Should sail and labour in a tossing sea,
And if the pilot's wit lay drenched in drink,
Who, being sober, should have saved the crew,
Would then, Empedocles swim in his own boat
And leave the ship to sink ?

EMPEDOCLES.

                You know my arm
Helped to strike down the tiger Thrasydaeus.

PAUSANIAS.

The arm that struck down one may help to strike
A thousand.

EMPEDOCLES.

        Ha ! I understand you now !
The people grumble, we shall have revolt ;
The thunder growls, anon will flash the bolt.
The thousand are no friends of mine ; but I
Am less a demagogue than an oligarch,
And as I grow from youth I farther grow
From hot unruly movements.   I do love

The people; but I stand too far apart
To touch their humour; I would coolly do
What thing I do; they with a violent plunge
Reel into change; and, all unreined, their right
Rushes to wrongness.   Like accepts from like
Its native guidance.   Boys should captain boys;
And old grey cats are out of date to head
Light kittens in their sport.   We do not seek
Sense from the centaurs, nor from drifts of men
Deliberation.   With the thoughtful few
Chaste wisdom dwells, and shuns the clamouring crowd
Who love not wisdom but in loftier phrase
To hear their folly echoed.   Whoso gives
Their thought in loudest replication back
Is styled their friend.   Fling the dear dog a sop,
And he will worship you !

PAUSANIAS.

                    You are much changed
From that Empedocles who, as you said,
Smote Thrasydaeus.

EMPEDOCLES.

                    Then I was young, and then
I carried in my breast the fiery stuff
Blazed up at every spark ; but, for that beast,
Did his foul presence now profane the air,
My wrath would spring to head, and burst upon him
Like spouts from rifted Aetna !   I cannot live
A Greek and be a slave !

PAUSANIAS.

                        Yet you despise
The people whom your hand holp to be free.

EMPEDOCLES.

I not despise them ; I suspect them ; rather
Suspect myself that I was never made
To captain a revolt, or rule a mob,
By waiting on its humours.   I will not be
A ruler of the people.

PAUSANIAS.

                        But the Thousand—

EMPEDOCLES.

I hate them !

PAUSANIAS.

        Why?

EMPEDOCLES.

                        Because they love themselves,
And take the children's meat to fatten swine.

PAUSANIAS.

Just so.   There spake my old Empedocles !
But who comes here?

EMPEDOCLES.

                        It seems a train of men
From Agrigentum.   Grant the gods that not
The Selinuntian plague hath taken wings,
And touched them with its foulness !

PAUSANIAS.

I know them now, all citizens and men
Of substance in the town.   I can discern
One of their oracles, Embadius,
A man of counsel, who might reap respect,
Did he not stage himself before the people
Too much like Jove, making his knotty staff
Play thunderbolt ; but here they come.

[*Enter a body of citizens from Agrigentum.*]

EMPEDOCLES.

Welcome, good gentlemen ; what is your business ?

FIRST CITIZEN.

Most honoured sir, we fear to steal the time
That being yours is sold to wisdom's work,
But we are urged by very grievous wrongs
To crave your ear a moment.

EMPEDOCLES.

                              Is the matter
Private or public ?

EMBADIUS.

What we come on is certainly of public, not of
private concern ; and yet of private also, for we who
are private persons are all touched by it ; and, indeed, public rightly interpreted is but the sum of all
privates. As a drachm signifieth only all the oboli
that it numbers, so every public wrong is the wrong

of all the private persons, whereof the public is constituted.

PAUSANIAS.

Speak more curt, Embadius; this is no forum for rhetoric; you will anger the priest, who hates above all things sounding sentences and big-bottled phrases.

EMPEDOCLES.

Well! let us hear.

FIRST CITIZEN.

High-sapient sir, the fact is simply this;
We by the oligarchy sorely galled,
And knowing you the people's friend, beseech
Your hand to break the yoke.

EMPEDOCLES.

                  I am not used
To meddle with affairs of state; you know
Where the shoe pinches.

EMBADIUS.

                In truth, sir, we do know: for it fits so closely, and is screwed down so tight, that we lack strength to draw it off. Thereto require we a strong arm, that is, with your liberty, your most excellent self.

FIRST CITIZEN.

'Tis even so; and therefore stand we here;
We are the twigs that ask a bond to bind us

And make us one.   We wield a thousand bows,
But, sans a head, we, like a blinded Cyclops,
Fumble for lack of counsel.

EMPEDOCLES.

What special wrong now stirs your discontent?
We bear no evils now but what we bore
These twenty summers.   The snail is used to bear
His house, so men their burdens.

EMBADIUS.

This is precisely the text of our complaint, that we
are not snails.   The burden which is laid on my
back, if Fate had made me a snail, that I will bear,
but being a man I bear only such burdens as to
man's nature appertain ; and being a man born, and a
free Greek to boot, I will not bear the yoke of vassalage.

FIRST CITIZEN.

Grave sir, 'tis very true : we know to bear,
And patiently have borne, till we can bear
No longer.

EMPEDOCLES.

　　　　Name your grievances.   I live
Without a murmur; why not you?

FIRST CITIZEN.

　　　　　　　　You are
So placed that their offence not reaches you,
Or, reaching, may be slighted.   We are poppies

That grow i' the open field, which they may lop
For pastime as they go, and no man blame them.
Such is their measure; and their measure makes
Our fate; but we say we are human kind,
One blood with them, and claim full brotherhood
Of civic right.　Our fathers won this soil
In common feud with the Sicanian hordes;
Our fathers drew the common sword against
The sea-marauding Carthaginians; we
With them drove out the tiger Thrasydaeus,
And now they fatten on the roods we sowed,
And for our wage they kick us!　Nevermore
May this consort with justice, that our backs
Be weighted with all fardels that they choose
To strap upon us.　They alone do make
The laws that lend them wings, and link our chains;
The council and the judgment-seat they hold
As private heirlooms.　In the rich man's cause
The rich man judges, and condemns the poor;
All favour, honour, privilege they heap
Upon their sons, and kin and cousinship,
While we stand by, and spill our blood, and cry
Huzza! to see them decked with dignities,
Whose flaring splendour from our bleeding wounds
Hath drawn its purple pride.　We were not made
That men should spit upon us, and expect
Low-crouching loyalty; we claim to share
The making of the laws, and so to bear
Apportioned burdens, freely with the free,
And with the equal equal.

EMBADIUS.

This, my lord, is precisely the posture of our plead-
ing; Liberty and Equality are the two points of our
charter, the two hinges on which our whole of citizen-
ship turns; and the one answers to the other as the
two shells of an oyster, or the two jaws of a mouth.
For, if we are all equal then are we all free, being
equal in the quality of freedom; and, if we are all
free, then are we all equal, being in the like measure
all gifted with freedom.

EMPEDOCLES.

Gentlemen, I have heard you to the end,
And well I know that not from empty air
You pluck your grievances.   'Tis the vice of power
To lord it o'er the powerless, as unpruned
A sturdier growth spreads rampant o'er the plot,
And smothers all the feeble.   If the god
Whose will I serve, and who commands my art
Wills that I lift my hand to strike again
I' the public cause, as once I struck before
When blood was hot in me, and wrongs were red,
In Agrigentum, and all Sicily cried
Aloud for vengeance, and the vengeance came,
I wait his mandate.   If he shall refuse
His sanctioning nod, my name may never be
Mixed with this new embroilment.   For yourselves
Work out your own salvation, prized the more
For that you spend your proper sweat, and blood,
And brain, and brawn to earn it.   Fare ye well.

[Exeunt Citizens.]

Pausanias, I will go consult the god,
And what he counsels do.   A stroke well planted
May shake a crazy palace ; when the pear
Is ripe, a little breeze may loose the stalk,
And strew the ground with plenty.   If I shake
The pillars, they from ruinous heap may pile
What building suits them.   I am not the man
To work their work ; but I may help their plan.

SCENE III.

*The Senate-House in Agrigentum, a committee of the Thousand
sitting in Council.*

PRESIDENT.

Well, worthy counsellors, who bear with me
The weight of thinking for the public weal,
Say with what humour do the people brook
The new adjustment of the common rates,
Our latest ordinance.

FIRST SENATOR.

                    As they always bear
What's for the general good, each from himself
Eager to shift the burden on his brother.
Self-counselled, each would for himself repeal
His rated service, till no rate remain,
And all agree to snap all bonds of order,
Banish all common store, and tumble back
To naked use of self-willed savagery,
Which knows no taxes.

SECOND SENATOR.

          And no ruler knows;
And so, being free and equal, they would all
Have equal right to claim what all desire;
And being free to fight for't, they would fight,
And hew each other down; then vote a king
Into the chair to still their own hubbub,
And save the remnant!

PRESIDENT.

          And their king would be?

SECOND SENATOR.

Tiger or fox; or one of mingled kind,
Both fox and tiger; certes not a lion!
The people never yet were wise to choose
Their master; but, like children, being sick,
From the confectioner take the candied death,
And spurn the leech's bitter-healing drug.

PRESIDENT.

Well said : the people, children, women, slaves,
Have one same need, firm-handed rule; and this
They get from us.   But for their present mood,
'Tis but the common grumble, I opine,
From fretful stomachs, which least peril bring
When least regarded; Nature's bubbling vent
We should not close: let them bescrawl the town
With slander, and make sacred dignities
A mark for public gibe,—but let them know
We hold the whip.

N

SECOND SENATOR.

   Trust me, 'tis nothing more
Than the old fret; the frogs make war with croaking.
Coax! coax!

FIRST SENATOR.

   I fear 'tis more than croaking:
Ætna will grumble twenty times before
He spits fire once. We must not sleep with snakes
Beneath our pillows.

PRESIDENT.

   Have you aught observed?

FIRST SENATOR.

I have observed what not to have observed
Had proved me blind. They wear a serious look
On their lean faces, and on holidays
At the street corners thickly congregate,
And look, and wink, and mutter. But t'other night
I saw Embadius, that booted pedant,
Talking, like sophist, to a wondering ring
Of sallow hearers, who devoured his words,
As starving fowls pick corn. I make no doubt
His speech had matter in't with danger fraught
To peace and public order, though I stood
Too far to catch its scope.

SECOND SENATOR.

   Pooh, he has talked
This way for years, and means no more, in fact,

Than to see himself on waves of plaudit ride
Before the mob.   I fear no man whose great
Tool is his tongue ; your silent men wear knives.

PRESIDENT.

Besides he's but a king of rabblement,
And leads the rats to battle.   There is none
Of mark or substance in the town who sell
Their ears to him.

FIRST SENATOR.

'Tis whispered that Pausanias and Acron,
The wise physicians, have been seen with him
In private parley.

PRESIDENT.

There may danger lurk.

SECOND SENATOR.

Pshaw ! fear them not !· a pair of peeping knaves,
Well trained to wander o'er the hill o' nights,
And cull strange herbs beslavered by the moon,
Or memorise the virtues of a patch
Of crusted lichen, torn from dripping rock,
And laid on for a plaster !—fear not them !
In the blind alleys of a frame diseased,
Their hand is drastic ; but on public stage,
And the broad day-light of large policy,
They show like moles uncustomed to the light,
And from the face of manful action creep,
Like road-side snakes that scuttle 'neath the stones,

When the stout traveller's knotted staff comes nigh.
Such men are harmless.

PRESIDENT.

    But Empedocles?

SECOND SENATOR.

Him I might fear.

PRESIDENT.

    But is he of them?

FIRST SENATOR.

They say that what Pausanias thinks he thinks;
And when Empedocles thinks, his thought will soon
Grow to a deed.

SECOND SENATOR.

       He lives not with the people,
And loves not us.   He keeps a soul apart.
Long months I have not seen him.   Rumour says
That he has doffed all state concern, and now,
Like leech Pausanias, affects a skill
In drugs and fumigations.   Some avouch
He's turned a poet, and gives his passion vent
In peopling parchment with sky-scaling dreams.

PRESIDENT.

Most like.   I knew him when a boy; he was
Always a dreamer.   I remember well,
Some fifty years ago, the urchin was

In the back garden of his father's house,
With whom I stood in serious talk upon
The house-top.   Well, we turned our eyes, and lo !
We see an altar in the middle green
Conspicuous piled ; and young Empedocles
Stood vested like a priest, and in his hand
Held stones, and fruits, and herbs of spicy power,
And wood of various splinter ; these he heaped,
Row after row, pyramidal, upon
The altar's top ; then looked in face of Heaven,
And voiced a prayer to Jove ; and then the child
Took from his belt a little rounded glass
Bought by his father from Sidonian men
Bound for Carchedon ; this he held before
The sun's bright orb, and by its potent virtue
Massed all the rays that fell upon its round
Into a point, which, with concentred heat
Flamed all the pyre ; and thus my baby-priest
Had done his sacrifice.

SECOND SENATOR.

O, rare conceit !

FIRST SENATOR.

And he is still a priest ; the boy's the bud
That blossoms in the man.   Men say he holds
Himself more surely than the Pythoness,
Apollo's mouth-piece, and with awful words
Speaks doom oracular.   With large promising
He vaunts to gag the winds, and fling his rein
On the imperious floods, and from the face

Of the hot copper sky bring spouts of rain,
To drench the gaping earth; he hath control
Of every element; his skill defies
Death; and the dark, long-shadowed pestilence,
Spell-bound by word of wise Empedocles,
Droops his black wing, and drops.

[Enter officer.]

OFFICER.

Most honoured councillors, a man demands
Admission to your session.

PRESIDENT.

Who is he?

OFFICER.

I know not; he is vested like a priest;
A man of presence and imperial port,
Most like a god to look on.

FIRST SENATOR.

'Tis himself—Empedocles.

PRESIDENT.

Let him come in!

[Enter Empedocles.]

Good morrow, worthy sage; what happy chance
Brings you, divorced from lofty communings,
To fellowship of trivial talk with us,
Who in the trodden paths of dusty life
Do vulgar service.

EMPEDOCLES.

My will obeys no chance ;
But like a ship well freighted I am bound
With message to your grace.

PRESIDENT.

From whom ?

EMPEDOCLES.

The god
Bids me declare his will.   Lend me your ears.

PRESIDENT.

What god?   Have you been missioned, and by whom
To Delphi or Dodona, or the shrine
Of hornèd Ammon in the Libyan sand?

EMPEDOCLES.

No man need travel far to seek the gods,
Who are as near us in our narrowest home
As when we wander o'er the spacious globe,
Who speak their will in nightly dreams, and in
The reverent silence of a bosom purged
From impure passion.

PRESIDENT.

Well, let the gods
Speak, or yourself.   The worship of this place
May not deny meet audience to a man
So wise reputed.

EMPEDOCLES.

First hear a parable
Spoke by the Phrygian sage, the friend of Solon,
Who knew the speech of beasts.   There was a man
Once travelled through a waste far-stretching plain,
When suddenly from out a shaggy wood,
Prickly with pine, and grown with ancient moss,
There rushed a bull with brazen bellowing,
And plunging head, and tail to fury lashed ;
What shall he do ? no tree is near, no wall,
No fence, no shelter, and his limbs are weak,
And weary from long march 'neath sultry skies ;
He spied a horse, some space apart, and said,
Good horse, if you allow me mount your back,
And use your legs, that I escape this bull,
I'll feed you in the grassiest lawn in Greece,
And you shall largely roam.   I'll keep your crib
High-heaped with corn ; you shall be free from goad
Of vulgar service, and the wearing use
Of heartless boors ; only on holidays,
Trapped in fine gold, and gay with heraldry,
Thou shalt be seen in front of all the pomp,
Bearing your master to the shrine of gods.
Well, said the horse, swear by great Jove, and I
Will serve you.   The man swore ; and on the back
Of the brave brute he mounted, and away
He scampered into safety.   Now attend.
The man stood faithful to his promise, firm and fast,
For twelve moons and a day, but after bought
A high-blood roan of pure Thessalian breed,
And gave it all his love.   The horse who saved

His master's life now scarce could save his own ;
His corn was stinted ; from the bleakest moors
He cropped the stiff grass ; every saucy knave
Might scourge his flanks, and yoke his pride to drag
Rubbish or offal ; he grew lean and lank,
And the flies fed their gory appetite
On his out-staring bones.   Upon a day
The favourite roan fell sick ; and now perforce
The master must content him to bestride
His ancient benefactor, for a short
But needful journey.   The most patient brute
Meekly uptook the rider, but in heart
Vowed sharp revenge.   The road lay by the sea,
Upon the edge of a high-toppling cliff,
Naked and sheer ; when at a sudden bend
The horse full deftly jerked his rider down
Into perdition, while himself escaped
With dusty speed into the wilderness.
Here ends my parable.

PRESIDENT.

       And where begins
Its pertinence to us ?

EMPEDOCLES.

      Jove stole your wits,
If this you see not.   Thou'rt the rider ; thou,
And these, thy grave compeers ; and, for the horse,
He is the people, whom you stint of joy,
To pamper your own pride.   The will of Jove,
From Loxias, prophet of his father, speaks

Now from my mouth.   Make free this people ; speak
Impartial dooms ; make equal laws ; embrace
With arms of love, whom now with haughty heel
Ye spurn : else have a care how the poor horse
May hurl you into Hades !

SECOND SENATOR.

Sir, you rave :
Your moody temper, fostered with cold moons,
Is cousin to hot madness.   You forget !

EMPEDOCLES.

Not I forget, but you.   When Thrasydacus,
That raging bull, tramped on all holy things,
Tossed right and statute with insensate horns,
To all the winds, gave to his hand free course
Through all men's pockets, and from every field
Reaped corn where others sowed, yea with such sweep
Of lawless haviour ramped, as the big world
Were all his toy to play with, or a cake
For him to slice ; this bull, this wolf, this bear,
Tiger, hyæna, viper, sum and soul
Of every beastly fierceness—him this hand,
And every hand that wields an honest tool
In Agrigentum, drave out from your bounds
And made you masters—for what fee ? to earn
Neglect, and scorn, and cold contempt, and airs
Of high disdainful eminence, and the right
To hoe, and sow and reap for you, while we
Are left to grub the out-field !   No, grave sirs,

This may not be; we must have equal laws;
Jove rules the world for all his creatures, not
For a few monstrous feeders; every Greek
Must help to make the laws which he obeys;
Thus saith the god I serve.

SECOND SENATOR.

                  My lord, we sin
Gravely against the duty of this place
To let this dreamer spew his frothy spite
Against the state we bear.   This cant he brought
From Athens, where, since Xerxes bowed his head
At Salamis, the naval people flown
With insolent esteem of their high worth,
Spurn ancient rule, and from most sacred seats
Cast down revered authority.   We who hold
By Doric use and strong consistency
Of due subordination, may not leave
Our ears, the warders of our wit, unhinged
To such seditious babble.   Call the officers
And bid them bind him!

PRESIDENT.

                  Ho! a traitor! seize
This man and bind him! officers!
    [*The officers come forward and proceed to bind Empedocles.*]

EMPEDOCLES.

Poor fools! your withes may bind me, but yourselves
Are bound already in the iron meshes
Of Justice, daughter of wise-counselling Zeus.

Here take my hand, and let your fetters eat
Into my flesh, my soul ye may not reach;
Freely I give my ankles to your gyves.
Poor fools! the barking of a thousand curs
Stays not Jove's thunder!

[*A loud knocking is heard without; then suddenly enter
Embadius and a great throng of Agrigentine labourers and
artisans, with halberts, picks, mattocks, and other instruments of
violence. They seize the councillors and bind them. The president and a few others escape by a hidden passage, through a
back door. They strike the gyves from Empedocles.*]

FIRST VOICE.

Down with the oligarchs!

SECOND VOICE.

Down! down!

THIRD VOICE.

To the crows!

FOURTH VOICE.

Strike for freedom! strike! strike! down
With the oligarchs!

EMBADIUS.

Now, my masters, thank the gods, we have made
quick work of it! There is no such cowardly beast
in creation as an oligarchy, that has usurped the
chair of a free people. Their strength lies all in our
lethargy: when we sleep they ride and rule; when
we awake they are straws and we are the hurricane!
A hurricane—yes! my valiant fellow-citizens, I have

said the very word; a god spake in me when I said it; in that word lies our strength, and in that word also, mark me, lies our weakness.

FIRST CITIZEN.

How our weakness?

EMBADIUS.

Timotheus, perpend. A hurricane is powerful to blow down, powerless to build up. We have now finished only the first act of the drama, and that the easiest. There remains to make a new constitution, a democratic constitution, a constitution that shall please everybody, and give just offence to nobody. Where is the man that shall curiously carve out and cunningly concatenate so marvellous a piece of enginery? Wilt thou, Timotheus?

FIRST CITIZEN.

Indeed, sir, I am, to speak with humility, a weak brother. I can see that we ought to bear equal burdens, but I cannot forge constitutions.

EMBADIUS.

Can you, Physcon?

SECOND CITIZEN.

In sooth, sir, my notion was, that, if the oligarchs were once fairly ousted, we might with small trouble rule ourselves. We are all free citizens, and, therefore, by natural right of man, all privileged to use our freedom, that is, to rule ourselves with freedom, and without taxation.

EMBADIUS.

Physcon, thou art a fool; there is more wit in thy paunch than in thy poll. That all men should rule all is impossible. Try it, and this our fair cosmos, which we call the state of Agrigentum, will resolve into chaos incontinently. Mark what I say: if a chariot, like the helmet of Pallas, could contain ten thousand warriors, there would still be but one charioteer: I propose, therefore, that, being now free to choose, we proceed to elect our charioteer; the charioteer of the democratic constitution—who shall he be?

A VOICE.

Empedocles!

ANOTHER VOICE.

Empedocles!!

A THIRD VOICE.

Empedocles!!!

GENERAL CRY.

Long live Empedocles and the constitution!

EMBADIUS.

[*Advancing to Empedocles.*]

Most sage and worshipful sir, you hear what your fellow-citizens say. They elect you archon of the democracy of Agrigentum. You are our head, our

hand, our spear, our shield, our everything.   Without
you we are, so to speak, a shoe without a foot, a mill
without a mill-wheel, a kitchen without a cook.

EMPEDOCLES.

Hear me, good citizens, and weigh my words.
Not from the prompture of mine own conceit,
Or spur of private vantage, I did freight
My shoulders with the task to speak for you,
And your Greek liberties.   What the god enjoined
I did, as works a slave his master's will,
My function but to voice the high command
Of Jove, the all-wise counsellor, to proclaim
The right of reason, to unlock the prison,
And set the captives free ; yours, being free,
To use that freedom easily.   If I knew
That wit in me to move the general heart,
And from the jar of harsh-contending claims
To charm forth harmony by smooth address
And wise device, and combinations fine,
I'd be the willing servant of your will,
Clept archon, aesymnete, or any name
The sweetest to your ears.   But I have lived
Some fifty changes of the moony year,
If less for others than my prayer desired,
Not vainly for myself.   I have surveyed
The length and breadth of what I ken and can.
I may not be a ruler.   I am sworn
To search of truth, and worship of the gods,
And witness of the harmonies of things
In wise discourse.   Within this bounded field

I move content, serene, and free from fear,
Vexed only by the dulness of my sense,
The briefness of our span, and the short range
Of mortal wit.   Therefore, dear friends, farewell.
I will to Aetna, being called to note
The workings of that potent central Fire
Which rends the iron bowels of the rock
With dread disruption.   For you, I pray the Father,
Upon that surgeful sea where you are launched,
To give you seaman's craft, and venture bold,
With wakeful caution.   This from me receive,
My latest word.   If you shall fail to keep
This new-won freedom, blame not the wise gods,
But your own folly.   Freedom's a glorious thing,
But 'tis a wine, which being largely used
Turns joy to madness, madness to despair.
Rejoice with trembling.   The excess of life
Lodges next door to death.   If ye shall fail
To rule yourselves with wisdom, Jove will send
New oligarchs to whip his naughty boys
With scorpions, not with scourges.   Fare ye well !

[Exit.]

FIRST CITIZEN.

He's gone ! a marvellous man !

SECOND CITIZEN.

Marvellous indeed ! one who will not taste a fat
pudding when it steams into his nose, and, when a
throne is set for him to sit on, lies on the grass like a
dog.

THIRD CITIZEN.

A most unaccountable man ! one who risks his
life to cut down a fruit-laden tree, and, when it falls,
is resolute to touch not with one of his fingers the
best apple that grows on it !

FOURTH CITIZEN.

One of your philosophers, an incalculable generation, who never do anything like other people.   They
may help us, but they certainly know not to help
themselves.

FIFTH CITIZEN.

I have heard it said he hath a magic mantle can
sail on the wind ; who knows but he may be supping
to-night with the Hyperboreans whom his god Apollo
loves, or with dart-rejoicing Dian on the horns of the
moon !

EMBADIUS.

He can do many things ; but this I know of him,
he'll stick to his purpose.   A little child shall sooner
draw his fingers out of a crab's pincers than any
mortal man turn Empedocles from the fixed mark of
his intention.   If he were now to say that he would
jump into the bowels of Aetna to see the secret brewst
of that Cyclopean cauldron, by Styx he would do it.
Meanwhile we must do what we can do without him.
It may be that he is right after all, perhaps a little
too good for us, and a little too dainty-fingered for
the rough work we have to do.

o

First Citizen.

Let's to the agora !

Second Citizen.

To the agora !

Third Citizen.

And Embadius shall lead us.

All.

Ioo ! Ioo ! long live Embadius ! Embadius and the Constitution ! to the agora ! to the agora !

[Exeunt omnes.]

ANAXAGORAS

Νοῦν δὲ τις εἰπὼν εἶναι, καθάπερ ἐν τοῖς ζώοις, καὶ ἐν τῇ φύσει
καὶ τὸν αἴτιον καὶ τοῦ κόσμου καὶ τῆς τάξεως πάσης, οἷον νήφων
ἐφάνη παρ' εἰκῆ λέγοντας τοὺς πρότερον.

ARISTOTLE.

ANAXAGORAS.

PERSONS OF THE DIALOGUE.

1. ANAXAGORAS, a Philosopher of Clazomenae, residing
   in Athens.
2. PERICLES, an Athenian Statesman.
3. ASPASIA, Beloved by Pericles.

SCENE.—*The house of Aspasia, in the suburbs of Athens.
Time sunset.   Aspasia discovered reclining on a couch, and looking towards the city.*

ASPASIA.

I wish the man I love were less to Greece,
And more to me; more to himself, and each
Dear friend that loves him. Whoso serves the people
Sweats for a hard taskmaster, who demands
All labour and no rest, for scanty fee.
Zeus has his cares : the vasty universe
Hangs on his nod; his thought is Fate ; but here,
In this Athenian world our Zeus, the Demos,
Knoweth not thinking, and my Pericles
To his wild will must be both brain and brawn,
And rule by studying wisely to obey.
Well ! well ! 'tis better so, no doubt, than love
A silken fopling, or a creamy-cheeked

Soft-bearded Ganymede, to watch my wink,
Swear me a goddess, deck me like a doll,
And lackey me with amorous services.
My Hercules must live to fight with lions;
Or bears, may be, sometimes—yes, bears,—while I
From the keen edge of expectation peer,
And with a lean and hungered outlook wait
To wipe the bloody trophy from his hands,
And hymn Athena's booty-bearing praise,
When he returns.

       [She rises, and walks about the room.]

                  What's here?—My lute.   Ah, no!
I cannot touch a string unless to work
His present pleasure!   Here's a book!   Right so!
The old theologer, Boeotia's boast.
I've had my fancies too about the gods,
Though I'm a woman; let me ruminate!
If that fat country makes not fat the wits,
Nor all the subtle glibness of the soil
The eel usurps in the Copaic pool,
There should be wisdom here.

[She unfolds the roll of the theogony of Hesiod, and reads.]

In the beginning had Chaos his birth, and then into
    being
Earth, broad-breasted, arose, firm footstool of gods
    who inhabit
High on immortal thrones the peaks of the snowy
    Olympus;
Earth and Tartarus dim in deep subterranean combs,
    and

Eros, fairest of gods, who with thrills of delicate rapture
Counsel subdues in the hearts of men and of gods
    immortal.
Then from Chaos was Erebus born, and the murky-
    mantled
Pitchy Night; and from Night sprang Ether and Day
    into being,
Fathered by Erebus mingling with Night in fruitful
    embracement.

Here I must pause; here's food for thinking, much
Beyond my stomach.   In distinctest phrase
He says, not *was*, but *had his birth*, and grew
And into being came; but why, and how,
Whence, and for what, the prophet gives no sign.
" *In the beginning*,"—when was the beginning?
Or how could things begin to be, and leap
Into this something from the womb of nothing?
All plants shoot from a seed; all mighty rivers
Are strained out of the clouds; all clouds do mass
Their volumes from the sea.

                    Then what could CHAOS,
With infinite waves of seething ferment, breed
But mere confusion?   Chaos breedeth Night,
And Night to Day gives birth; what means he here?
Sooner could love from hate, and fire from frost,
Milk from sharp vinegar, sweet from the sour, and
    reason
From distraught madness, fulness from the void,
And every thing from nothing, than that Light,

The blessed Light, from hated Night be born,
Which is in fact mere nothing, being naught
But sheer defect of light.   Here is no hope.
If this is all that grave theologers
Can teach a questioning and curious girl,
I'll take to levity again, and strum
A catch of the old Teian.

[She takes up her lute.]

But who comes?
I hear a footstep.   Let me see!   'Tis he!
Right sure 'tis he!   Adieu theology!
And welcome Pericles!

[Enter Pericles, who embraces her.]

PERICLES.

Well, queen of beauty, have you entertained
The hours with light-winged fancies since I left?

ASPASIA.

Partly; but partly, touched with moodiness,
For want of better company than myself
I plunged into a book,—but you,—how went
The slippery game to-day with that wild beast
Which knows your bit?

PERICLES.

O! to a wish! sing forth
Loud pæans to the gods; *ἰού! ἰού!*
For I have slain mine enemies, and now
Sparta doth count two kings, and Athens one.

ASPASIA.

Thucydides?

PERICLES.

Is ostracised.

ASPASIA.

                              And all

His faction down?

PERICLES.

                    Down; bruised and battered all
Flat as a toad, squelched by a weighty wain,
And quenched in its own venom.   I am free
To pitch this Athens in the general eye,
The cynosure of Greekdom, where the hate
Of Persia lives, and Freedom flaps her wings,
And to the Maiden goddess, whom all Greece
Adores, conjunct with her wise-counselled sire,
To pile a fane in pillared state beyond
The scope of small ambitions, that shall draw
The worship of all people, and out-dure
In strength of marble majesty severe,
The Memphian wonders.   Athens votes free use
Of all the Delian dues.

ASPASIA.

                        O wise decree !
A fierce, and yet a very facile beast,
I always knew the Demos.   You may lead
The wild boar by a string, if you but sound

The lion's march, and bid all beasts bow down
To their huge sovereign ; but I always said
That you could noose their necks, and make them bite
Your bit with pleasure.   Though I am a woman,
I knew that Pericles was Fate's chosen child
To tickle the tiger.

PERICLES.

O yes ! you women know
All things ; where Jove first tasted Hera's lips,
Where Aphrodite keeps her zone, and Mars
His sword, and Mercury his cap !   Some day
I doubt not you'll aspire to grow our beards,
And vote with pebbles, and engrave your hates
On damnatory shells, expound the law,
Surgeon the wounded, renovate the sick,
Command the agora, harangue the people
On war and policy, and shrewd device,
To foil the Spartan.

ASPASIA.

When you were a boy,
And mighty Xerxes, like a locust drift,
Swept with his wasteful myriads o'er the land,
There was a woman followed in his train,
So wise in counsel, and in field so brave,
That, had she been the head, and he the hand
Of that huge host, all Greece, from high Olympus
To Taenarus, were now a footstool planted
For insolent Persia's golden-sandalled foot ;
But Xerxes was a fool.

PERICLES.

Thank Heaven for that !

For Artemisia——

ASPASIA.

Never would have leapt .
Into the net spread by Themistocles.

PERICLES.

And glorious Salamis had been the key
Of Hellas to the Mede.

ASPASIA.

And Pericles
Had been a pretty page with ministrant hand
To hold a golden trencher to the king !

PERICLES.

Who knows what might have been, if Greeks were not
Greeks, and barbarians not barbarians.   But
Tell me, thou fairest of fair womankind,
Unchartered wisdom, and tenth Muse that failed
To top the nine, say in what lettered roll
You plunged your searching nose.

ASPASIA.

You have it there.

PERICLES.

Hesiod !

ASPASIA.

Even so.

PERICLES.

And did he teach you much?

ASPASIA.

Nothing, and less than nothing! With my blind foot
I stumbled on the threshold of the shrine,
And galled my flesh, and called the oracle
A fool, and turned my back upon the god.

PERICLES.

As I have done before, and all the men
Whom I call wise in Greece.   What else could be?
Boeotia had one Pindar; but I fear
The sober old Ascraean's homely wit
Helped your Ionian subtlety to more
Puzzle than progress.   It can calender
A shepherd's shearing or a reaper's sheaves,
Tell when to bait a fish, or lime a bird,
Warn a rash sailor from a rainy star,
Or from unlucky marriage-day a maid;
But that's his utmost.   Homer has a glimpse
At times of deeper truth, and in his sweep
Of old Pelasgic legendary drift
Brings down some precious gem that shows
Like a big golden nugget in the sand.

ASPASIA.

The poet sings the praiseful deeds of men,
But Hesiod is a grave theologer
And makes the gods his text; and we should look
To learn from such.

PERICLES.

                    Not till Pentelicus
Shall top Parnassus, and Ilissus swell
To Achelous, may Aspasia learn
From Hesiod.

ASPASIA.

                    I have heard Pythagoras saw
Once in the under world where he had been
Not once before, the old Ascraean bound
To a brazen pillar, moaning piteously,
Doomed to such torture for unseemly words
About the gods, far-wandering from the truth.

PERICLES.

I know not; for Pythagoras is a name
Round which there gathers every monstrous tale
That fools could dream, or itching fancy feign
In Hellas; but, fair sage, more sage than thou
A friend comes here to-night.

ASPASIA.

                              One whom I know?

PERICLES.

You've seen him once.

ASPASIA.

                    Or twice, perhaps?

PERICLES.

                                    Or thrice ;
But seen him only as you see a swallow
That flits across the eaves, or as you see
A traveller at a cross-way, where you change
A civil word and pass ; you never looked
Into the mirror of his soul, to know
The pictured wonders there.

ASPASIA.

                          Whom may you mean ?

PERICLES.

All Athens holds but one who could affect
To teach Aspasia.

ASPASIA.

                   Nay, I am not learned ;
But from the wise can glean some random truths,
As from the deep flood where huge monsters swim,
A little child that sits upon the brink
Can fang a stickleback with pin for hook.
But whose your friend ?   I'm sharply set to know.

PERICLES.

Guess.

ASPASIA.

      Well ; belike the man you mean is that
Odd son of Sophroniscus, whom we found
The other evening glowering moodily
On the departing sun, and looking like

A young Silenus, with snub nose, and eyes
That seemed to wander round his head, and see
All possible things.

PERICLES.

       No! sweetest.   No! not he;
He's in the bud; the man I mean hath cast
The summer blossom of his power, and bears
The autumn fruit of wisdom.

ASPASIA.

       Then you mean
The Clazomenian, whom the hierophant
Of boon Demeter called an atheist
But yesterday.

PERICLES.
Even so.

ASPASIA.

     He's very grave.

PERICLES.

And so am I, save when I look on you.

ASPASIA.

'Tis well he comes; we shall have sport anon;
But first he'll brush the cobwebs from my brain
I caught from Hesiod. Lo, he comes! I hear
The rustling of his beard.

    [*Enter Anaxagoras.*]

PERICLES.

Good even, friend !

After the blustering storms, and venomed spite,
And bitter ferment, and hot-blooded brawls
That vex the Pnyx, thy tempered face, serene
With mellow thought, attunes me like the breath
Of this sweet eve, and the mild-mingled hues
Of yon soft sky.   Aspasia, know the man
Who fathers more of good in Pericles
Than did the sire who gat him.

ASPASIA.

You're welcome sir ;

You have been known to me, as are the notes
Of a wood-bird to him that sits at home ;
And oft I wished to levy from your stores
The tax that knowledge owes to ignorance.

ANAXAGORAS.

I

Know nothing, lady, but a hundred guesses,
And half a score of reasoned truths that lend
These guesses grace.

ASPASIA.

Men say you know all things ;

But chiefly can interpret, as a book,
The starry scripture of the sky, each phase
Of changeful seasons, and the speechful sense
Of every portent that confounds the heart
Of apprehensive man, shakes into fits

Old-seated Powers that hope no good from change,
And from their stable basements pluck, like weeds,
Time-rooted thrones.   Sir, if you love my lord,
Do me this kindness : let the overflow
Of your much thinking pour into my dust,
And make me sapful !   Can you tell me why
The flaming face of the all-seeing sun,—
You well remember,—some three months ago,
Even at the top of noon, his brightness dimmed
And flung a tremulous leaden veil athwart
The sickened earth.   They say you can foretell
The fainting fits o' the moon.

Anaxagoras

         Well, I have tried.

Aspasia.

Men say the bright gods, frowning on the fault
Of sinful men, their brightness veil, and thus
Eclipses come.

Anaxagoras.

     Men say they know not what.

Aspasia.

Then make me know.

Anaxagoras.

     You see this lamp?

Aspasia.

         I do.

P

ANAXAGORAS.

Mark with how clear and stout a cone it shines;
But let me move my palm between your eye
And the full radiance—now you see it winks,
And shows but half a face, as children do
Peeping behind a door.

ASPASIA.

     Or beacon lights
Swept by a mist.

ANAXAGORAS.

   Well, now you comprehend.

ASPASIA.

Is this the whole?

ANAXAGORAS.

    What more need be? the moon
Travelling serene through silent wastes of air,
Sails with her spotty sphere between your eye
And the sun's disc; and curtained thus we feel
Darkness at noon.

ASPASIA.

    How simple, yet how sage!
And is this all that shakes the hearts of kings
With fever fits, blanches the rose of hope,
Staggers all calculation, lames all speed,
Cracks the strong nerves of stout-thewed enterprise,
And makes the imperious march of conquerors
Reel backwards, like a stream that meets a tide!

ANAXAGORAS.

Fair lady, man is proud, but man is weak;
We are the slaves of powers we may not know,
And on the vacant chair of knowledge throned,
Usurping Fancy flaps her busy vans,
And with the shadow of their own conceit
Affrays the boldest; as a little child,
Left by its nurse in the lone darkness, fears
The touch of nothing.

ASPASIA.

Can your ken discern

All things as plainly as you saw what masque
Dims the sun's glory?

ANAXAGORAS.

Lady, human wit

Knows, safely creeping, but makes guess with wings.
Some things are certain; many things are dark;
All things mysterious in their primal spark.
But what a thoughtful man, who lives for truth,
Of true may know, and things most like the true,
As the gods show to me, my duty bids
Impart to who inquire.

ASPASIA.

What is the sun?

ANAXAGORAS.

A glowing sphere.

ASPASIA.

A glowing sphere! how large?

ANAXAGORAS.

The chain, fair lady, no smith yet hath linked
To measure that ; but, for a modest guess,
That lustrous orb that to our vision shows
No bigger than a shield, and wheels his dance
Daily from rosy east to rosy west,
O'er azure fields with starry flowers besprent,
Is larger twice, or thrice, or four times more,
Than Peloponnesus.   If a man could ride
Like Ganymede upon an eagle's back,
And soaring sunward with unwinking eye,
Engaze the radiant round, he'd see it grow
Bigger and bigger, as a sailor, when
With nearing keel he ploughs the browner flood,
Sees the dim spot, that through the whiteness loomed,
Swell to a continent.

ASPASIA.

What hold you of the moon ?

ANAXAGORAS.

The moon's a land with mountains, rivers, caves,
Peoples and cities, even as our earth,
And, like our earth, made luminous by rays
From the all-permeant sun.

ASPASIA.

Our poets sing
That the Nemean lion from the moon
Came down to roar at Hercules ; is this true ?

ANAXAGORAS.

I know not; stones have fallen from the moon
As large as lions.

ASPASIA.

Stones?

ANAXAGORAS.

Yes; large and hot,
And hissing from some Aetna in the moon;
Doubt not.

ASPASIA.

What man hath seen them fall?

ANAXAGORAS.

The priest
Who salved them where they fell, and sacrificed,
And rained his prayers upon them, and made smooth
The lustrous trunk of the new god with wealth
Of slavered kisses.

ASPASIA.

Have you seen such stones?

ANAXAGORAS.

Yes! a good dozen; like an iron mass
They showed, all brown and burnished and harsh-
grained
From forge Cyclopean.

ASPASIA.

Wonderful!

ANAXAGORAS.

                All things
Are full of wonder.

ASPASIA.

        Tell me, what should be
The milky way?

ANAXAGORAS.

        'Tis but the softened light
Of thickly clustered stars, the most remote,
With interflowing rays, not overblazed
As at bright noon by the all-mastering sun.

ASPASIA.

Your words have likelihood; and as his foot
Proclaims all Hercules, so one word from the wise
Well said, gives note of many yet to say.
Dear Pericles, I pray thee hold me not
Oblivious of your presence, if I urge
This Delphian with more questions.

PERICLES.

                Beauty stoops
To pick a charm beyond herself, when she
Is found at Wisdom's feet; for mine own self,
Redeemed from that crude babble in the Pnyx,
With such high doctrine sounding in mine ears
I feel like one from bedlam rout uncaged,
And by sure wingèd ministry of Jove
Whipt upward to a green and gardened land,

Where I may sit and muse, the breezeless night,
Lulled by the songs of nightingales.   Talk on.

ASPASIA.

Well, if the windy Mimas ever blew
To fair Clazomene's sea-cinctured isles
Fine inspirations, like the voiceful oaks
In hoar Dodona, I shall gain from you,
Most learned sir, swift riddance of some doubts
That vex my reason.   I have here a book
Of lofty scope and high theology,
Which says that Chaos was the first of things.
[Shows him Hesiod's Theogony.]
Shall I accept it?

ANAXAGORAS.

Hesiod is, like many,
Half wise, half foolish ; like a sculptor's block
Cut on the one side into shapely lines
Of apt significance, on the other left
In unhewn blankness.   Chaos surely was,
And yet may be, where needful wisdom fails
To draw from the crude-mingled brewst of things
Like drops to like, and from all possibles
Make something real, and many somethings marked
Each with his regnant virtue.   You have seen
The harsh-grained rock before the rude assault
Of windy buffets, and the gradual siege
Of softening dews and slow-consuming rains,
Slide from its nature into speckled sand,
Formless and colourless, nor black, nor white,

Nor green, nor red, but all with all commixed.
Here Chaos grows before your eyes ; and what
The thing becomes when shaken from its joints
It was before the jointing.   With his wheel
A potter turns a lump of shapeless clay,
And makes a shapely jar ; your servant goes
At sunrise to the well, and stumbling breaks
The cunning form, and it is dust again.
Infinite Chaos is the bed from which
All being grows, and in each part of Chaos
All possible being sleeps.

ASPASIA.

How mean you this ?

ANAXAGORAS.

In a mixed heap of black and white, each part
May become black or white, which now is neither :
And oft-times what no eye perceives lies spread
With large infection through the floating mass.
A drop of ink into a bowl of milk
Being dropt, is present allwhere through the white,
From the creamy top to the thin waterish dreg,
But nowhere seen ; so all in all, believe me,
Lies hidden, uncognised ; for nothing springs
From nothing ; and what each thing now contains
Lay in the general womb and seed of things,
Else had not been at all.

ASPASIA.

This I believe ;

But whence grew Chaos ?

ANAXAGORAS.

> Chaos nowhere grew ;

It *was*.

ASPASIA.

> But my theologer says it came

First into being.

ANAXAGORAS.

> There he errs.   The world,

Not Chaos, had a birth.   The primal stuff
From which all being is compacted knows
Nor birth nor death, still equal to itself,
Through the long masquerade of changeful forms
Changeless. Thou see'st how water, charged with heat,
Is viewless vapour ; reft of heat becomes
The hoar and frosted rock which men call ice.
All firmness comes from fluency ; from air
All watery flow ; the form of things departs,
The power remains ; no force is lost in Nature ;
But all substantial being is conserved
With every various virtue, form, and hue,
By right of its own essence.

ASPASIA.

> This I see ;

For nothing comes of nothing, and by mere will
To make a garden bloom forth from no seeds
Beggars the wit of gods ; but this I ask—
How from this jumbled welter of all possibles
Came forth the fairest possible, the World ?

ANAXAGORAS.

Here Hesiod halts ; but any child may teach you
The link he lacks.   What made the world is MIND.

ASPASIA.

How prove you this?

ANAXAGORAS.

                    It was but yesterday
I chanced in the Piraeus to be cheapening
Some saffron from Cilicia, when I saw,
Close by the shrine of Zeus and Pallas sitting
A little maid, a most industrious imp,
With eyes like stars, and hair like flowing waves
Of boon Demeter's gift in harvest month ;
She with nice craft had moulded from the clay
A panoplied Pallas, and in her hand had put
A long straw for a spear.

ASPASIA.

                    Well, what of that ?

ANAXAGORAS.

Suppose I had not seen that pretty maid
Into the goodly likeness of a god
Moulding the clay, but stumbled on the work
As she had left it, what then had I said ?

ASPASIA.

                    Some child had made it.

ANAXAGORAS.

With her fingers?

ASPASIA.

Ay.

ANAXAGORAS.

And with her fingers only?

ASPASIA.

No; her hand
Was but the tool with which her genius toiled.

ANAXAGORAS.

Such genius is the MIND that made the world;
Such Mind from Chaos' seething cauldron charmed
All this fair order.

ASPASIA.

Sayst thou that mind may be
In hurricanes, and whirlwinds, and the swing
Of tossing torrents, and the air-rending claps
Of terrible thunder?

ANAXAGORAS.

Lady, you have mind,
Not only when you measure thoughts with me,
As a cool fencer measures stroke to stroke,
But when you trip the graceful maze, and in
The dizzy whirl of your light twinkling feet
Sweep the admiring gaze. Believe me, lady,
'Twas mind that made the world a world at first,

And only mind upholds it, being made.
All torrents, tempests, squalls, and hurricanes,
Loud-rolling thunders, and huge tidal swells,
Which over-sweep our ease, and rudely shake
The tenon from the mortise of our lives,
Are in the vast admeasurement of things
Part of a balanced whole, as nicely true
As the fine tactics of your mimic men
Upon the chess-board.   What we mean by world
Is order, and all order comes from mind;
Else might the letters in a school-boy's box
Leap into sense, and Homer's rhyme be piled
From a sick baby's dream.   All things are slaves
But Mind which, strong by autocratic right,
Moulds and controls, musters and marshals all.
Matter with matter mingles, dust with dust,
With water water, till the confluent drops
Swell to an ocean; but from mixture free,
Like Jove, remote from all the throng of gods
Mind sits enthroned, even as an army counts
Thousands of hoplites, but one general,
And all the uncounted troop o' the radiant stars,
One sun.   Mind being one fills all
The multiform with oneness, wandering else
In babblement inane, and spent like spray
In barren dissipation.

ASPASIA.

You behold
This rose : how came it not to be a lily?

ANAXAGORAS.

There are who talk of puissant circumstance,
Fine combinations, born of dateless time,
Formative forces, self-evolving laws,
Consistent sequence, and perdurant form,
From chanceful-falling dice; but these are fools,
Who please their ears with pomp of cunning phrase,
As strange to reason and the law of thought
As is the mumbled shibboleth of a creed
To God-discerning piety.   I have
One answer to such questions; in the chaos
Nor rose nor lily lay; but when the power
Of mind in plastic circles swept the tide
O' the infinite germs of things, as amber rubbed
Draws straws to itself, or as the magnet makes
Iron from sand disparted form in threads,
So from confusion order rose, and things
By dominance of kindred particles
Took each his separate feature and his type.
That which makes difference in things is mind;
A block of wood becomes a stool, a chair,
A spoon, an oar, a sceptre, or a god,
As in the cunning carver's shaping soul
The type was gendered.   Shape is but the stamp
Of quality imposed on formless stuff,
Which else were all, or nothing.   To create,
We needs must separate, and like to like
Welding, strike out the measured marks that make
Classes and kinship.   Thus the Cosmos grew
Out of rude Chaos, and still growing spreads

To difference more rich and vast, and swells
The simple cuckoo's note to thundering sweep
Of Titan harper on uncounted strings.
Mind is the harper, and the harp the world,

ASPASIA.

But a good harper makes no jars; the world
Is full of jarring.

ANAXAGORAS.

                    There again you speak
Not like Aspasia. Who knows but the midge
That buzzes o'er the bubbling marsh esteems
Aspasia's lute. a discord, when she sings
The praise of gods and heroes to the march
Of Pindar's Muse?

ASPASIA.

                    Thus in the sum of things
You swamp all difference, if worms may rank
With serpents, man take measure from a midge.

ANAXAGORAS.

Blame me not, lady; man and midge are both
Great by comparison, or small; a fly
Is small to you; the Thunderer in the sky
Holds you a minim; in the wimpled wave
A floating bubble, breaking with a puff,
Is to great Ocean as Aspasia's soul,
Or mine, or any human soul that thinks,
To the great soul o' the world.

ASPASIA.

                    In this wise
Your wisdom plucks the plumes from our conceit
Right royally; and king or beggar thus
Is but a dot to Jove.

ANAXAGORAS.

                    Weak swimmers need
Bladders to float them, and delusion feeds
Weak stomachs that reject unsugared truth.
Man is most little then when least he knows
His littleness, and blares his mighty nothings
Into a breadth of trumpeted display,
Which tickles children, and makes mirth to Momus.
All things are small but God, and all things great
In his great purpose.   We are great by being
Part of the mighty thought that shapes the whole.

ASPASIA.

Well spoke, high-honoured sir.   Apollo's priest,
Who from the Clarian well makes pure the blood,
To course with prophet virtue through his veins,
Never spake wiselier.   I could lecture now
On high theogony with tripping tongue
As glib as Gorgias; I could sell my words
For gold, and make dear market of my wit,
Like many a famous sophist: let me see!

   [*She retires with Hesiod in her hand.*]

ANAXAGORAS.

What means she now?

PERICLES.

Wait; 'tis her wont, you'll see.

ASPASIA.

[*Returning after a little.*]

Yes! now I have it.

In the beginning was Chaos; then Mind, the mighty magician,

Strong, with circular sweep set the mingled atoms in motion,

And in concentric whirls was monad from monad disparted,

Seeking divergent homes, and moulded to opposite natures;

Some were heavenward sent, the light, the wingèd, the fiery;

Some to drops were condensed, and formed wide ocean; and some were

Hardened to rock, and became the crusted face of the broad Earth;

Like came rushing to like, and countless forms of existence

Massed in limited types, were marshalled in beautiful order.

Thus the Cosmos arose—

PERICLES.

Bravo! bravo!

ASPASIA.

And Mind was monarch of all things.

PERICLES.

Thus the Cosmos arose, and Chaos was conquered
for ever!

ASPASIA.

Bravo! bravo! and formless Chaos shall reign again
never!

ANAXAGORAS.

I too say bravo! would I oft might find
Such apt disciples! Sophroniscus' son
Not from my flask more greedily drained the oil,
When first I trimmed his lamp. But I must go.

ASPASIA.

Nay, you remain; a glass of Pramnian wine
Waits for you in the arbour.

ANAXAGORAS.

                        Lady, wine is good,
And, seasoned with the sweetness of your wit,
Is named with nectar.

ASPASIA.

                        Sages too can flatter;
But you must sup with us.

ANAXAGORAS.

                        Fair lady, no!
I'm bargained to Euripides to-night,
Who in his plays is fond to prink the verse
With shining granules from the golden sand
Of our philosophy.

ASPASIA.

He should have been
A sophist; he hath much delight to make
Parade of speeches, and unfolds his case
Even as a practised pleader 'fore a jury,
With pleasing amplitude of polished phrase,
To entertain their dulness.

PERICLES.

Ay; myself
Sometimes have filched his phrases; Socrates,
Who noses all fine qualities, declares
A play of wise Euripides as good,
Better, perhaps, than tractate most profound
On Nature by our sagest!

ANAXAGORAS.

Even so!
Verse is the very mintage of our gold
That gives it currency; we thinkers dig,
But neither buy, nor sell;—Good night to both!

ASPASIA.

Good night! and come again.   When you lack ears
To listen, think on me.
[*Exit Anaxagoras.*]
Well, Pericles,
Bright stars with bright keep company, and the wise
Herd with the wise.

PERICLES.

He is a man of thought,
And as he thinks he acts ; he might have been
For wealth the foremost in Clazomenae ;
But, counting gold a hindrance to his scope,
Unfettered by the small economies
That peg proud speculation's wing, he lives
To search deep-reasoned truth, and to proclaim
Its harmonies to men ; he taught me much.

ASPASIA.

And me.   You saw with what a flashing edge
He clave my dulness, and gave me a sense
To spell my Hesiod.

PERICLES.

So it chances aye :
With eyes we see not, and with ears not hear,
Till, touched with salve of high philosophy,
We lift our lids, and lo ! all Nature shines
With flaming miracles.

ASPASIA.

The gods be praised
That we are Greeks, and wisdom dwells where you
Rule wisely, schooled by Anaxagoras wise ;
But mark me well, and let me prophecy !
This your wise friend, whose life enriches yours,
Will not live long in Athens.

PERICLES.

Not live ! for why ?

ASPASIA.

He is too wise and good: his wisdom shows
Here, like a sharp invasive ray that cleaves
The general dark, whose questioned sovereignty
Will cast him out.   Himself hath taught me this;
Like draws to like, and bird with bird is paired;
'Tis bruited much that, like Protagoras,
He is an atheist.

PERICLES.

Protagoras, I potently believe,
Is a most pious man, though far from wise
In that he blazed into the vulgar view
Of purblind peepers, truths as apt for them
As noon-day glare for owls; he doth deny
The gods, the people say; and so, indeed,
His book says to the ear, but to the sense
Of him who thinks, and thinking reads, his word
Denies not gods, but what weak mortals deem
Or dream about the gods.

ASPASIA.

    Belike; but he
And Anaxagoras are atheists, both
In the intolerant tyrannous conceit
Of our poll-counted demos, who, you know,
Do rate themselves the very crest and crown
Of Greekish piety, and this town the loved
Abode of gods, and fortress of immortals;
In whose esteem the man whose clearer sight
Hath spied a flaw in their high-lauded faith

Is but the stinking fly within the pot
Of their most fragrant ointment; they have the power,
And will not lack or will or skill to cast
The offender out.

PERICLES.

We cast Thucydides out!

ASPASIA.

That was a chance by wisdom wisely used.

PERICLES.

Have you no faith in our Athenian men?

ASPASIA.

Yes; but as men.   In monkeys I have faith
That they will mow and mock and grin; in bears
That they will growl; in dogs that they can nose;
I do believe in hens that they will cluck
And run from rain, and store the straw with eggs;
In cocks that they will crow, and strut, and fight;
In Persians that they sweep the streets with silk;
In Spartans that their arms can brandish steel,
And that their fingers love to stick to gold;
And in Athenians I believe that they
Can talk, and laugh, and dance, and sing, and flash
With points of wit, like light on shimmering seas,
Or stars in cloudless skies, but not that they
Can leap out of their skins.

PERICLES.

              'Tis ever thus;
You women paint, in black and white, and find

Your chiefest bliss in hugging hot extremes,
Trusting in all points, or in all suspecting.

ASPASIA.

So be it! Pericles is king of Athens,
And brooks no NO to-night: but mark me well,
Women can prophesy; and I shall be
Cassandra to your fate and Pythia now;
You'll have a wrestling-bout with Demos soon
For Anaxagoras, and yourself, and all
The friends that love you.

PERICLES.

    The gods make true your word!
A goodlier death I could not choose to die,
Than with my sword drawn for what most I prize,
Aspasia fair and Anaxagoras wise.

ASPASIA.

Well, fights are always splendid when we win,
And easy when we dream.   But let's go in!

  [*She leads him out into the supper room.*]

SOCRATES.

I. ARISTODEMUS; OR, THE ATHEIST.

ὠγαθέ, κατάμαθε ὅτι καὶ ὁ σὸς νοῦς ἐνὼν τὸ σὸν σῶμα ὅπως βούλεται μεταχειρίζεται· οἴεσθαι οὖν χρὴ καὶ τὴν ἐν τῷ παντὶ φρόνησιν τὰ πάντα ὅπως ἂν αὐτῇ ἡδὺ ᾖ οὕτω τίθεσθαι.

XENOPHON.

ARISTODEMUS; OR, THE ATHEIST.

PERSONS.

ARISTODEMUS, A young Athenian.
CHAEREPHON, an Athenian, Disciple of Socrates.
SOCRATES.

SCENE.—*A Street in Athens.*

[*Enter Aristodemus.*]

ARISTODEMUS.

Protagoras was right ; if there be gods,
Or if there be not, overjumps my ken ;
But this I know, I am a man, and take
Of things that be the measure for myself,
And things that be not.   Each man for himself
Is God in his own world, his world the hour,
And what it brings—all else is blank and void.
The moment and its thrill of soothèd sense
Is heaven to man and moth.

[*Chaerephon appears in the distance.*]

But who comes here ? oh ! 'tis my boxwood friend,
My yellow face, my bloom of asphodel,
Who feeds on moonwort and on meditation,

And hangs on Socrates, that quibbling pedant,
As children on their nurse's skirts, and curs
On heels of them that kick them.   Yet I ween
He is no pudding-pated fool, no dough
That lends itself with apt servility
To the first hand will knead it; he hath bone
And stiff upstanding bristles, being roused,
And firm-set will, and tough persistency;
And, when he claps the spur to his conceit,
He'll ride the battlefield of argument
Fierce as Achilles, and with fearless chase
Out-gallop all the Furies.   Jove knows how
A fellow full of nerve and fire, and made
To head a rattling charge of cavalry,
Should get him so entangled and enmeshed
In that old proser's quirks and quiddities!
How now, good comrade, whither drives your speed?

CHAEREPHON.

To Socrates.

ARISTODEMUS.

        To Socrates! what can you hope to learn
From him?

CHAEREPHON.

    All things.

ARISTODEMUS.

            O yes, all things he knows,
Like that Margites, of whom Homer sings,
Who knew all trades, and all trades badly knew.

CHAEREPHON.

I fear you know him not, the godlike man ;
Else had you loved him.   Hast thou drawn thy breath
In this wise Athens, and not felt his power
As broad and gracious, as when Phœbus draws
From lawn and hill-top, and from bosky dell,
Bright flowers to strew the pathway of the spring.

ARISTODEMUS.

O yes; I know him; but not know to use
Your fragrant fine similitudes, and tropes
That smack of nectar.   I have heard him called
The great man midwife of our Attic youth,
Who brings to birth each green and crude conceit
Of men, whose waking business is to dream.

CHAEREPHON.

You know him wrong.   The Delphic oracle——

ARISTODEMUS.

Bah ! who believes in oracles?   I have heard
Our politicians buy their prophecies,
Like other wares, with gold.

CHAEREPHON.

I know not; but I know the Pythoness
This answer gave to me, and got no gold—
Your Sophocles is wise ; wiser than he,
Euripides ; but wiser far than both
Is Socrates, the son of Sophroniscus.

ARISTODEMUS.

I'm sick of him; his wisdom were no harm,
Would he but keep it to himself, and ride
His hobby in the riding school; but now
He makes the public square his training floor,
Haunts the palaestras, and infects the streets
With his snub nose, and big out-standing eyes
That walk about, and see all round his head.
One cannot miss him in the agora
More than the henwives, when they bring their hens
Well-cooped to market; would he too were cooped !

CHAEREPHON.

What harm does he?—he loves all men and wears
A smile for every comer; fair or foul,
He's ever bright.   Apollo knows a cloud,
Socrates never.

ARISTODEMUS.

       He hath a wealth of smiles,
As ever on good terms with his sweet self.

CHAEREPHON.

Not without cause: wise men are happy men.

ARISTODEMUS.

The cat is happy when it plays a mouse;
The angler when he lands a lively trout;
So this old quibbler when in verbal noose
He traps a simple wit, and tortures him
On hooks of contradiction.

CHAEREPHON.

You mistake;
The man I venerate traffics not in words.
Not his the craft to thrash the wind, or sow
The barren sea, or twist a rope of sand,
Or measure slippers for a flea, or take
The cube root of a mustard seed, or roof
A tent with beetle's wings, or plant a cone
Upon its apex by the dexterous craft
Of words well set in rank and file. Not he;
Euclid of Megara might cobwebs weave
For flies; but who would fish for souls of men
Must twine his meshes of a stronger cord.
My master brooks no jugglery of phrase,
But tears the swelling purfles of your speech,
And shows the naked frame, or fair or foul,
With every pin and pivot of your thought,
Bare to the day. He's a brave fellow too,
And when hard blows are needful deals in blows.
I've heard old grey-beards tell, when all the rest
Fled like a whirl of snow-drift from the fight
At Delium, he, like Ajax, his retreat
Footed as nicely as a dancing-girl
May time her paces. 'Tis a rare thing that men
So deft of tongue can with such cunning wield
Their limbs, and with such brawny forwardness
Launch out their arms to action.

ARISTODEMUS.

He's a cool dog, and looks you in the face
With a fixed stare, as blushless as a bull;

Oft-time I've wished to slap him on the cheek,
And pluck his beard.

CHAEREPHON.

              And, if you did, you'd reap
A barren triumph. Water shall sooner wet
A water-fowl, or fish be drowned in sea,
Or birds in air, than insult or reproach
Fret the fair summer softness of his soul.
He knows not wrath, and scorns hostility,
As Phoebus in his April increase laughs
At the sour drift which baffled Winter flings
On his enforced retreat. I well remember
When a rude fellow heaped him with abuse,
He turned aside and said—This bitter blast
Warns me seek shelter; with a north wind keen
He fighteth best who plants a hill between.

ARISTODEMUS.

He is well schooled to bear all contumely,
And from a scolding woman's tongue hath learned
To vail his crest in meekness.

CHAEREPHON.

              There you are right.
Whoso would sit, like Centaur, on a horse
Takes not the dull, demure, down-trodden hack,
But the high-blooded, mettlesome, and apt
To throw his rider; this he tames, and sits,
And rides secure upon the skittish brute,
As on the storm an eagle. Even so

I choose my wife, said Socrates, for this end,
To learn to manage her, and manage thus
The worser steed, myself.

ARISTODEMUS.

          O, he's perfection !
Right pious too, I understand, and prays
To Pallas, Jove, and all the host of gods,
Of whom the baby-world erst fondly dreamed
When Homer rocked its cradle !

CHAEREPHON.

          Here he comes !
Of Homer and the gods you may discourse
At large with him : he'll give you line, believe,
And leave you flouncing on a muddy shore,
Like an old eel, when the deep pool is dried
Where it grew long and fat.
       [*Enter Socrates.*]
          Good Socrates,
Here is a friend who gladly would be taught
The power and virtue of the gods from thee.

SOCRATES.

Hail, noble youth ! the fountain of all good
Is Jove, and reverent piety the root
Of all the virtues.

ARISTODEMUS.

Virtue is good ; but, for your piety,
Who worships Jove worships he knows not what.

SOCRATES.
Who taught you that?

ARISTODEMUS.

Protagoras, and all
The famous sophists who from town to town
Make knowledge travel by contagious power
Of wise discourse.

SOCRATES.

I know Protagoras,
A very just, well-worded gentleman;
Who knows him not? to round a sentence well
Lives not his equal from the rugged Thrace
To fruitful Sicily; but, for the gods,
If he denies them, then, for once full surely
A wise man's mouth hath brought forth foolishness,
And from sweet fountain bitter water flowed.
Come, answer me.

ARISTODEMUS.

Right willingly, so be
You use plain speech, and deal not over subtly
With my untutored wit.   I think as men
Think in the field and in the market-place,
And know no paces but what bear my limbs
To where my business calls me.

SOCRATES.

That is wise;
You'll find no man-traps in the agora
Nor in my speech.   Now this thing tell me first,

Who, by your reckoning, were the wisest men
In Athens?

ARISTODEMUS.

Well, I fancy he who found
His heritage a wilderness, and left it
A garden to his children.

SOCRATES.

There my wit
Sails close with yours.   Now, further say wherein
This wisdom lies, more than in other works
Of the much-labouring race of deedful men.

ARISTODEMUS.

Why, to make much of little, and to bring
Blossoms from barrenness, and from hideous scars
The blush of beauty, surely this must be
The witchcraft of high thought.

SOCRATES.

Even so.   'Tis Thought,
Plan, Calculation, Purpose, that creates.

CHAEREPHON.

And, when I find a wilderness, and say,
Here from this bog I'll drain the stagnant tide,
And lead it kindly o'er the thirsty heath,
And make it trickle down the arid rocks
In fertilising rills, and from this parched
And shingly slope I'll teach the white-stemmed birch
To fling her graceful tresses, and the pine

R

To spread his broad green fan, and in this nook,
Where spiteful Boreas droops his baffled wing,
I'll plant my cottage, and I'll plough my field,
And of this wide and wasteful moor I'll make
A grassy lawn, and pile my mansion here,
Cinctured with roses, and with leafy shield
Of laurel shaded and of sycamore ;
I speak with Reason's prophecy, and all
I do is Reason ripened into deed.

ARISTODEMUS.

Just so ; he fills his mouth with tropes, and makes
My sense look bigger ; what I said, short-summed
Was this, that fruit of wisdom chiefly shines
When Thought brings order from confusion, and
Growth from decay.

SOCRATES.

Our Solon thus was wise,
Who twixt the stout and overlusty lords,
And their poor bondsmen growling discontent,
Made sweet accord of well-poised government.

CHAEREPHON.

And wise was he who from the babblement
Of multitudinous voices, and the strange
Wild intertanglement of sound with sound,
Which we call language, framed an alphabet ;
By whose high-reasoned order all the vast
Luxuriant storm of moulded speech becomes
As clear and measurable as the rank and file
Of a well-marshalled host.

ARISTODEMUS.

                Yes! Cadmus was wise,
Phoenician Cadmus or Egyptian Thoth,
Or both together; for most like our stream
Flows from barbarian founts, and vainly we
Deem ourselves earth-born, native to the soil,
Like rocks and oaks. Not wisely may the tree,
Which the sun kisses on its breezy tip,
Despise the darksome far-fanged root by which
It stands and grows.

SOCRATES.

              Bravo! you too have tropes.
I am no poet, but a plain-worded man
That would live wisely, and help men to live;
Yet much I love true thought that for itself
Shapes an apt body in a pictured phrase.
Now tell me this: If Solon was most wise,
Phoenician Cadmus, and Egyptian Thoth;
If Polycleitus, Zeuxis, and his hand
Who made the formless and insensate block
Breathe forth the awful majesty of Jove,
And the bright terror of his daughter's eyne,
Know you none wiser?

ARISTODEMUS.

              Well; I cannot say.

SOCRATES.

If Polyclete and Phidias were wise
To type the living in the lifeless, say

Who made the living prototype must be
Wiser by much.

ARISTODEMUS.

       Belike ; but no man knows
This hidden Maker.   Chaos and old Night
By secret throes of primal Eros stirred,
And bound by bonds of strong Necessity
Brought forth—so our theologers bravely sing—
This struggling, blustering, battling, whole of things,
This bubbling pot of crude hostilities,
Which men call life, or rather life and death,
To endless scuffle damned.   I cannot see
Much wisdom here.

SOCRATES.

       If mid the dust and heat
Of a far-spreading battle, whose wide lines
Outreach the eye, some soldier, posted far
In the extremest flank, should know no more
Of the great plan and purpose of the fray,
Than a strange wanderer through a pathless wood
Knows of the marks which guide the forester,
Not less the artful captain knows the how
And why of every calculated move
That wins the game o' the battle.

ARISTODEMUS.

           Very likely.
But, if he recks not me, nor spares my life,
And I am kicked about from risk to risk,

Even as a ball that makes the children sport,
And with a blind obedience led to woo
The slashing sword, harsh barb, and pointed spear,
Why should I love him?

SOCRATES.

Curb thy hasty tongue;
Deem'st thou that thou and I are in such wise
Entreated of the gods?   O say not so,
Unless, belike, my teeth were made to ache,
And every breath of wind brought hellish smoke,
To smart mine eyes.   I pray thee cast a thought
Upon that goodly framework, called thy body,
So curious-piled, so cunningly composed,
So strong to bear, so jointed well to bend,
So quick to move with every various thrill
Of pleasurable power.   That little eye,
Whose circlet holds the vasty world in view,
Who made it was an architect, and wise
To roof it with a moving pent-house lid,
And guard it with the cornice of the brows.
Bethink thee also what a wealth of sounds
Wends through the technic chambers of the ear,
Nor this for luxury only, but for need
To sentinel what danger from behind
Might steal unseen.   The teeth with reasoned skill,
These to divide, and those to grind were made;
The mouth, where sight and scent might indicate
The healthful food received well-ordered place;
While, from each delicate sense removed, what failed
To nourish life from life was cast away.

Deem'st thou this workhouse of assorted tools,
This stately pile of nicely-portioned rooms,
Was tumbled into form by chance, as when
A dicer throws the highest throw three times,
And marvels at the kindness of the dice?

ARISTODEMUS.

Well, there does seem strange wisdom in these things;
But this fair order with disorder foul
Is paired; sweet honey with sour vinegar
So madly mixed, one knows not with what name
To bless or ban the potion.

SOCRATES.
Rein thy tongue,
Young man; nor blame my free speech when I say
Thy words run wild, and from the Muses far.
Shall sun and moon, and every trooping star
Stoop from the shining battlements of heaven
To pleasure thee? and, if a little chink
Gapes in thy boat, belike from thy neglect,
Shalt thou blaspheme the carpenter, whose hand
Timbered the floating house?   What thou dost call
Disorder is but order more complex,
And plan too vast and multiform for man's
Baby-conception.   Chance is nowhere found,
Or all chance is divine: a god commands
The gusty blast, and twists the chambered shell.

ARISTODEMUS.
But I not see this god; the blast to me
Is but a terrible confounding force.

SOCRATES.

And when Aristodemus flaps a fly
From off his nose, his flap to the poor fly
Is but a terrible confounding force;
And yet Aristodemus is a man,
And, if his mouth might truly voice his thought,
A very proper man.   You do not see
The gods, you say;—pray do you see yourself?
Or can I see the thing that is yourself,
The soul that is the king of what you call
Your body?   Soul is nowhere seen, but felt.
No revelation of the mighty Jove
Can be, but the fair world which he hath made,
Indwelt by him, and fashioned as befits
The immortal vesture of immortal Mind.

ARISTODEMUS.

Well, be it so; but why should I besiege
His throne with prayers, and mock his mightiness
With the poor ministrations of a moth?
He needs not me, nor recks my little breath,
More than the chariot-rider recks the fly
Caught in the whirling fervour of his wheels.

SOCRATES.

Most natural thought, and yet ill-sorted.   You
And I have no concern with flies; but God
Makes them, and wings them, when with rare delight
They weave their sportive dances in the sun,
And, if they die upon a whirling wheel
Or in a honey-pot, there is no harm:

They've had their joy ; all mortal things must die ;
But if you deem the gods need not your prayers,
'Tis true ; the need is yours to pray to them
With kindly trust, even as a little child
Hangs by its mother.

ARISTODEMUS.

     But, when I shall pray,
Will the gods answer?

SOCRATES.

     Chaerephon and I
E'en on that theme wove very grave discourse
But yesterday.   Perhaps he'll give you now
The fruit of our debate.

CHAEREPHON.

     Right willingly.
Casting our eyes upon the breathing wealth
Of life in the vast-heaving world, we found
All kinds, all types, all faculties, all forms,
In rich gradation ; from the slimy worm,
The blind earth-burrowing mole, the fluttering fly,
To the keen-scented hound, the stately steed,
The sun-confronting eagle, the vast troop
Of glancing swimmers in the swarming deep,
The brindled strong-jawed tiger, and the tramp
Of huge-limbed elephant by Ganga's flood :
All these by inspiration from the gods,
In every guise of beauty and of power,
Walk the broad-breasted earth, and with their being

Praise mighty Zeus.   But of all creatures, Man
Stands forth pre-eminent; in him great Jove
Hath capped and summed his wondrous workmanship,
As in the bright-hued bloom the plant beholds
The crowning joy of its transmuted green.
All other kinds that walk the earth declare
Prone-faced their earthy kinship; he alone
Looks upwards from the ground, and with proud glance
Holds converse with the stars; his pliable limbs
By dexterous shaping make the world his slave;
And, where his strength may fail, his subtle wit
Commands an army of Promethean tools,
That make earth, fire, and water work his will,
To ride in triumph o'er the subject globe.
And, if the light air-winnowing birds outrun
His earth-bound movement, Jove hath gifted him
With magic of far-travelling thought, which swift
As lightning darts from pole to pole, and scales
The flaming battlements of the universe
With fearless wing.   But, crowning all the gifts
Wherewith the gracious Fate hath richly dowered
High-favoured Man, the chiefest is that he
Alone can know the gods, and own the source
Whence his rare greatness flows. Hence prayers ascend,
And hymns of grateful praise, and temples rise
Conspicuous far in each well-peopled land,
And creeds with various phrase that strive to lisp
The wonder of our being.   Never brute
Had thought of God (brute knows not thinking, nor
Can say, I KNOW); though in his outward form,
And in the pulpy volume of his brain,

The tricksy ape oft time hath seemed to claim
Close brotherhood with man.   So great a gap
Betwixt the reasonless and the reasoning life
A favouring God hath set.

ARISTODEMUS.

                         Hold now, my friend !
You play the painter; and I must admire
Your range of pictures; but my question was,
Will the gods answer, when I pray to them?

SOCRATES.

Aristodemus, that is simply said.
When in the pillared Parthenon we pray
The grace of the strong-fathered, flashing-eyed,
Spear-shaking Pallas, not like starving beggars
We beat the doors of her white-fronted shrine,
Nor, with the greedy piety of curs,
Fawn for the customed crust.   Our hymn of praise
Spontaneous mounts like the lark's matin song;
And, if we ask a boon, we ask it thus:
" O Pallas, or whatever gods there be
That love this spot, grant me a soul within
Pure and chaste-thoughted; and, for outward things,
May they hold harmony with inward power
To grasp and to enjoy them; rich let me be
In wisdom chiefly; and, for gold, of that
Give me what ration I can wisely use
To make life sweet and help a brother's need."
Pray thus, and make no doubt the gracious Powers
Will drop their grace like dew upon your vows !

ARISTODEMUS.

Yet such are not the prayers we mostly hear.

SOCRATES.

That matters not ; wise men have their own prayers.
A fool will pray, for that he sails to Rhodes,
May Jove make all the winds his ministers,
And for some petty merchandise divert
The airy currents that invest the globe
With tides of vital virtue unconfined.
Thou doest well from such presumptuous prayers
To keep thy lips.   To every human prayer
The Alpha and the Omega be this,
Jove's will be done!   But from their frosty use,
Who nip the bud of prayer, and rudely snap
The bond of fellowship 'twixt men and gods,
Abstain no less.

ARISTODEMUS.

          Thou seemest to speak well.
I will bethink me of thy words, when next
I hear Protagoras discourse.   Meanwhile,
This answer me, how know we that the gods
Have such a form, such human features, and
Such signs and badges, and accoutrements,
As Homer sings, and god-like Phidias moulds,
And Polycletus paints ?

SOCRATES.

          What matters form
To God's pure essence ?   A form is but a sign

Outward of inward power; a naked sword
The Scythian worships; Hellas bends the knee
To harnessed Mars; in spirit Greek and Goth
Do reverence to the same.   But I must go,
And share a festal sacrifice to-day
With Plato's father, for the love I bear
To sire and son,—a very marvellous boy,
Dear to the gods.   Some other day with thee
And Chaerephon I'll hold a high debate
Of shape and dress significant, and all
The symbols of the gods, which godly Athens
Delights to heap with honour.   [*Exit.*]

CHAEREPHON.

                              The sage is gone.
I hope you find yourself affected now
More kindly to him.

ARISTODEMUS.

                              Yes; I must confess,
He cheats opinion strangely.   He's a bee,
All honey without sting.   I never knew
So mild a disputant; so courtly kind,
And so like other men in all he says,
No cloudy notion, and no prickly phrase.
Sure Aristophanes wittier was than wise,
Who swung him up for laughter in the skies.

CHAEREPHON.

Now, let us go!—I've business at the Pnyx.

SOCRATES.

II. ARISTIPPUS ; OR, PLEASURE.

Τῶν πόνων πωλοῦσιν ἡμῖν πάντα τἀγαθ' οἱ θεοί.

EPICHARMUS.

ARISTIPPUS; OR, PLEASURE.

PERSONS OF THE DIALOGUE.

SOCRATES.
CHAEREPHON, an Athenian, disciple of Socrates.
ARISTIPPUS, of Cyrene, founder of the Cyrenæan Sect.
Young Men of Athens.

SCENE.—Before the temple of Theseus in Athens. Socrates and Chaerephon discovered sitting on the lowest steps of the temple. Enter a company of Athenian young men.

FIRST YOUNG MAN.

Here sits that old eccentric gentleman,
Whom all men love, and no man understands,
On the steps o' the temple.

SECOND YOUNG MAN.

Whom all men love? Not so. I know a few
Who hate him inly.

THIRD YOUNG MAN.

    And for why is plain.

FIRST YOUNG MAN.

Not plain to me; unless mine eyes might learn
To hate the sun.

THIRD YOUNG MAN.

Owls hate the sun, and bats.
This son of Sophroniscus hath a trick
That men don't like.

FIRST YOUNG MAN.

What trick?

THIRD YOUNG MAN.

He deals in truth,
And though 'tis fenced oft-times all round with thorns,
And stings like nettles, and as hard to bear
As bitter drug or surgeon's ruthless knife,
He flings it lightly under each man's nose,
As it were dust of roses.   You cannot drop
A word with him but he will pick it up
And weigh it well, and look it through and through,
And measure it all round ; and, if it fail
A jot of nice propriety of art—
His triple joint of *if*, and *but*, and *therefore*—
He damns it for false coin, and you who passed it
A forger or a fool.

FIRST YOUNG MAN.

That's hard to bear
For fools and forgers ; but an honest man
Turns to the truth, as flowers turn to the light.

SECOND YOUNG MAN.

Such honest men are few.   If he goes on
In this large way to ferret out conceit

From each pretentious fool who entertains
Porch or palaestra with the quack, quack, quack,
Of croaking Muses from his bubbling brain,
He'll sow a seed of enmity, and reap
A crop of curses ; and, for that he takes
No silver for his broad-cast tutoring,
They'll deem a cup of hemlock for his supper
May fee him fitly.

FIRST YOUNG MAN.

No fear of that.
Thank Jove we live in Athens, not beneath
Tyrannic yoke in bonded Syracuse.
If an Athenian may not wag his tongue,
Fowls shall not fly, nor fish shall saw the sea,
Nor eels grow fat in slimy Copais.
But say, to-morrow is, I think, the eighth
Of Pyanepsia.

SECOND YOUNG MAN.

Indeed it is ;
And we shall have a jolly feast of beans,
To honour Theseus.

FIRST YOUNG MAN.

Yes, I see the shrine
Already all bedecked with festal pomp,
To greet the feast.   Our Attic joys were bought
With toils of Theseus.   Let us honour him !

SECOND YOUNG MAN.

Come, then; the sun is westering.

s

FIRST YOUNG MAN.

                              Let us stroll
Down to Phalerum, where the hero's sons
Have a fair temple.

THIRD YOUNG MAN.

Just so.   Let us go!
[*They pass on.*]

SOCRATES.

What's all the stir to-night?

CHAEREPHON.

                              It is the eve
Of Pyanepsia.

SOCRATES.

I should have known it.

CHAEREPHON.

Indeed you were not wont to stint your praise
Of Theseus and the godlike Hercules.

SOCRATES.

Sons of the gods!   I tell thee, Chaerephon,
There is no feast in all the calendar
Makes such rare pleasure travel through my veins
As this our Pyanepsia.   In the name
Of mighty Theseus all his sons rejoice,
And every worthiest man in Attic bounds
Rejoices in a worthier than himself,

A name that overtops his topmost worth,
As the tall pine the thistle.   Such worship lifts
The humblest worshipper, brings down the proud,
And makes all brothers.

CHAEREPHON.

                    Tell me in what kind
You rate our Theseus highest?

SOCRATES.

                    At Troezene,
You know, he spent his boyhood ; and, when years
Brought round the day should bring him back to
    Athens,
He might have shot across the gleaming gulf
In a light shallop, as a sea-gull flies,
Or plumy seed that with light wafture rides
On the back o' the breeze from random field to field ;
But this he chose not.   Why?   For that he scorned
To do what any fisher-boy could do,
As well as Theseus.   At his heart there gnawed
A noble hunger for the manly deed,
The toilsome venture, and the stout exploit ;
And so he spurned the easy way, and chose
A path thick sown with peril.   All the road
From Epidaurus to Eleusis then
Bristled with savage and club-bearing men,
Who made the guileless traveller their prey,
And either bartered venal ruth for gold,
Sparing a life where murder gained a loss,
Or with strange unimagined tortures glutted
Their tiger natures.   Never thought of fear

Flung shadow o'er the assurèd soul of Theseus ;
But on he went, careering, like a god,
From bright to brighter, making every foe
Writhe like a wounded worm, caught in the firm
Unwavering grip of his heroic hand ;
And thus by sweat and toil of one brave man
Brought joy to thousands, and for lawless rule
Made right prevail, and gave the smiling coast
Into the golden guardianship of peace.

CHAEREPHON.

And thus I sum your eulogy ; by toil
To snatch success from danger's iron throat
Is virtue, excellence, and good of man ;
But who comes here ?

SOCRATES.

       I guess it is our friend
The Cyrenean, whom we met last night
With Critias at the banquet.   His light step
And airy look declare him.

CHAEREPHON.

        You are right.
Pity he came not sooner to imbibe
Your praise of Theseus ; for, in sooth, his soul
Needs hardy discipline.   He's not the man
To pluck confronting Peril by the beard,
And swerve from flowery path, to have a bout
With bears or burglars.   He doth love delight,
And says that pleasure is man's only good.

I fear divine philosophy for him
Will grow but earthly fruit; albeit his ear
At the Olympian games, some moons ago,
Through all the din of dust-upwhirling cars,
Heard only thee, and the soul-winning voice
Of thy high-reasoned wisdom.

SOCRATES.
                        He is a man
With a strong smack of sensuous delight,
Which runs to rankness.   It may be some taint
Of Afric blood, with fervid passion fraught,
From hot Cyrene's verdurous terraces,
Hath fired the Doric chasteness of his veins.
But rather this I love than meagre hearts
Whose watery tides swell with no quicker pulse,
When beauty's full-rigged splendour sails in view.

CHAEREPHON.
Ay! there are barren soils where basest weeds
Disdain to grow; and where the land is fat
A thousand weeds spring with the gorgeous flower,
In rival superfluity to pluck
Bright honours from the sun.   But here he comes!
                [*Enter Aristippus.*]

ARISTIPPUS.
Well met! what knotty point did you debate
To-day?
                CHAEREPHON.
            A point that well beseems this place,
And the bright eve of Theseus' festal day.

For Socrates has just been praising Theseus,
And of his praise this sentence is the sum,
To snatch success by strength and sweatful plan
From danger's throat, is the chief good of man.

ARISTIPPUS.

That sounds sublime, and for a hero's praise
Most fit; but for myself and common men
An humbler wisdom hits a lower mark,
Which, planted higher, were no mark for us.
It shows right brave in things that tread the ground
To talk of wings and sky-assailing flights;
But creeping things must creep; and things that walk
Can only tempt the breezy element,
To eternize their folly with their fall.
I would not soar above the state of man,
And pleasure is the highest good I claim;
To toil and sweat must ever be a pain,
And uphill roads are hateful to the horse.
There are who scale sheer-fronted heights to view
A glittering desert of untrodden snows;
Some to hear harmless thunders 'neath their heels,
And some to break their necks in tumbling down;
Some for they know not why, and some to boast
That they have stood more nigh to frosty Jove
By four or five or good eight thousand feet
Than other men, who on the common clods
Clatter their boots. Such sweaty vaunts I hate;
For sweetest flowers with brightest tincture grow
Down in the valleys: and the high-throned Sun
Brews rarest juices from the lowliest herbs.

I'll have no toiling, struggling, panting life;
No juggling fiend shall beck me to my ruin
With shows of bliss remote. The fruit I find
On mine own garden wall shall pleasure me,
More than all golden berries hung sublime,
That I must plant a ladder to approach,
And, when I claim the guerdon of my toil,
They stretch their thorns into my shrinking flesh,
And pluck mine eyes out.

SOCRATES.

By the dog, well said!
But tell me this, before our talk may branch
Into a random rankness undefined,
What thing is pleasure?

ARISTIPPUS.

Nay, good Socrates,
I pray thee spare me now this word DEFINE!
I leave it to your Megarensian friend
To build a dainty definition, fenced
With forecast thought and wary-chosen phrase
Against the rude assault of contradiction.
Your definition is a skeleton
In every joint compact; with skeletons
I use not to consort; but what I know,
The flushing body of the breathing thing
Instinct with power, in beauty panoplied,
That I will tell. There's pleasure in all life,
Free and unhindered, where no clogs impede,
Or modish false proprieties confine.

There's pleasure to the race of summer flies,
When in the luminous ocean of the air
They flit about in multitudinous maze,
And tune their chorus o'er a breezeless brook;
There's pleasure to the finny race of fish,
Or lolling lazily in a deep brown pool,
Or darting deftly up the glancing rush
Of virgin streams rock-born.   The snow-white
    lamb
Footing the noiseless velvet of the grass,
That fills the solitude with tremulous baa,
And finds its dam, and frisks about, and drains
With eager tug the creamy wells of life,
Hath choicest pleasure.   Every flower hath pleasure,
That leaping from its darkening sheath salutes
The glorious sun, and revels in the day.
The green woods ring with pleasure in the spring;
The fragrant branches wave it; all the sky
Thrills with delight, when fervid Phoebus flings
His quickening virtue o'er the teeming earth.
And man, much-labouring man, when dust-besoiled,
On happy holiday he bursts the bond
And deadening dulness of enforcèd toil,
And on soft bank, flower-carpeted, lies down
Beside the foam-bells of the silver brook,
With eye and ear and every sense agape,
Then cunning Nature harps upon his heart,
And makes that music on the strings of life
Which men call pleasure.   From his grimy den
Bring forth the captive long immured, and let
Some glorious prospect rush into his view

Of hills, and waving fields, and gleaming firths,
And islands sown like stars upon the deep,
And white-empurpled orchards, and the strength
Of pinnacled heights, in living gold aglow,
His widowed eye now finds his natural mate
And lives in rapture.   Take the brooding boy,
Expectant on the threshold of sweet life,
And let the image of his inmost thought
Of fair perfection, slumbering long, at length
In virgin grace incorporate pass before him ;
Rapt in mute ecstasy of gaze he stands
At sight of that he sought, nor knew he sought ;
His creeping nature straight usurps the air,
And floats on pinions of delicious dream.
And when the lovely worshipped form replies
With answering thrill, and like a god descends,
Life of his life, and fills the vacant shrine,
Then Aphrodite's perfect work is done,
And Pleasure blossoms to her crown, in Love.

SOCRATES.

O Pan, and Hermes, and Apollo ! sure
Some god holds haunt in breast of Aristippus,
And moulds his lips to music !   I must praise
Thy praise of pleasure ; pleasure's a good thing ;
But there are divers pleasures not a few
That make no concord with the chord you
    touch ;
And puff-cheeked Boreas, when he fills his conch,
Feels ecstasy no less than soft-plumed dove
That coos on lap of golden Aphrodite.

Chaerephon.

I always thought a dove was rather stupid,
And should prefer an eagle for my Cupid.

Socrates.

And I full many a hunter keen have known,
That had more pleasure to course down the hare,
Than others had with roasted hare for dinner.
But, tell me, Aristippus, if you had
A prince to train,—and to your feet the gates
Of kings are wont to gape with willing hinge,—
How would you breed him,—strong in sturdy act,
Or in the arms of softness?

Aristippus.

Strong to endure
What all men must, who would by strength prevail.

Socrates.

Strong to deny each dear delight of sense,
And drown the natural calls of appetite
In swelling surge of business.

Aristippus.

Even so;
Else, when he took his sleep, some burglar might
Make breach in the walled palace of his power,
And steal the sceptre.

SOCRATES.

                And from love's close embrace
Confirmed to tear him, and with an iron foot
To quash sedition.

ARISTIPPUS.

        Aphrodite shuns
Sweet converse with the man who sternly rules.

SOCRATES.

Then with his thought a kingly man must toil
To map and register the state's resources,
Its points of vantage, chinks of danger, all
That makes him strong to thrust, and wise to parry;
And he must know the weakness of the foe,
Both how to strike and where to plant the blow;
And he must take true measure of the strength
Which he defies; else——

ARISTIPPUS.

        ·   O ! of course, of course !
Jove must know all things, or all things would not
Be ruled by Jove.

SOCRATES.

                Then, mark well what I say ;
All powers that rule in Earth or on Olympus,
Hold no account of pleasure; every ruler
That wisely sways a prosperous land maintains
His kingly state by trampling under foot
What you call chiefest good ; and thus 'tis true,

Kings know no pleasure, Pleasure knows no kings,
But rules sole sovereign over servile things.

ARISTIPPUS.

And thus you preach that all are slaves of pleasure
Who love it?

SOCRATES.

    I but preach the naked fact;
It is a witchery steals in from without,
And through the unguarded portals of the sense
Invades the soul, and takes the reason captive.
No man can rule the world, or rule himself,
Who vails his casque to pleasure.   Both men and gods
Who mould and shape all things to their desire
Do so by power; and power is his who works
By strength of reason and by scorn of sense.
Would you not be a king?

ARISTIPPUS.

     By Jove, not I!
I would not govern slaves whom I despise,
Nor freemen, who with feverish faction strive
To hold the substance of the sway, and leave
To me the shadow.   I could make a sport
To tame the tiger, or to charm the snake;
I could flog wisdom into mulish boys;
Make tittering girls preach grave philosophy;
Or in his foaming madness chain the mad
Till he grew baby-mild; but for the trick
By force of sovereign reason to unite
To some great end that motley regiment,

That huddle of wild helmless human wills
(Whose reason serves but to enhance the beast,
And make stupidity fearful, being armed),
That million-throated monster with one bray,
Which men do call the people, to unite
For reason's sober service to one end
That holds no bribe to passion—this to do
Baffles my function.   Therefore I have made
The world my country, and Cyrene knows
Me now no more than Corinth, or your own
Fair Athens, violet-crowned.

SOCRATES.

But thus you float,
A straw upon the current of the time,
Useless.

ARISTIPPUS.

The unbound breeze hath uses too,
And helps the strong firm-rooted plant to grow.
A wise man hath his country everywhere,
And, like the wind, brings seeds of wisdom with him.
Wisdom's too good a thing to stay at home,
Unless, like Helios, she could hold her seat
In heaven, and with warm radiance sweep the globe.

SOCRATES.

I love thy aptness to fling back the word
On him who threw it, as in dexterous sport
Ball answers ball.   But this tell me, friend,
Ruler or ruled, at home, or far from home

Wandering rootless, for one only price
The gods sell all things ; that price thou must pay.

ARISTIPPUS.

Speak plainly.

SOCRATES.

   Thus wise Epicharmus saith :—
Seek other worlds who without sweat would smile,
On earth the gods sell everything for toil.
And to the same tune Hesiod :—
Vices are cheap ; a doit will buy a load.
Near is the house of error, smooth the road ;
But who would scale fair virtue's height sublime,
Both long and steep the sweatful path must climb,
Stony at first and hard, but soft and sweet,
When near the gods you plant your practised feet.

ARISTIPPUS.

All this I know, and all can well endure ;
'Tis but the natural fee we pay for pleasure.
But to fling pleasure's self away, and all
The sweetness of sweet life, for some conceit
That hangs i' the air, some wilful, self-imposed,
Thorny, and fruitless march of blood and tears,
This I disown ; I cannot truly shake
Hands with grim Death, and call him my good friend.

SOCRATES.

Yet 'tis our being's law that we must try
What being tried may bring us near to die.
Who lives must venture, and who ventures not
Must die at home, a sluggard and a sot.

ARISTIPPUS.

Talk not to me of laws; the law to me
Is what I feel.   If I like honey, well;
If you like vinegar, well not less for you;
And for the world well, that each may hold
His separate love, and what he loves enjoy.
Reason of any form nice reason draws,
Can tell the nature and declare the laws;
But of what things I feel with pain and pleasure
My sense to me is the sole proof and measure.
I knew a man who said the trees were blue;
And when I lived in Megara I tore
My tunic on a bramble bush, where I
Was hunting rabbits with a little dog;
Forthwith I gave my rag, being saffron-hued,
To my good hostess' daughter, pretty maid,
Who stitched the rent with red, and when I blamed
The motley tissue—" Nay, but sir !" quoth she,
" 'Tis all one red !"   So to our diverse tongues
Sweet may be bitter, bitter may be sweet.
There is no law but Nature's need; the wind
Is good to him whose sails it fills; the shoe
To whom it pinches not; and every fly
That points its base proboscis into dung
Hath right, with choicest epicures, to thank
The gods for pudding.   That is most divine
To each, to which each mostly doth incline.

SOCRATES.

And if I do incline to quaff strong wine,
Till I have drowned my senses in the draught,

And, for a moment lifted to the gods,
Subside into a beast, what call you this ?

ARISTIPPUS.

Nay, there you do me wrong, good Socrates !
'Tis an old saw of sages, who were wise
Before your Solon gave you laws, that harm
Lies in extremes, and safety in the mean ;
So pleasure is not pleasure, being spurred
Beyond what Nature wills, or sense receives.
As in the sea when wave doth fight with wave,
In yeasty trouble tossed, such thing is pain ;
But as when light winged breezes gently drive
Ripple on ripple to the pebbly shore
With silvery break, such to our sense is pleasure.
And when in waveless calm dull ocean lies,
This, imaged in our bloods, as mostly haps,
Is neither pain nor pleasure, but a thing
Indifferent.   In these three kinds our whole
Of being stands ; our craft of happiness
To hit the pleasure and to shun the pain.

SOCRATES.

Well, Aristippus, boots not to prolong
Discourse to-day ; but, if the blue-eyed maid,
Daughter of Jove, from whom all wisdom flows,
Shall please to shower her kindly grace on thee,
The mellow power of time that ripens wine
May change thy quality of thought to mine ;
And, ere ten summers shall increase the measure
Of rapid rolling years, thou'lt find that pleasure

Is but the grease that oils the wheel of life,
Not the strong racer in the glorious strife.

ARISTIPPUS.

Who knows what may be ; contraries may kiss,
Even as two streams that issued from one head
And wandered far apart, nor mixed again
And flowed together, till with confounded flood
They greeted Ocean, so your way of life
And mine one day may meet.   Meanwhile I am
The man I am, and use the blooming hours.
Farewell, this night Aegina is my home :
A boat waits for me now at the Piræus.   [*Exit.*]

CHAEREPHON.

Poor youth ! he drinks from Circe's charmed cup.

SOCRATES.

Judge him not harshly, he is young and rich ;
His will is wanton, but his thoughts are high ;
He will not drown him in a sensual stye.
These men are oft-times better than they seem ;
Their pride forbids pretension, that they rather
Stint the profession of their worthiness,
Than limp behind the worth that they profess.

CHAEREPHON.

This night he goes to Lais.

SOCRATES.

        Is she here ?

CHAEREPHON.

Ay, in Aegina, where he entertains
The summer hours with her.

T

SOCRATES.

                              He entertains
His soul with danger, who with lawless love
Wantons unreined.   Brief is the keen delight,
The limb-dissolving ecstasy of sense,
Which Aphrodite gives to passioned blood.
She sells her raptures for a languid life
And cushioned soft recumbency, which dulls
The edge of enterprise, and lets each chance
Of fair achievement slip unheeded by ;
While sceptred grace, and majesty and power,
And shaping energy divine, belong
To Jove, and to his daughter flashing-eyed,
Who shares his counsel and his thunder wields.
But let us hence.   I see the rosy bands
Of boys and girls that, with to-morrow's prime,
Will teach each street of Athens to resound
With praise of Theseus, and his toilsome mate,
Stout Hercules, who therefore joined the gods,
For that above all mortals he abounded
In fruits that on the soil of labour grew,
Watered by sweat and blood.

CHAEREPHON.

                              And we, I wis,
From hymns of rosy boys and girls to-morrow,
Praising strong Theseus and stout Hercules,
Will reap more wisdom, and a purer joy,
Than he from that Corinthian fair who baits
Fools with her smile, and sells her kiss for gold.
                    [*Exeunt.*]

SOCRATES.

III. THE DEATH OF SOCRATES.

Ἥδε ἡ τελευτή, τοῦ ἑταίρου ἡμῖν ἐγένετο, ἀνδρὸς, ὡς ἡμεῖς φαῖμεν
ἄν, τῶν τότε ὧν ἐπειράθημεν ἀρίστου καὶ ἄλλως φρονιμοτάτου καὶ
δικαιοτάτου.   PLATO.

THE DEATH OF SOCRATES.

PERSONS OF THE DIALOGUE.

SOCRATES,
SIMMIAS,
CRITO,   } Disciples of Socrates.
CEBES,
APOLLODORUS,

SCENE.—*The Prison—Athens.*

SOCRATES.

[*Discovered sitting.*]

Well friends, the Delian ship hath now performed
Her sacred voyage.

APOLLODORUS.

        She hath been detained
Beyond her wont by stiff contrarious blasts.

SOCRATES.

A better bird shall beckon on the bark
Which now I launch. I go to meet the gods,
And fear no adverse buffets. But here comes
Our Theban friend, by Philolaus trained
In the pure lore of sage Pythagoras.

[*Enter Simmias.*]

Hail, good Cadmeam! Thou art right welcome, now
I would that all my friends were here to see
My vessel ride into that brighter sphere
Which your wise Samian pictured.   Where is your
   brother?

SIMMIAS.

He will be here anon.

SOCRATES.

And where is Plato?

SIMMIAS.

He is sick, good master.

SOCRATES.

Would he had been here!

He hath a look of quiet strength about him
That makes me stronger.   I see in him a bud
Of thoughtful flower that soon will burst in summer,
And make all Greece a garden to his praise;
And, when I fling sometimes a happy thought
Upon the ground, as a good god inspires,
He picks it up, and by strange charm of thinking,
Transforms it to a palace, based on rock,
And all ablaze with gems.

SIMMIAS.

In sooth he hath

A marvellous grasp, and holds all knowable,
As Heaven doth clasp the Earth.

SOCRATES.

           Nor only holds,
But what he holds adorns, making all grey
Green with his touch.   Where is our Libyan friend,
The bright-eyed, pleasure-loving Aristippus?

SIMMIAS.

He's in Aegina.

SOCRATES.

      Fitly planted there!
'Mid the rich greenery of tuneful groves,
And the sweet hum of peaceful-plashing waves,
More pleasureful to his luxurious whim
Than these grey walls.

SIMMIAS.

       He's a light-feathered bird,
And may not fly with weight upon his wings;
But here comes one, in palace or in prison
Thy friend the same; the noble Crito comes.

[*Enter Crito.*]

Well Crito, have you seen the women home,
And the dear child?

CRITO.

I have, good master.

SOCRATES.

          'Tis well;
At deaths and battles women suit not; for
They, with their wailing, make men wear blank looks

Whose hearts are stout.   I wish to meet the gods
With a bright face.

CRITO.

Your face did never wear
A native cloud.

SOCRATES.

I had no cause for gloom.
For sixty years and nine I've walked the earth
I' the sun's face with sunny-hearted men,
And every joy that godlike reason brings
To reasoning men, was meted full to me ;
I had two wishes, one to know the truth,
Such truth as men, being men, may claim to know ;
And t'other to proclaim it.   Both were granted.
I die as one who from a feast retires
Pleased with the fare, and grateful to the host.

CRITO.

But they do kick thee rudely from the table,
As one uncalled for.

SOCRATES.

That brings blame to them,
Not pain to me ; and anyhow the threads
Of the nice-woven web of life are snapt
Not without rudeness.   Better thus, I deem,
Than to outlive the joys of life, and dwine
With stiffened sense through slow delightless years,
Coffined in feckless flesh, at last to drop
Like a sear leaf, that rots in dull decay

From sapless branch in Autumn.   But see where
    comes
Another friend,—your brother, Simmias.

[*Enter* CEBES.]

Good morrow, Socrates.

SOCRATES.

       A right good morrow;
For now you find me free, who yesterday
Sat here a bonded slave: you see my gyves
Are struck off.

[*He sits down and rubs his legs with his hands.*]

       Well, 'tis strange, 'tis passing strange,
To think how ever in this chain of things
Pain begets pleasure, pleasure fathers pain;
So now I had not known the rare delight
Of limbs unfettered but for these harsh bonds:
So light from darkness springs, and peace from war,
And war from peace again.   Thus evermore,
In a great round of contraries, doth run
The cycle of existence—enemies,
That still will hate, and still are fond to love;
A daily riddle, by the dog! a theme
For Phrygian Æsop's beasts to talk about,
In wiser parle than reasoning man can weave.

CEBES.

Thank you for this; I wished to talk of Æsop,
For I was told you had been writing verses,
And from his low pedestrian pace had raised

The Phrygian slave to mount your Pegasus.
What may this mean ? oft-time I heard you say
If crows were nightingales, and saws were flutes,
Then you might talk in metres.

SOCRATES.

Very true.

Tell all your poets my death-song will never
Cheapen their laurels.   What I wrote I wrote
From conscience and religion, not at all
From inspiration.

CEBES.

How so? you are not wont

To spur reluctant Nature, when she kicks.

SOCRATES.

Thus it bechanced.   Once and again I dreamt
In diverse guise with one significance ;
And still the dim night-wandering vision spake :—
" Up, Socrates, and court the Muses !" I,
Well-knowing my infirmity, and far
From forcing what my natural bent denied,
Deemed that a voice from Jove had heartened me
To court the Muses in the search of truth,
And service of divine philosophy,
As I was wont.   So formerly ; but now,
Here as I lay in prison, the vision came
With the same message, but more serious charge ;
And I, that I might leave the world with no
Debt to the gods that might be justly due,
Assayed the rhyme ; this short hymn to Apollo,

And this from Æsop's prose trimmed into verse,
Ungainly, like a precious purple robe
Snipt by a botching tailor—rags were better.
There, take them ;
                    [*He gives the papers to Cebes.*]
                        they may not concern me now,
For I depart to-day ; my hour is come.
You, when the gods invite, obey the call.

APOLLODORUS.

There are some men in Athens now were willing
To go with you uncalled.

SOCRATES.

                    Speak pious words ;
Uncalled may none go hence who fears the gods.

CEBES.

How mean you this ? sayst thou no pious man,
Wearied of life, may fling the load away
He hath no strength to carry ?

SOCRATES.

                        Ay ; even so :
As you, by Philolaus taught, should know.
We are but chattels of the gods, and wait
Our masters' pleasure, when and where, and how
To serve their uses.

CEBES.

                    What you say accords
With most devout submission to the gods,

And we must live like soldiers, with no will
To march or stand but at the Captain's word.

SOCRATES.

And when the word goes forth, then we depart
With forward face, firm-footed.

CEBES.

                Yet, in sooth,
The best men seldom open wide the door
To death as to a friend, but bar him out
As landsmen bar the flood tides, while they may;
And wisely.   We are slaves and chattels here,
But slaves of kindly masters; from the gods
Why should we gladly flee who tend us here
So lovingly?

SOCRATES.

           I praise thee, friend, for this;
Like a coy damsel thou art slow to say
Yes with thy mouth, though more than half thy heart
Assents.   Thou with an holy jealousy
Dost keep strict watch against the chance of error,
As one who fears an ambush, or as one
Who sees a friendly light shine through the dark,
And fears to follow, lest the marsh-born fiend
Decoy him to his ruin.   But bethink thee,
Our masters here, and who await us there,
Are one.   I know to whom I go.   The change
Is not from distant clime to clime, but only
From room to room of old familiar halls.
If here, on earth, I leave a wealth of friends,

A host of heroes in Elysian fields
Awaits my coming.   And, if these should fail,
(And who will surely speak of things unseen?)
At least the gods, I know, will welcome me,
Their faithful servant.   All who serve the gods
Faithfully here may hope to find them there,
Approving masters.   To the good belongs
This hope, not to the bad.   Long years of thought
Have taught me this, with reasons most assured.

SIMMIAS.

Assure me too ; your cause and its defence
Be common to your friends.   We wish to stand
For life or death on one sure ground with you.

SOCRATES.

Right willingly, if what convinces me
Is proof to you.   The goods of friends are common.

CRITO.

Nay ; but you shall not speak.

SOCRATES.

Not speak—for why?

CRITO.

The man who brews the drug declared to me
That much discourse doth rouse the blood to make
A stiffer stand against the hostile force
Of the o'ermastering juice, which then must draw
His reinforcement from a second dose,
Or if need be, a third.

SOCRATES.

Let that fear sleep !
His office is to work by death, my work
To entertain the time till death shall come ;
Which cannot be, I deem, more worthily
Than by discourse of what belongs to death.
And if what Crito says be very truth,
It matters little to the darkened lamp
If with one puff the light went out, or two.
Be ye my judges, then ! and I will make
Before your worshipful authority
My soul's defence, and show 'tis good to die.

SIMMIAS AND CEBES.

Proceed, good master.

SOCRATES.

Well then, this I deem,
The life which wise men live in fleshly case,
Is from the cradle to the urn but one
Long exercise of dying.   Should they grieve,
When what they sought they find ?

SIMMIAS.

How mean you this ?

SOCRATES.

If we would argue wisely, ask me first
What thing is death ?

SIMMIAS.

By all means.

SOCRATES.

Simply this,
That soul and body from long fellowship
Part company.

SIMMIAS.

I accept it so defined.

SOCRATES.

Then mark me this—Is the soul parted thus
Better or worse? of needful tools deprived,
Or freed from gross incumbrance?

SIMMIAS.

Answer thou.

SOCRATES.

I know, and you, and every man may know,
That as a clog about a deer-hound's neck,
So is the body to the soul; nay more,
It fouls our fountains of pure thought, and brings
Quick fuel to our lusts; beclouds our light;
Smothers our reason; clips our wings; and lays
Us level with the brute.   What but the body
Works deeds of violence, rapines, murders, wars,
And horrors against Nature, that the Sun
Averts his face, and the incensèd gods
Curse their own creature man.

SIMMIAS.

The tragic scene
Is full of tales that prove your reason good.

SOCRATES.

Next answer this : Does flesh and fleshly sense
Instruct us in the noblest truths, or rather
Brew mists to blind us ? does a man behold
Virtue, or truth, or wisdom with his eyes,
Or with his soul ?

SIMMIAS.

                    Mere sense could never raise us
Above the oxen, which have Hera's eyes,
But not her godhead.

SOCRATES.

                    Plainly then the soul
Gains from the body nothing, but is forced
To make sharp war on the rebellious flesh,
To vindicate his kingship.   Thus we live
A daily fight to keep the body down ;
And, when it falls in dusty death, we stand
Free from its bonds, and o'er its dragging weight
Victorious.   Thus in death men win the prize
For which they sweated in the long career
Of their life race, and from our wings we shake
The clay that clogged them in our fleshly slough,
And, being purged from sense, our spirits rise,
By quality of nature, from dull zone
Of human grossness to the pure serene
Of gods and demigods.

SIMMIAS.

                    But few are pure.

SOCRATES.

'Tis an old saw, ' The men who bear the badge
Are many, but who know the god are few.'
Only the pure may find the pure ; with earth
Remains the soul that's soaked in earthly lust.
Wise were the old Pelasgic priests, who gave
The consummating power of mysteries
To Greece, and taught god-fearing men of yore
That souls impure and uninitiate
Sunk in deep Hades shall for ever roll
In swathes of mud voluminous ; but they,
Who through the sanctioned grades of holy rite
Were led to vision of the lifted veil,
And pictured hopes of life from death re-born,
Dying, shall brook the fellowship of gods
In blissful fields.   Thus have I pled my cause ;
Ye Judges ! judge me now if I am wrong,
Who mount with pleasure from this fleshly cage,
On whose harsh bars my soul, poor bird ! oft-times
Hath torn her plumes.

CEBES.

       Well hast thou spoken now,
As ever ; and, while thy eloquence holds my ear,
I or believe or would believe the thing
Thou preachest, true, or worthy to be true.
That they are wise who o'er the mutinous flesh
Assert the soul's imperial mastery,
And to liege Reason's chariot bind in triumph
The train of passions, subjugate and tame,

U

I potently believe.   But still the doubt
Whispers within me, What if that be true
Which many fear, and some aloud declare :
What if the soul no separate being knows?
But from its brittle shelly crust flies off
Like smoke, by death with rude-disturbing stroke
Dissolved and dissipate, and nowhere found.

SOCRATES.

Well cautioned, Cebes ; thinking men are slow
To yield their reason to seductive show
Of flattering truth, and then most slow when truth
Jumps like an eager trout, or seems to jump,
To the first fly we fling.   Pursue we then
The theme well started, looking honest doubt
With brave heart in the face ; and surely none,
Not ev'n the light comedian, who buys
Laughter with slander, and with lies applause,
Will vote me now a garrulous gossiper,
Weaving such serious talk with serious friends,
To serious season suited.

CEBES.

                    Not they will judge
You by your deeds, but by the itch which pricks them ;
Like tumblers, who, to please a gaping crowd,
Walk on their heads, they make all nature grin
To glass their humour.   Boys in tricks delight ;
And with the juggle of their shallow jests
These wits amuse the town.

SOCRATES.

If my round eyes,
Bald crown, and satyr face, and ways apart
From vulgar use, can help them to a laugh,
I grudge it not, so laughter be the food
Best for their apish stomach.   But, for the theme
We now were handling, hoar tradition tells
That souls of men not here are born, but travel
From the great home of shades into our earth,
And hence again to Hades; thus the chain
Of life from death, and death from life runs on
In endless cycle.

CEBES.

So the wise have taught.

SOCRATES.

Take it more widely.   Said we not before
Pain begets pleasure, pleasure fathers pain;
So life from death, and death from life may spring,
As waking comes from sleep, and sleep from waking.
'Tis a strange world, stuffed with the unexpected,
Where a fair show oft veils an ugly sin,
And a foul outside masks a fair within.
The peasant on the dry unfruitful sand
Spreads rottenness and refuse, and the rank
Ferment of putrid humours; and behold!
From all that life abhors, and beauty loathes,
A flush of greenness leaps to greet the sun,
Life from the festering death.   'Tis Nature's law
That makes us wonder, being ignorant;

Belike that she sometimes may cheat her children,
That they may marvel more.   When underground
A cunning engineer hath pierced the rock
And forced a path through darkness, take a child,
A little child, into the lightless void,
And he will shrink, and to your guiding hand
Cling fearful, till familiar light press in
From the near exit.   Even so the gods
Lead us from light to darkness, and from dark
To light again ; delighting still to soothe
Our fears with contraries, and make to spring
Rare transport from despair.

CEBES.

                          And, if we pass
From death to life, as life to dying leads,
'Tis like we bring some memories from the home
Of souls that wait for bodies, as yourself
Oft-time have taught to me and Simmias,
That all our learning is what once we knew,
Old truth, recovered and refurbished.

SOCRATES.

                          Just
As, when we see a face we ought to know
But cannot name, we beat the brain about,
As one that lost a jewel in the sand ;
With patient search now here now there we probe,
Till in some hidden nook we find the link
That knits the present to the past, and then
We cry, *I know !*   Thus we, in very fact,

Know nothing but from seeds of knowledge brought
From pre-existence with us, as a delver
Trenching the sluggish clod, unbars the grave
Of loveliest flowers, whose seeds long summers there
Lay sunless and sopite, which straightway leap
Into the sun's embrace, and spot the fields
With sudden wealth of blade.   If we conceive
That we from sense the simplest germ derive
Of thought, we largely err ; the sense can show
Two things, or equal or unequal matched,
Each for itself discerned and nicely marked,
This any dog more sharply does than man ;
But to compare two things and take their measure,
To say that one is more or less than t'other
By so much swerving from equality,
This baffles sense ; the faculty to know
Is brought, not born ; we carry it within,
From spirit-country travelling into flesh ;
And, as the equal, so the just, the true,
The beautiful, we learn, not taught by sense,
But recognise and hold them by a force
Which we not got but have, and, having it,
Must bring it from a birth before our birth.
This is my doctrine, often taught, which says,
Knowledge is reminiscence.

SIMMIAS.

Cebes now,
Though vastly pleased to kick against persuasion,
Might grant with me the kindly likelihood
That our poor human birth bears speaking trace

Of godlike parentage; but still the fear
Recurs (as human hearts are nests of fear)
To blind our blinking hopes, that after death,
Its fleshly tenement dissolved, the Mind
Flies off like smoke, and mingles with the wind.

SOCRATES.

Excellent doubters! take a post, and run
Through all Hellenic, all Barbarian ground,
Till ye shall find a charm to exorcise
These fine self-torturing *Buts*.   Ye cannot spend
Your gold more aptly than to find the man
Whose potent incantation shall soothe down
Such stout objectors.   Meanwhile this I say,
Who am no prophet, but a sober man
Seeing and seeking; Mind is not like smoke.
Only a thing of many parts compounded
Can by a blast be blown and dissipated.
A little child may shake a box of dust,
And send its floating atoms far apart,
Seized by contending airs, once and for ever
Divorced from union.   But a simple thing,
One undivided, indivisible
(And souls are such), no force or strife of forces
Can of its own essential unity
Disrobe and dispossess.   As in the field
A mighty army, huge as Xerxes' host,
May drift, like flies, before a hurricane,
And be a host no more, but who commands,
Fighting or fleeing, is a king the same;
So soul is one, of myriad facts the king,

On awful throne, or in a captive cell,
Essential lord.

CEBES.

These words are in my soul
A goad no trick of shifty sophist's tongue
Will make to budge.   If any truth I know,
'Tis this—the soul is one, and, where it works,
Stamps all things with its own grand unity.

SOCRATES.

'Tis well ; all souls, the pure and the impure,
Are in their nature indivisible ;
The mortal blow that cracks the bodily shell
Divides not them : yet souls that cannot die
May by contagion of much grossness grow
Into gross quality, and, when they pass
Into another life—so Fate decrees—
Be clothed in form, to their own baseness kin,
Ass, fox, or wolf, ferret, or slippery snake,
Or ravenous vulture, or some spectral thing
That flits with bats and owls, where no light dwells,
And gibbers o'er the waste of dead men's graves.
'Twere well for such, if they were blown away
To smoke and nothingness ; but souls are souls,
And to their own substantial oneness bound,
In bliss or bane must live for evermore.
      [*A considerable silence intervenes.*]
Well, Cebes, and you Simmias, you seem
Scarce satisfied ; as with hungry guests, the sop

First served but whets the zest for what's to come.
You look as one who would and who would not.

SIMMIAS.

'Tis even so.   Our doubts are hydra-headed,
And do pursue us, like a routed ghost,
Still fleeing, still defying.   But we fear,
In such excess of your calamity,
Like beggars at a rich man's door, to vex
Your ears with iteration.

SOCRATES.

Say not so.
My friends should know me better than to call
My present hap a sore calamity ;
I thank the gods I have no cause to weep ;
If others have, may sorrow make them wise,
Washing their foul deeds with atoning tears !
For me, I rather, like the tuneful swan,
Greet death with hymning, being near the gods.
Ask without fear ; he only knows who tries ;
Who smothers doubt gives rightful range to lies.

SIMMIAS.

Well then, good master, hear me.   Some have taught
The soul is as a lyre with many strings,
Now tempered well to dulcet harmony,
Now stretched to grating sharpness, or to dull
Tameness relaxed.   What if the soul of man
In all its functions, feelings, offices,
In fine accord, be even as a tune

Played on the stringèd harp we call ourselves ;
A tune, unseen, invisible, and one,
Though of the many born?   Now, if a man
Should wrench the lyre's compactness, rudely dash
The resonant board to flinders, harshly snap
The eloquent strings, and fling it on the ground,
Like a ship stranded on a rocky shore,
Where now is gone the rich concentuous strain,
Fine viewless essence of light-floating joy?
Nothing and nowhere is the thing that thrilled
The ear with tip-toe ecstasy, and subdued
The heart to sweet subjection ; even so
The fine articulation of the thing
We call ourselves, thoughts, feelings, functions, all
One blow may dash, and the rare tune it played
Be lost for ever !

SOCRATES.

[Looking at him with a fixed gaze.]

       Well, I will answer you ;
But take my reasons as a cautious vendor
Takes coin, and ring them well, once and again.
Be apprehensive for the truth, not me.
Suspect my speech then most when sweetest-tongued
It steals into your faith, lest with the sweet
I dose your wits, and, like a bee, depart
Leaving a sting behind.

SIMMIAS.

       Thou never didst
Impose thyself upon us, as a tyrant

Rides with strong laws the people whom he rules,
But from the inner witness of our souls
Thy kindly converse gently drew the truth
Seemed ours no less than yours.

SOCRATES.

       Consider then
How lightly this rare knot may be untied.
Who called the soul a tune forgot, I trow,
That all the parts which make a harmony,
Nor each with each, nor with the whole may war;
The nice adjustment of the concord knows
Within itself no power contrarious
To plant a *No* against a mutinous *Yes;*
But in the soul imperial Reason stands,
Controls, diverts, warns, threatens, contradicts
The impetuous passion billowing to and fro,
As a strong swimmer breasts the tide, and cuffs
The tempest's lordly crest.   Laertes' son,
You well remember, in the Odyssey,
When hard beset, holds commune with himself,
And beats his breast, and bids his heart stand up
Against a sea of sorrows.   He who called
The soul a harmony understood not this;
But the wise poet knew that Siren strains
Within us, or without, are not ourselves.

SIMMIAS.

I grant thee victor here.   This doubleness,
This strange confronting trick of self with self,
Is nothing like to harmony.   We rather

Conjure ourselves against ourselves, and are
Pilot and tempest, rudder and sail in one;
I fail to grasp the mystery of the soul.

SOCRATES.

Who owns the mystery of life is wise;
Who would explain it, or by harmonies,
Or by careering atoms up and down,
Mingling in love and strife, is as a man
Who says the house is burned by fire, nor knows
Whence the spark came.   We know in part; to look
Into the face of truth direct, and put
Our finger on its fount, doth far outreach
The narrow God-set limit of our ken.
As they who scan the changes of the sun,
When darkness cuts his rim, regard his orb
Through coloured glass, or water, lest his ray
Received direct should strike the gazer blind,
So we directly cannot know ourselves,
Nor God, nor any primal force that is;
But outward show, and sensuous flourish lead
By natural divination to their cause.
There is one cause to all the things that be,
Eternal MIND; and herein lies the key
To solve thy doubts, good Simmias. Sense may never
Or make or mar what stands above all sense.
And high above all dissolution throned,
Lives the great Thought that moulds the world, and
        types
All things that be.   All soul retreats before
The touch of death, and lives, because to live

Is its essential nature.   God can not
Himself destroy, nor will the image blot
Of his own reason in high-reasoning man.
This is my faith, and in this faith I die.

SIMMIAS.

It should be mine too ; but my weak assurance,
Behind the proud scope of your argument,
Flags like a poor clipt bird.   I fear to rate
Our mortal stuff so high, that we should dare
With tainted lips to taste immortal cups,
That make the blood of gods.

SOCRATES.
                        Now, by the dog,
I praise thy modest measure of thyself
In Truth's despite ! in Athens, here, not many
Will make their score with Simmais, casting count
Of their own virtues !   But, for thine honest doubts,
Have them, good friend, nor fear to entertain
Their presence kindly.   Doubt's the pioneer
That leads each man to so much of the truth
As profits him.   All things we may not know ;
But what we know with manly grasp to hold,
And what we hold with reasoned skill to use,
And make it parent of immortal deeds,
This is true wisdom.   He who drives a stag,
With toil and sweat, o'er field and fell, and through
Far-winding glens, and over stumps and stones
And miry sloughs, and brings it nobly down,
Is the true hunter ; not into whose aim

The antlered troops are driven by a slave,
That he—the lazy lord who rules the wild—
Ensconced behind a rock, with facile shaft
May pierce them as they pass.   A hundred truths
Are barren in his hand who never sought
With honest sweat for one.   Search then; and what
To human wit a kindly god may give
My Simmias will find.   We cannot will
Conviction or the weather to our need;
But both will come to those who wait and watch
Wisely the hint of Jove.   A petted child
Is he who, worsted in his first conceit,
Deserts from reason and despairs of truth.
Who, being cheated once, or twice, or thrice,
Calls all men swindlers, we call misanthrope;
Misologist we name, who being tossed
In a Euripus of conflicting thoughts,
Drops reason's rudder—safety of the wise—
And woos a shallow vain companionship
With sneers, and gibes, and laughter's barren brood.
Not so my Simmias; he will bravely bear
What doubts to this high argument belong;
As when a traveller in a mountain land,
When from a glen he breaks on open moors,
Sudden beholds his diverse-forking way
Wreathed with huge mists, and leading through black
      bogs;
He stands, and waits, and marks, and calculates,
And weighs each dubious step, till from the hill
Either some shaggy shepherd from his hut,
Or wandering merchant of the lonely braes,

Or, through the foul investment of the cloud
Peering victorious, the all-seeing sun,
Inform his footing.   Such be thou, my friend,
Tracing the obscure path which opes to thee
The nature and the destiny of souls.
One thing is sure ; if souls are deathless, they
Must be of priceless value.   Being here,
The good man tends them well, and reaps the fruit
Of a well-ordered life.   Beyond the grave
We carry nothing but our naked selves,
Which, being tettered with the leprosy
Born of gross carnal itch, may never find
Good guidance from the gods, but wanders wide
From bliss divorced, through labyrinthine reach
Of long recurrent cycles ; while the hand
Of the kind god that ruled their earthly life
Conducts the good, by sure and easy path,
To happy homes, thence, in the appointed time,
To rise to stages of a higher life,
Enlarged and purified.

SIMMIAS.

I would gladly know
More nicely of those homes.

SOCRATES.

Surely to know
Of that grand unseen world is given to none
In mortal frame enshelled ; but ancient myths,
Made in old times when gods with men conversed,
Give high assurance of what we divine

By likelihood of reason.   What we call
The earth, from the inhospitable sea,
And Phasis, Colchian river, to the West,
Where stout Alcides raised his pillars, all
Is but the dregs and grosser sediment
Of that true world above, which is to this
As air to water, breezy, light, and pure,
Peopled with stars, and interpenetrate
By native glory.   But beneath this crust
Whereon we tread are chasms many and deep,
And hollow caverns, and dark tunnelled ways,
Where rivers roll of mud, and some of fire
With winding spires voluminous, and fierce
As currents bursting from the ruptured flanks
Of the flame-belching Aetna.   Hugest and last
Of these dark chasms is the deepest deep
Of Tartarus, whose horror-breathing name
Blind Homer knew, and he who told the roll
Of gods in Ascra.   In the swirling pot
Of this abyss all the dark waters meet ;
Hither they flow, and hence they are disgorged
In sempiternal billowy torture tossed,
Inhaled and exhaled, like the uneasy breath
Of a sick body.   Of these subterrene streams
The greatest, and whose tideful waters flow
In the extremest circle winding wide,
Is Ocean.   With opposing current next
Flows Acheron, which through barren wasteness rolls
Its slow funereal flood, until it reach
The Acherusian pool, where the great crowd
Of bodiless souls their diverse seasons wait

Of destined incarnation. In the midst
Of these two rivers Pyriphlegethon
Outpours his tide, and near his cradle falls
Into a mighty basin wreathed with flame,
And makes a lake bigger than our Greek sea,
Bubbling with mud and water; issuing thence
He winds with many a tortuous link about
The lowest Tartarus, and oft-times upcasts
Torrents of burning mud and molten rocks
Where the cracked earth gives vent. Cocytus next,
Vocal with wails, feeds with his woeful flood
The black blue hollow of the Stygian pool,
And issuing thence upon the adverse side
From Pyriphlegethon, with many a bend
Rolls under ground, then into Tartarus leaps
Precipitous. Now, when souls of men arrive
Unhoused from mortal lodgment to this place,
His guiding god conducts each to the judge,
Who with infallible doom, to good and bad
Their diverse lots declares. Those who had lived
Indifferent well, nor soaring high to seats
Of lofty virtue, nor in seas of crime
Drowning the godlike germ that makes them men,
These mount the wain that waits their special use,
And fare to Acheron, where they pay the fines
Due for their faults, and for their fair deserts
Reap fair rewards, and from the taints are purged
That years of sinful act in carnal case
Had grained into their souls. But they whose sins
With venomed tooth into their core of being
Had gnawed corrosive, eating out the seed

Of good past bettering, they who dared the worst
Against both gods and men, in hot career
Of wilful violence, and all-grasping greed,
For these deep Tartarus by all-righteous doom
Yawns, and down swallows, and engulphs them there,
Hopeless, incurable, never more to rise.
Some souls there be who murderous deeds have dared
On sudden gust and squall of passion, not
Confirmed in fell intent and stout device
Of wicked will, these—for no lesser doom
The Fates allow—must with the rest descend
To deepest hell, and for twelve moons remain
In durance there, till or Cocytus, or
Red Pyriphlegethon take them to his flood
And roll them on to Acheron, where they
With outstretched arms and piteous cries beseech
Their shades whom living they had rudely wronged,
To let them rise and mingle with the crowds
Who brook purgation for repented sin.
Then, if their quest be granted, from the flood
They rise, and cease from torture ; but, denied,
The fiery torrent sucks them back, and sweeps
Into the gorge of Tartarus, thence again
Doomed to emerge at stated times, till they
With prosperous iteration of their prayer
Shall win the dear redemption from the mouth
Of whom they wronged ; for thus the Fate ordains.
But whoso lived above the vulgar herd
In manful struggle and high-hearted deed,
Them no unkindly durance underground
Detains ; but they by natural upwardness

Remount to earth, and live new lives of men
In purer shell encased ; while of these pure
The purest, whom divine Philosophy
Purged from all grossness, now discharged and free
From fleshly service, in disbodied bliss
Dwell with the gods for ever.   Wisely then,
My Simmias, we strive, even as we strive,
To leave this mortal life, participant
Of virtue and of truth.   Olympia boasts
Her laurelled racers, but to us much more
Noble the contest and the hope sublime.
These things, or some such things (for what wise man
Will myths interpret like a chronicle?),
Seem fitting to believe about the home
Of human souls from human flesh disthralled,
And such words, like a charm of power, I sing,
Launching my bark to Hades.   Wise is he
Who, armed with justice, piety, and truth,
Waits the dim voyage to that distant land,
When Fate shall call.   You, Simmias, and the rest,
My dear loved friends, abide your hour ; me now
My destiny—so a tragic bard would say—
Calls to my end.   I must go to the bath.
'Tis better so, than, having drunk the drug,
To leave the women—an unhandsome gift—
My corpse for last ablution.

CRITO.
                            Even so ;
But, ere you go, say is there nought that I
For you or yours could do, to prove our love
In face of your departure?

SOCRATES.

        This one thing
I ask of you, and of all friends that love me ;
Take to your heart the truths that I have taught,
And live as who believe them.

CRITO.

        This we promise ;
But for your due disposal, being gone,
We wait your will; how choose you?

SOCRATES.

        As you please ;
That is, if you can catch me !
      [*To Cebes and the others, smiling.*]
        Ye behold, good friends,
How all my talk was blown, like idle wind,
About the ears of Crito !   Still he deems
The soulless trunk that I shall cast behind,
Having drunk the draught, is very me who speak,
And what I said, that I should straightway join
The blessedness of blessed shades in Hades,
I spoke to ears that heard not.   Speak to him
With words of comfort, and impledge yourselves
That now indeed I do go hence, and no
Cold prison walls shall hold me ; nor need he
Give his dear soul to grief, to think that I
Feel pain when flame consumes, or earth conceals
What men called Socrates.

[*To Crito.*]

       Trust me, best of friends,
We train our tongues for arrant juggling knaves,
To rob us of our wits.   Our current trade
We make with words that have no bones ; as if
A foolish merchant should for ringing gold
Take a gilt paper promising to pay,
Or I should see a stretch of weighty cloud
Massed into towers, and call it Babylon.
Use no such trickery ; know that I am gone ;
And, for my body, mine no more, give it
Disposal as your own conceit may please,
Or custom of the State.

   [*Exeunt Socrates and Crito.*]

APOLLODORUS.

[*Who had been sitting in a corner of the room for some
time with his face covered.*]

O Jove, Apollo, and Athena, why
Do the bad live, and all the best men die ?

CEBES.

He goes like to himself ; or, like the sun,
More glorious in his sinking than in all
The pride of topmost noon ; he weeps no tears
For his own woe, nor needs ; but we must weep,
Poor orphaned children, soon no more to look
On our dear father's face !

APOLLODORUS.

      Our father's face !

SIMMIAS.

There is more weighty argument to me
Of immortality in his great life
Than in the subtle, finely-woven web
Of his most high discourse.

[*Enter the* OFFICER *of the Eleven.*]

I am come
To do the duty which the State enjoins;
Where is your master?

CEBES.

He is gone to take
His last ablution, and the last farewell
Of wife and children; he will come anon.

OFFICER.

I wot it well.   There lives no man in Athens
Whom he kept waiting.   Lo! even now he comes.

[*Re-enter Socrates and Crito.*]

O, Socrates, I come with subject feet
That go not where I will, but where I must;
Ungrateful service, with no gracious words
Mostly rewarded by the men whose ears
Drink my ungracious message; but from you
I never heard a murmur, and I know
Thou wilt not blame me now.   I am the dog
That at the shepherd's call must bark: the bell
That rings alarm when he who holds me fears.
I know thou wilt not blame me, Socrates,
The best of men that ever lodged within

These' hated walls.   Thou know'st my message ; thou
Need'st not my counsel.   To the Almighty MUST
All necks must bow.
                              [*He weeps.*]

                    SOCRATES.

                    Farewell, my worthy friend ;
And we what the hour bids will blithely do.
                    [*Exit officer.*]
A most true-hearted, mellow-blooded man !
So was he ever kind to me, and now
He tides his grief in tears.
                              But, Crito, come
And let us do our duty.   Bid them bring
The poison, if 'tis rubbed ; or, if 'tis not,
Let some one rub it !

                    CRITO.

                    The sun is not yet set ;
He hath some space, before he veil his face
Behind the purple hills.   I have seen men
Ere this within these walls, and by such drug
Depart from life ; and they, I wis, drew out
Their time to the latest dregs, and did invite
Their friends to sup with them, and died with wreaths
About their brows, and sweet wine in their veins,
And songs of merriment ; as who had vowed,
Not sinking like dull brook in sandy beach,
But like the last scene of a stately play,
With full-sailed pomp to die.

SOCRATES.

And wisely so,
Belike for them, who hoped for nothing more,
And to the dregs would drain the cup which held
For them their all.   But I, whose quality
Of bliss is diverse, diversely must choose.
I would not hug the shadow of the life
Whose substance is departed, would not gnaw
The shell that holds no kernel.   Tell the boy
To bring the hemlock.

CRITO.

Go, boy, tell the man
That Socrates awaits him.
[*The boy goes, and returns immediately with the man,
who administers the cup.*]

SOCRATES.

Hail, worthy friend ! tell me—for thou must know—
What yet remains to do.

JAIL SERVANT.

'Tis simply said :
Having drunk the draught, to walk about a little,
And when you feel your legs grow heavy, then
To lay you down.
[*He gives the cup to Socrates, who takes it cheerfully ;
and then, looking the man steadily in the face, says :—*]

SOCRATES.

What say you of this cup ;
Is it the use to drink the whole, or may
Some part serve for libation ?

SERVANT.

We rub enough for drinking, and no more.

SOCRATES.

I understand ; but pious use commands
That we implore the gods with happy bird
To speed our emigration ; and I now
Implore them so.   Jove, and all blessed gods,
Grant me a smooth departure !

[*He drinks off the draught ; whereupon all the company cover
their faces with their cloaks and burst into tears ; especially Apollodorus, who had been weeping the whole time of the discourse,
and now breaks out into loud sobs.*]

SOCRATES.

O, strange disciples, who your master love
More than the lore he taught you !   Sent I not
The women from the place, for that we ought
To die by harsh protesting undisturbed,
That cuffs at Jove's high will ?   I pray you keep
A manly cheer, and, as I lived in peace,
So let me die !

[*Feeling his legs beginning to grow heavy, he lays himself down
on the floor on his back, and covers his face.   After a little while
the jail servant comes up, and begins to feel his body.*]

SERVANT.

My hand presses your feet ;
Say, do you feel my touch ?

SOCRATES.

No; I feel nothing.

SERVANT.

[*After an interval.*]

Now I press his limbs;
You see he makes no sign; his legs are cold.

SOCRATES.

I feel no pain here, when I press my finger
Upon my thigh.   When the cold creeping taint
Shall reach my heart, I die.

[*Apollodorus sobs, and after a pause.*]

SOCRATES.

[*Uncovering his face.*]

Crito, we owe a cock to Aesculapius;
I would not die in debt to any god.

CRITO.

Myself will pay the vow, with fitting speed.
But say, hast thou aught else?

[*No answer is given; Socrates covers his face, and, after a
short pause, with a convulsion dies.   The jail servant, advancing,
uncovers him; and Crito closes his eyes and lips.   The scene
drops.*]

PLATO

Ἔρως ἀνίκατε μάχαν,
Ἔρως, ὃς ἐν κτήμασι πίπτεις
ὃς ἐν μαλακαῖς παρειαῖς
νεάνιδος ἐννυχεύεις
φοιτᾷς δ᾽ὑπερπόντιος ἔν τ᾽ ἀγρονόμοις αὐλαῖς.
καί σ᾽ οὔτ᾽ ἀθανάτων φύξιμος οὐδεὶς
οὔθ᾽ ἁμερίων ἐπ᾽ ἀνθρώπων, ὁ δ᾽ἔχων μέμηνεν.

SOPHOCLES.

PLATO.

PERSONS.

Plato.
Alciphron, a young Athenian, his disciple.

Scene.—*The gardens of the Academy, near Athens. The philosopher discovered sitting in an arbour, with books and papers on a rustic table before him.*

Plato.

How soft the summer sleeps upon the hill;
How sweet the lazy wafture of the breeze,
With the free pillage of redundant growth,
Comes richly laden !   Aphrodite's term
Is gone but yesterday, and now bright May
Assumes her grace, and stands like blooming bride
With veil new lifted, making common good
Of hoarded smiles, and bliss too wide to brook
The bars of one poor breast.   On such a day,
Albeit now perched on the grey brink of time,
And stretching forth my hand beyond the gulph
Of sensuous shows to grasp the great unseen,
Not less I feel the bonds of mother earth,
And with a filial fond endearment cling
To her that bare me, old but ever young,

Lavish in beauty, scattering waste of life,
And dowered with deathless virtue to repair
Her annual loss, making all loss a trick
To double gain.   On such a day sometimes
I feel the thought within me stealing back
Into my prime of life, before I knew
That holy wizard, who with fine-reasoned talk
Charmed universal Athens into bonds
Of high discipleship, and free vassalage
To Jove-born wisdom.   For in that green time
With liberal swing of fearless venturing vans
Out-vaulting dull sobriety, I oft
Would leap into a dithyramb, and besing
The ruddy Dionysus crowned with joy,
And golden Aphrodite's fervid bliss,
And limb-dissolving rapture.   At that tide
My friends would ply me, saying : Plato, now
The wreath is flung for thee, which noblest Greeks
Have worn before thee ; stoop and pick it up !
What weighty Aeschylus, mild Sophocles,
And wise Euripides bore like a star
Upon their godlike fronts, the tragic crown,
Mid the far-billowed resonance of praise
From most religious Athens, waits for thee
As for its rightful heir !   But from that voice
I turned aside, to their great wonderment ;
For in the life of holy Socrates
A stronger Siren sang—so let it stand !
Our lives are wise interpreters from Jove
That spell our destinies.   I am loftier thus
Than in the race with poets to contend

For prizes, at the crude arbitrement
Of mobs with venal ears, whose praise we stoop
To buy with well-glossed falsehoods,—but who comes?

[*Enter Alciphron.*]

My bright-eyed Alciphron, the hopeful boy,
The pride of Athens, walking in the light
Of purple youth and flow of native joy,
Whose beauty makes me glad, when I behold
The bloom of love and reverence in his face
Still looking sunward.   Alciphron, my boy !
Why, what's the matter?   You have lost yourself!
What evil genius, jealous of your bliss,
Hath blurred your front of gladness with a grief,
That looks as foreign there as inky mutes
At marriage feast?   What grieves thee, Alciphron ?
You look as mouldy as a pool in June
Whence Sirius sucked the humour.   Be thyself!
Look up and smile; divine Philosophy
Is sun to all things.

ALCIPHRON.

I have lost a friend.

PLATO.

Just cause of grief, but not so just as theirs
Who have no friend to lose.   But thou art rich,
And one friend gone leaves many friends behind ;
All Athens loves thee.

ALCIPHRON.

> But he was to me
> No wayside flower, which one may pluck and wear,
> And make parade of for a festive hour,
> Then fling aside ; our lives were twined in one,
> And in the sweet exchange of common joy
> We shared like brothers, building up our lives
> With common cares, and growing like twin trees
> Whose roots do interlace with mouths that drink
> A common brook ; but now he knows no friendship,
> Or holds it vilest brass to that fine gold
> Which he calls Love, and I, perforce, must call
> A madness very strange and very sad.

PLATO.

> Why sad ?

ALCIPHRON.

> He lived in heaven some blissful weeks,
> No doubt ; but since that tide he lives in hell,
> Or nowhere.

PLATO.

> Is he dead ?

ALCIPHRON.

> Yes ; dead to me.

PLATO.

> Droop not, dear youth ; for Eros is a god
> That hath his tricks, like Hermes ; what you lose
> By him, you 'll find again when he shall choose
> To wave his wand.   Who was the friend you loved ?

ALCIPHRON.

Erastus, son of Sophroniscus, he
Who carved the winged Eros at the gate
Of your Academy here.

PLATO.

      A goodly youth.
I hope no harm has chanced him ; let me hear
The tale that brought both bliss and bane to him,
And left you mateless. Time and thought may bring
Some happy healing. None who lives despairs.

ALCIPHRON.

You know Callippides, whose brother gave
The year its signature, being archon then,
When the great Theban soldier bowed to Fate,
And 'neath the piny brow of Maenalus
Bought victory with death. Well, this proud wight
Has a fair daughter passing all conceit
Of beauty in our common mortal mould,
So mingling queenly state with natural grace,
That now she seemed the bride of Jove, erect
With stately port, treading the Olympian floor,
And now a shepherd girl that twines a wreath
For a pet lamb on holiday ; and now
A nymph of Dian's kirtled troop ; and now,
With every line to yielding sweetness tuned,
Mere Aphrodite ; now a paragon,
Compact of all the four. Her father brought
The maid to Sophroniscus, that his hand

Might teach the Parian block some part to breathe
The wonder of her charms, and help her father
To feed on her dear counterfeit, when she
Were far away, to some high-blooded lord
Well-mated.   To his father's chisel trained,
The young Erastus—better half of me—
Oft eyed the maiden, as she came to lend
Her features to the mould, and drank delight
From the fine visible music of her form,
Which slid into his soul, like gentle rains
Into the bosom of the purple blooms
By maids and matrons delicately culled,
A gift to Proserpine in Trinacrian meads,
For vernal crowns : a pure delight at first,
Like that which stirs the sculptor's nerve with thrills
That flow into the block ; but soon, alas !
The light that sunned him warmed into a flame,
And the rare honeyed sweetness which she brought
Now left a sting behind.   My poor Erastus,
I knew him mine no more ; he was not seen
At the Palaestra ; in my sports and toils
He shared not ; in my room he was not found,
As was his wont, like some familiar bird,
That loves his cage beside a lady's lap,
More than the ample air.   He walked alone,
And listened to the cuckoo's note, or plash
Of wavelets breaking on smooth beach, or croon
Of silver waters by a thymy brae,
Where he lay stretched from morn to lazy noon
In high-wrought fancies rapt ; then, on a thought,
By sudden inspiration caught, would start,

Like whom the Nymphs possess, and make the wood
Ring with his fitful rapture.   When he heard
My step approach, or any social tread,
Even as a wounded hind he slunk away,
And hid him in the thicket; and so lost
To friendship and to me, by that strange madness
Which men call Love.

PLATO.

All this is common chance,
Mere fever in the hot blood o' the world,
Like sultry heat in Scirophorion; change
Comes with the changing moons.

ALCIPHRON.
Pray it be so!
But mark the end, how this hot summer bore
A bloody harvest.   'T is ten days now gone,
There was a feast of Artemis at Brauron,
Where from old ancestry Callippides
Owns an estate of many fertile roods,
And here, by sacred usage of the place,
Behoved his daughter's grace to lead the pomp
In honour of the goddess.   All Attica
Thronged to enjoy the season and the sight;
And young Erastus, winged with love, outraced
The sun to greet the feast; myself was there
With early morn; and sure it was a sight
For gods to look on, and to envy men;
All the choice youths and maidens of the land,
The blood of Codrus and of Solon, led

By fair Antheia, fronted like a star,
In one long line of blooming purity,
Like flowers that flush the bank and climb the brae,
Marched from the beach, to where chaste Artemis
Sways from her far-viewed throne. Thou would'st have thought
    have thought
Herself, the huntress of the woods, was there,
With all her nymphs, they were so habited
With bow and quiver from fair shoulder slung,
And stole succinct, for nimble spring prepared,
And booted shins, and with a silver moon
Upon their brows.   Antheia in the van
Peered like a lioness for the festive car
Of towered Cybele; her rare wealth of locks
In undulant fulness overflowed her neck,
With golden gloss dependent, and her eye
Showed like the queen of what it looked upon,
And yet not haughty.   At which view enrapt
Some cried, 'Tis Dian's self! and some fell down
And kissed the ground with worship.   My Erastus
Stood like a stock in rooted ravishment,
And eyed Antheia, blind to all beside.
That hour had signed his doom.   With no more thought
    thought
Than a wild ox that runs with lashing tail,
Stung by a summer fly, he seized a style,
And to the haughty, high Callippides
Sent a sealed tablet furnace-hot with love
For his fair daughter; and himself, he said,
Might fitliest claim to be her husband, bred
To that fine art which Phidias used, and taught

Our Pericles to make Erechtheus' rock
A citadel for gods.   Callippides
Made little score, I trow, of his hot blood;
But laughed, then fumed, and flung an oath or two
Into the air, and said, The boy is mad!
And I were doubly mad if I should wed
My gem of daughters to a Hermes-cutter,
Tainting the high descendence of my blood
With such a puddle.   Then, with a stinging NO!
He flung the scornful answer to his quest,
And flapped him off, as one would flap a fly,
That, having battened on a dunghill, now
With dainty insolence will pitch his nose
Into our pudding.   Since which time I fail
To find Erastus; Athens hath no clew
To track his whitherward; his poor father weeps;
His mother pines; we know not if he lives
To look on light, or wanders with the Shades;
But this I know, the friend I loved is lost.

Plato.

Thy sadness is a witness of thy worth.
The worthy live by love, as rivers swell
By drawing in new waters.   But believe
Thy friend is hid, not lost; the blast hath nipt,
Not killed his bud of manhood; he will live
To call thee friend, and thou to bless his madness.

Alciphron.

I know not; in the lunacy of love
Some men have dashed their lives away, and some

Lived in stale apathy of life, and some,
Like thundered milk, have turned the sweet to sour,
And murdered whom they hugged.　I may not deem
This rage a good, nor him a god who spurs
His moonish votaries to make war on reason,
And, even as pouting children break their toys,
Rive the sweet bonds of life.

PLATO.

       Speak soft, my boy !
Not wise against the gods who stirs his tongue,
Ev'n in a whisper ; and of all the gods
Most ancient, honourable, in virtue prime
Is Eros, fathered nor by Jove supreme,
Nor hoary Kronos, unbegotten ; whence
Sprang the exhaustless progeny of Time,
Still changing, still the same.　Thus Hesiod taught,
Acusilaus and Parmenides,
And all the wisest of old bards, inspired
Not by the tinkling plaudits of the mob,
But by the brooding silence which informs
True thought from Jove.　A mighty god is Love,
Whom, if thy tongue blaspheme, a countless host
Of Hellas' sons and daughters, fairest famed,
Shall rise to flout thee.　Peleus' son ; and she
Who for her lord the king of Pheræ's life
Yielded her own ; and he, the Cean youth,
By Dian's grace who saw and loved and won
The fair Cydippe ; and that valiant pair
Who with their good swords wreathed in myrtle drave
The hated home-bred tyrants from their seats,

Whose tombs you passed to-day upon the road ;
All these Love's vouchers stand, beyond the craft
Of sophist to redargue.   The gods prove
Their truths by facts, 'gainst which our dialectic
Butts with blind horns in vain.   And sooner shall
The sun desert the pole, and all the power
That spheres the world with fire be caked in ice,
Than Love shall cease to stir the heart of things
With plastic pulses, which fish-blooded men,
Prisoned in lobster crust of cold conceit,
Call madness ; but the wiser poet sang,
I will, I will be mad !   And so sing all
True worshippers of Love.

ALCIPHRON.

                    But Love brings pain ;
And pious bards the blest Immortals praise,
" Givers of good things."   Pain is not divine.

PLATO.

Blame not sweet Love for bitterness it brings ;
Evil dogs good, as low by lofty lies,
Shadow by light, and death where life may be.
No pleasure without pain ; the bright-faced heaven,
With the sure change of the swift-wheeling hours,
Shows pitchy black ; only the deathless gods
Live in unclouded sun ; themselves are suns ;
We, being shined on, shine a little space,
Then pass to shadow.

ALCIPHRON.

My beloved Erastus
Must needs be pained, being exiled from the view
Of that most fair perfection, on whose charms
He fed, as flowers feed on Hyperion's blaze,
Not without reason, though his yeasty soul
Turned the sweet wine to sourness.   What he loved
Was worthy of his love, if love may wear
A wise man's livery; but I have known,
And now I know, a very proper man
Caught by this phrensy, young Alcidamas,
You know him, once a passing prudent youth,
With a bold front of speech, and words exact,
Grave propositions, and conclusions just,
Weighed in a balance very right or wrong;
But now he talks in tropes like any poet,
For why? he is in love with little Thisbe,
The blooming daughter of the blowsy dame
That sweeps the floor and smooths the bed to Damon,
The sooty charcoal burner at Acharnae!

PLATO.

All men are poets, though bald prosers born,
When Love shall touch them; as, when Helios thaws
The close-ribbed ice on Pindus' gleaming ridge,
Long prisoned Nature bursts her wintry bars,
And loveliest blossoms 'neath the frozen rim
Peer with hot blushes!

ALCIPHRON.

          This not causeless comes;
And fair Antheia well might Fancy move
To break her shell, where with numb wing she lay
In proser's breast; but young Alcidamas
Raves without reason.   Would you heard him talk!
His admiration is a theme for laughter,
Like love that ladies spend on snarling curs,
Or mothers lavish on mis-shapen brats,
Or curious scholars waste on sapless books;
Earth grew no woman worth a glance till Thisbe
Sprang at the roots of Parness; other corn
Has chaff, but she is chaffless; other ore
Takes rust, but she is gold, accepts no taint
From air or water, but adds grace to all.
Her eyes, he swears, out-lustre all the stars,
Her smiles out-blossom all the wealth of summer,
Her step is Hera's, and her delicate hand
And foot are Hebe's, her little waist is bound
With Aphrodite's cest, her voice is sweet
As summer waves that break on silver shells,
Which Nereids gathering from the bleachèd strand
String into necklaces; all the gods have showered
Their grace on this Pandora; and himself
Hath heaped her with a century of gifts
Ten mountains high; such gifts as women love,—
Milesian coifs, Sicilian shawls, and what
Amorgos markets of translucent stuffs,
Boeotian shoes that show the tiny foot,
Rings, brooches, jewels, tassels, snoods, and zones,

And all the bravery of woven gold
That marshy Elis breeds.   He'd fling the ore
Of all Pangæus pounded at her feet,
And swear the dust was honoured by her tread ;
He'd dance on swords to please her, and declare
The ground was strewed with violets, so high
His madness runs ; and yet the maiden is,
To my poor thinking, but a comely wench,
Strong to draw water, wise to milk a cow,
Not sickly-hued, and not ashamed to laugh ;
Frank, and free-handed ; not afraid of men ;
And looking rather nice, when nicely dressed,
Like many another.   Women, flowers, and birds,
Are Nature's broadcast currency in the mart
Of Beauty.   I can smell a perfumed bloom,
And not get drunk on't ; but this juggling imp,
This angler Love, that with a maiden's curl
Trims flies to hook strong men, and leads the wise
From wisdom with a wink, and blunts the edge
Of manhood with a smile—what thing is Love?

PLATO.

I said he was a god ; but why ask me?
There are who worship Aphrodite better.

ALCIPHRON.

Thou art my teacher, guide, and oracle ;
Thou knowest all things ; all things that I know
Were culled from thee, as children gather fruit
From shaken groves in autumn.

PLATO.

All mine is thine that by long thought I know ;
But to know Eros thou hadst wiselier gone
To that fair Lesbian marvel, whose rare life
Was one fine fervid flame of sacrifice
To golden Aphrodite sparrow-drawn
On rosy car through ether, or to him
Who praised her fragrant beauty violet-crowned,
Sweet honey blossom of light wingèd smiles,
But feared to speak his wish.

ALCIPHRON.

     Why did he fear?
We fear not what we love ; Love killeth fear.

PLATO.

Pure love hath fear, lest with presumptuous touch
We wrong the thing we reverence.

ALCIPHRON.

     Is Love worship?

PLATO.

Not all Love ; there be many Loves ; one hot,
O'erwhelming, tyrannous, fierce, which wild beasts
  know,
And men more wild than beasts ; one mild and pure,
And loyal as a flower that bows its head
In duty to the sun. Love is a thing
So wide that vilest things must share it, tasting
Good, tempered to their vileness : only Death,

That hideous yawning mask of things that were,
Knows not Love's witchcraft.   Our theologers join
Uranian Aphrodite with the praise
Of her whom pigs, if pigs could pray, would greet
With grunting adoration,—whom men call
Pandemus, by the swinish multitude
Supremely honoured.

ALCIPHRON.

Call you her a god?

PLATO.

All things are gods, or from a god, that pass
The wit of man with tools of rare device
To make or mar; we cannot breathe without
A god, much less new life from old evolve,
Link after link in lines of long descent
From Infinite to Infinite, without
The procreant Eros.   There is love of bodies,
And love of souls; the one a sensuous thrill
Which any dullest slimy thing may know,
The other bright with winged intelligence,
The heritage of gods, and godlike men.

ALCIPHRON.

Pray tell me of them both: if both are gods,
I would not ban what Plato bids me bless.

PLATO.

I do remember, when I was a youth,
Some twenty summers on my peachy cheeks,

In sweet discourse with Socrates, one night
In Hecatombaeon, when, with stinted stream
Lazy Ilissus drew his lisping thread
Beneath the blanchèd stones, he, like a bee
Well bagged with honey, talked of mighty Love,
And of an high discourse in Agathon's house
In praise of Eros, at a banquet given
By the young bard, what time he gained the crown,
First in the tragic song, in that red year
When Athens murdered Melos.   In his turn
Each guest did aptly eulogise the god ;
And Eryximachus, the wise physician,
Of the Pancosmian Eros made discourse,
Which in his wide embracement comprehends
Pandemian Aphrodite, and all love
Of body for body.   This wondrous frame of things
We call the world, he said, this universe,
Is of contrarious powers compaginate,
With curious balance ; and what simple seems,
Is of most jarring elements combined
Into a peaceful amity : the sweet Force
That welds the diverse, and transmutes their hate,
Mortals call Love.   Thus liquid finds the dry ;
Cold marries heat ; and sweet the bitter tames ;
And thus of two imperious fierce extremes
Each from the other takes the bridling rein,
And gives, by losing half his former self,
A genial' mildness and a safe restraint.
By this high law of cosmic love we live,
Counting the rhythmic pulse of healthy blood,
Not into hostile alternation tossed

Of fever and sharp ague.   Our great head
Asclepius knew this, and conquered Death :
This mystic truth the thoughtful son inspired
Of Blyson, by Cayster's reedy banks,
Beloved of cranes.   No realm of bliss may be
From that fine reconciling force divorced ;
But chiefly Music, voicing procreant joy
From plumy breasts in spring, doth preach its power,
Or, winging hymns from hearts of blithesome boys
In praise of gods, the givers of all good ;
Or, with the measured breath of resolution,
Fluting the Spartan to the ordered fray ;
In these, and all the witchcrafts of sweet sound,
The high and low, by Nature contrary,
Being counterpoised, with nice adjustment blend
Into concentuous oneness, and forth draw
Concordant tremors from opposing strings.
Even so, from war of passions in the breast,
There is a touch that knows to bring sweet peace,
And spell them into Music.   In the strife
Of seasons too, and war of winds and waves,
The wise admire the mystic force of Love,
Now tempered well, now with loose-shaken rein,
Extravagant, rushing into fervent waste.
Plagues, frosts, and mildews, and the lashing hail,
The blasting levin, and the sulphurous bolt,
Are all but skits of crudely-mingled air,
Whose elements the harmonising power
Of Love hath left, which, but for gracious Fate,
In violent plunges of dissentious rage
Would bring back chaos, and insanely smite

All Nature with disease, strangling dear life
With suicidal clutch.   In Titan times
When earth-born, serpent-footed Power prevailed,
This war of lawless, wild, distempered Forces
Fevered the sphere, and shook the thrones of gods ;
But since what time the son of Kronos reigns
With Metis, strong in counsel, for his mate,
These powers are bound, and with safe vent discharge
Their snaffled wrath at Jove's high beck ; and now
Love holds all fast; and by constraint of Love
The constant seasons wheel with measured change
Of shifting beauty ; through the vasty void
The flaming couriers of the blue serene
Speed their fair sequences, and deftly thread
Their unentangled ways, and on green earth
The furious pulses of impatient growth
Being wisely reined, are moulded into forms
Of beauty, bursting in exuberant bloom,
Yet, in full pride, still bending to the law
Of lovely limitation, which redeems
Wild force from chaos.   And this law divine,
Of harmonising contraries, prevails
In loves and marriages of men and plants,
Where nothing single hath the plastic power
To procreate itself, but always male
And female, kindred but in diverse kind—
The active with the passive aptly paired—
Produce their like.   Thus the physician spake
And every couch applauded.

ALCIPHRON.

                    I too applaud;
But in this reasoned cool discourse I hear
No voice of comfort for my dear lost friend,
Transported out of reason's bound by love.

PLATO.

Your friend is young.   We, who are old, expect
The mellow fruitage with the mellowing year,
Sour juices with the crimson flush of Spring.
Our nature is too feeble to endure
The keen enlargement of immortal love
Beneath our narrow pale of flesh, without
Fearful disturbance; imped with untried wings
The soul must flutter ere it find a poise,
Like little boys in eagerness to swim,
Who beat the flood with palms undisciplined,
And sink themselves with hurry.

ALCIPHRON.

                      Socrates
Was there too, I presume, and, being there,
Would speak; alway he largely did profess
Himself a lover of all lovely things,
·And by a Mantinean prophetess
'Clept Diotima, was instructed well
In love's philosophy.   What said Socrates?

PLATO.

Of course being there he could not choose but speak,
Like brooks that babble while they flow, and like

The brooks his speech was music; but I heard
The argument not from himself, but from
Apollodorus, who in the recital
Seemed lifted somewhat from that drooping vein
Which he affects,—or, kindlier to phrase it,
Which affects him.

ALCIPHRON.

   I greatly long to hear
The words of Socrates.

PLATO.

    What talk he held
At Agathon's banquet you shall know hereafter;
But for your present need I will rehearse
His high discourse to Phaedrus, held in praise
Of the Uranian Aphrodite, strong
In souls of men and gods—the which to me
Seems worthiest of the theme; and Phaedrus said
He never saw the harp strings of his soul
So swept with godlike rapture. Would you hear it?

ALCIPHRON.

I drink your words.

PLATO.

   Well, thus the lecture ran.
All spirit is immortal. That which moves
Another, but from some precedent takes
Its source and spring of motion, fitly dies;
But with essential motive virtue dowered
Soul needs not borrow what it has, nor can

Part with its self of self.   Dull bodies move,
When they are moved, the lifeless clod, the block,
The stone, the stock, the lumpish aggregate,
Blind inorganic hinderment, mere mass
Unsignatured, uncharactered, from all
Feature divorced, these, from the boundless vague
To win the fair redemption, must receive
The shaping energy of plastic power
From the fine mobile Essence uncreate,
Source of all force and form, which men call Soul.

ALCIPHRON.

What is the Soul?

PLATO.

Dear boy, what in itself
The soul may be transcends all tongue to tell;
But for our sensuous need that knows by types,
'Tis pictured wisely as an airy car
Drawn by a brace of wingèd steeds, and helmed
By skilful charioteer.   The steeds that draw
The chariots of the gods are goodly, both
In form and fleetness, and with native ease
Own the wise rein; but to our mortal cars
The uneven Fates an ill-paired yoke assigned,
Cross and contrarious, as with good the bad
Holds concert never.   The one is tall, erect,
With kingly neck well-arched, and rounded limb,
And joints with nice articulation framed
For suppleness and strength, dark-eyed, but fair
In glossy felt, and with a nose that looks

Well out into the air, and to the rein
Obedient, without whip.   The other huge,
Unwieldy, crookèd, with neck thick and short,
Flat-nosed, dark-skinned, and with an angry eye
Of flaring blue, with shaggy ears, and deaf
To the rider's cry, of random plunges full,
Cross-grained, and going where his pace should go
By sheer must be, and mastery of goad.

Thus far of souls, and of their diverse kinds
In men and gods the heaven-taught master spoke ;
Then to the journeys of the souls he passed,
Their wheeling chariots compassing the girth
Of the illimitable spaces, far
Beyond the starry vault, at measured terms
Of festive high occasion, when they leave
Their customed posts and ordinary charge
Beneath the blue concave.   The splendid pomp
Of this procession of the souls is led
By supreme Jove, whom all the host of gods
Follows in marshalled sequence ; only Vesta
Remains at home to watch the Olympian hearth
Then with their fervid steeds on flashing way
They mount the steep of Heaven, until they climb
To hypercosmic fields upon the back
Of the fire vaulted sphere, then draw the reins
Of their obedient steeds, and feed their gaze
Upon the shining vast expanse of things
That are the substance of the shows we see,
Our sight their shadows.   From this fount the gods
Drink truth and knowledge, justice, temperance,

The native food of souls, which to their wings
Gives crescent virtue, plumy grace, and strength
Of venturous vans.   And, when their blood is rich
With virtue from this supermundane view
(Which chances when their steeds with willing feet
Have paced the whole career above the stars),
Then to his customed station every god
Returns, and with new strength administers
His cosmic charge, and works from hour to hour
With fruitful silence, and unhasting speed.

Thus far the gods.   But souls of mortal men
That followed in the starry march return
Not crowned with triumph, but with limping act
That mocks their purpose.   For the native vice
Of the contrarious cross-grained steed in each
Checks their smooth speed, perplexes wheel with wheel,
Plunges awry, and with rebellious rear
Sends perturbation through the file, and clogs
Their path with sheer confusion.   For which cause
They lag behind the gods and fail to reach
The line of prospect ; some but with their heads
Outpeer the starry rim and gain some part
Of the celestial vision ; some below
The vault are dashed, now visionless, and now
A point regaining, where they snatch a glimpse
Of things beyond, then downward jerked again
They reel precipitate ; others plomb as lead
Fall earthwards, with their wings all torn and crushed,
Their gallant charioteers all maimed and bruised ;
All from the perfect vision of the truth

Back-thrown, remain condemned to live on earth,
And feed on husks of vain opinion, fleshed
In various types of man, by strong decree
Of Adrasteia.   He who closest tracked
The chariots of the gods in guise appears
Of thoughtful sage, or passioned worshipper
Of beauty, lover of all lovely things,
With soul entuned to harmony divine
By songs that charm the cosmos.   After these
Who saw most of the truthful vision lives
On earth a king who rules by chartered right,
Or a brave warrior with victorious sword,
Who spends his blood for liberty and law;
And third in rank the statesman comes, the just
Administrator of affairs, or who
Is skilled by faithful stewartry to give
Increase to money wisely husbanded.
Fourth comes the trainer of our fleshly frames,
Gymnast, or healthful leech; and then the souls
Whose earthly mission is from guilt to shrive
By mysteries, initiations, charms,
Or clear the dubious path by oracles
And slippery divinations.   Sixth in rank
The poet comes, slight fancy-monger, pleased
With fine conceits in superficial play,
Or whoso, brothered with the rhyming crew,
Lives careless, monkey-like in mimic show.
The seventh in order is mechanical,
Who shapes the inform matter by his tool,
Or with his spade upturns the pregnant glebe
To sniff the vital air, and drink the beam

Of genial day.　Below these types of souls
Two basest classes stand, who in the race
Fell heaviest from the sphere : the sophist crew,
The democrat, and who, to please the mob,
For the slow silent growth of ripening truth
Gives fence of glittering phrase ; and him, beneath
The lowest type of low humanity,
The tyrant, naked from all rags of good,
Who, to englut his monstrous maw, usurps
The bleeding world, and swallows all in self.

ALCIPHRON.

Excuse me, if I break into your speech
With an unseasoned question.　From your words
The quality of souls I comprehend,
And how, hedged round by sensuous shows, we draw
Our high conceptions of substantial good
From seats beyond the stars ; but what of Love ?

PLATO.

Attend, and you shall hear.　The soul of man,
In walls of flesh encased, not lightly dares
To leap its prison.　Some their prison love,
Like birds that, bred in cages, fear to fly :
These serve the moment, little raised above
The earth-perusing brute :　Some burst their bonds
A space, and then with drooping wing return
To hug their chains : some with persistent poise
Float on brave wing, and in the body live
Above the body : these the sense-bound throng
Call madmen, dreamers, and enthusiasts, fools,

That to the marked and metalled road prefer
Helmless balloonings in the pathless air ;
Nor without cause prefer : for well they know
Their madness from a god, by whom indwelt
They rise proud-wing'd above the lowly stage
And narrow scene of life, and move apart
Conversing with the gods.   These men are prophets,
And purifying priests, and priestly bards,
Like Epimenides, whom Athens called
From Crete to clear the State from guilty taint;
Empedocles, who rode the winds, and reined
The water-courses, and disarmed the plague ;
Orpheus, and Linus, and Musaeus, men
Whose songs were sunbeams, by Apollo's grace
Shot through the dark.   More nobly mad than these
Are lovers, by the incarnate splendour caught
Of the Eternal Beautiful, revealed
In chiselled feature and in rounded limb,
In delicate hue, and queenly gait, and power
Of speaking eyes, and the rare glamoury
Of smiles that play about the mobile mouth
Like sportful children in a flowery mead.
For Beauty hath this power above all forms
Of godlike excellence to mortals known,
It may be seen ; it doth invade the sense,
Possess the reason, overwhelm the gaze,
And takes the gazer captive when it stands
In corporate strength before him ; other goods
Must be searched out, and to the constant toil
Yield of the straining chase ; but God hath spread
His living mantle round the glorious globe,

Broidered with beauty, that all eyes may drink
Its catholic goodness, and the stoutest yield
His reason thralled before its potent charm.
Now, in that high procession of the gods,
Of which I spoke, the souls of mortal men
Followed the track each of some god, and caught
Contagion from his nearness, and a snatch
Of his peculiar quality.   Some from Mars
Borrowed the fiery fierceness : some from Jove
The instinct of command : the grace of youth
From light-foot Hermes some : and others took
Soft plumy luxuries from the Cyprian queen :
Whence all men, born into this realm of sense,
Housed in their mortal rind, bring deathless seeds
Of Heaven-born instincts, aspirations proud,
And upward gropings in their several kinds,
Bright dower from lucid supersensual seats,
The cradle of all souls.   Hence divers loves
In diverse souls the diverse memory wakes
Of that pre-natal vision ; and by force
Of fiery Mars possessed, the fiery soul
Springs with intemperate fervid spur to clasp
The thing it loves ; but souls who followed Jove
In that high race, close to his kingly car,
In whom they love, love kingliness, and show
All loyal chaste obedience to their love :
So each with innate preference, and free
Elective choice discriminates, but all
By that celestial memory transported
Beyond their present selves, and stirred to high
Prevision for the future.   The crushed being

Of the poor spirit dragging earthly cares
Drinks in sweet dewy nurture from his love,
And grows and spreads, and with fine-thrilling pains
Bursts into liberal plumes, and stands redeemed
From aimless longings and from blind desires ;
The soul now finds its mate, and with its mate
The food it feeds on ; loved and lover grow
By mutual breathing in of excellence,
Ungrudged, unstinted ; and now either takes
His likeness from the other, as the light
Shines on the brazen mirror and returns.
Thus Love achieves his perfect work, beyond
The sensuous rudiments of the bodily form,
And from the pictured vestibule conducts
With genial hand into the inmost shrine
Of radiant gods, before whose grace to bow
Is better than to hold all earthly thrones
From Ganges to Gadeira.   This is all
My memory of the words of Socrates.

ALCIPHRON.

I would it had been more ; these godlike words
Possess my soul like memory of a hymn
Heard through an echoing fane.   But I must deem
The love men talk about in Athens here
Is to the picture in thy speech as like
As sooty Vulcan is to Vulcan's wife.

PLATO.

This is mere weakness of our mortal kind,
Who seek by groping, and by blundering find.

No facile work the gods assigned our race
To hold the track of right, nor touch the line
Where fevered passion madly vaults, beyond
All poise of seemliness, and spurs itself
Into a fault.　Our lofty lust to fly
Oft flings us from the back of our conceit
Into the mire, while he who lowly walks
Walks safely.　Beasts are never less than beasts,
Being never more.

ALCIPHRON.

　　　　　　And I must be content
To lose my friend, because he leapt beyond
His lowly state, maddened by mighty Love.

PLATO.

And, if he had not leapt, what better then?
He might have kept the wheelwork of his life
As true as tortoise to its morning crawl,
Or settled into mouldiness by sheer
Privation of the spur of proud desire,
Or wallowed in a swinish stye, and rotted
Into a sensual grave!　But now he loves
A thing that lifts the level of his life
Above all low regards; or, should he die
(Which gods forefend!) like her who sought and found
A briny death from the Leucadian cliff,
All men will weep, none harshly blame the deed.
'Tis human that we die; but, being crowned
With kingly grace above the brutish kind.
'Tis fit we die with crowns upon our head,

Not beg our way dispurpled to the grave.
Your friend hath caught no baseness from his love.

ALCIPHRON.

This thought shall comfort me.

PLATO.

       And add this other;
The weight of daily tasks, which men call life,
Sweet friendship lightens; but to lift ourselves
Above ourselves, and to behold the gods
Behind this visual screen of fleeting shows,
Who from immortal types of beauty weave
The shifting figures in the loom of time,
This is the gift of Love; whom know, and thou,
Like Diomede, unfilmed, shalt pierce through all,
And walk through gloom in glory.

ALCIPHRON.

        I have heard.
Henceforth my tongue from hasty blame be far!
Mine eye, with lowly worship fraught, be near
To every form of loveliness that treads
The flower-bespangled earth! Farewell, good master!

NOTES.

———◆———

PYTHAGORAS.

P. 3. CHORUS OF MAIDENS.—The idea brought out in this chorus, that Jove, by marrying Μῆτις or *Counsel*, commenced a new era in the history of cosmical progress, was familiar to the ancients. The dynasty of Jove is the dynasty of order ; order proceeds from number and proportion ; and this, being the watchword of the Pythagorean philosophy, forms a natural bond of connection betwixt the chorus and the philosophical exposition which follows.

Pp. 4 and 5. The mythological allusions to Hera and her sacred marriage with Jove are taken from Homer's *Iliad*, xiv. (with my notes), and Pausanias Argolis.

Pp. 10 and 11. The facts, or rather traditions, about the life of Pythagoras, are taken from Diogenes, Porphyry, and Jamblichus. There is a considerable smack in them of the silly miracle-mongery of the mediæval lives of the saints.

P. 13. In the Pythagorean objection to swearing (Diog. 22, and Jamblich. 9), we see a distinctly Christian element. Generally speaking, the ancients, both the vulgar and the sage, had no special scrupulosity about oaths.

P. 14. The Pythagorean test of character by physiognomy was as famous in its day as the craniological one in the skull-philosophy of Combe, and, as I believe, much more practically valuable ; Porphyry, 14.

P. 15. The traditions about Theano, and other sisters of the

Pythagorean society (Jamblich. 32, Porphyry, 19), are consistent with Doric society, as opposed to the usage of Attica. Plato inherited this apostleship from his great prototype ; and J. S. Mill, and other advocates of women's rights in these latter days, should not have forgotten the sage of Samos as the first Greek prophet of their gospel.

P. 21. The superiority of Egypt to Greece, in respect of early intellectual culture, is a favourite theme with Plato (Timæus, 22, B.), with the church fathers and Josephus.

P. 22. I have represented both Pythagoras and Diogoras as quick-witted enough to foresee the mischief that would be done by the generation of fluent talkers, called Sophists, who appeared in the chief cities of Greece shortly afterwards. For the refutation of Mr. Grote's views on the Sophists, see my *Horac Hellenicae*.

P. 22. The Pythagorean maxim—ἐν δακτυλίω εἰκόνα θεοῦ μὴ περιφέρειν, is quoted in Diog. 17, and Porphyry, 42.

Pp. 32 and 33. Number being the shibboleth of the Pythagoreans, of course, like other shibboleths, led to a large expatiation on the subtle properties and imaginary excellencies of certain numbers. Of these I have thought it sufficient to enlarge on the trine. Of course I do not say absolutely that Pythagoras ever enunciated the peculiar significance of the theological doctrine of the Trinity expressed in the text ; it only appears as a very obvious illustration of the general doctrine ; and I have little doubt that the Platonising fathers of the early Greek church believed in some intelligible Trinity of this kind, not in the unintelligible jabber of the Athanasian creed. On the supposed Trinity of Homer, see my notes to *Iliad*, iv. 288.

P. 37. The simile here used by Diagoras, to justify his theological conservatism, is a well-known Pythagorean maxim, —στέφανον μὴ τίλλειν. Porphyry, lxii.

P. 42. The Darwinian theory of the imperfection and helplessness of the primitive man, set forth in this chorus, was extremely familiar to the ancients, and will be found in Diodorus Siculus, book i., and not a few fragments of the most ancient speculators in Ritter and Preller.

THALES.

Thales chronologically stands before Pythagoras, and may be tabled in the memory with Solon, 600 B.C., in round numbers. The other sages in my list stand in chronological order. Socrates died 400 B.C., at which date his disciple Plato was twenty-nine years old.

P. 49. The Greeks early displayed a genius for mathematics, though of course the Egyptians preceded them both in the arts of field-measuring and star-measuring. The proposition about the rectangularity of the angle included in a semicircle (Euclid, iii.), belongs by historical tradition to the great Milesian Diog. La. i. 1, 3.

P. 52. The story about the star-gazer falling into the ditch is accompanied in Diogenes (i. 1, 8) by the question put by an old woman—*O Thales, if you cannot see what's before your nose, how can you pretend to read the stars?* Silly; the fact being that just because a man is looking at what is distant he cannot at the same moment be regarding what is near.

P. 52. For the story about the tripod fished up by some fishermen of Miletus, and ordered by the oracle to be given to the wisest of the Greeks, see Diog. i. 1, 7.

P. 54. To the ancients Egypt, as to us China, was the home of all oddities and eccentricities, some real, some imaginary. The instances in the text are from a well-known chapter in Herodotus, ii.

P. 59. The exploits of Miletus, as a mother of colonies, form one of the grandest themes in the early history of Greece. Some idea of their range is attempted to be given in the chorus.

P. 65. The verse of Homer, quoted here, is evidently a fragment of some pre-Homeric elemental theogony. See *Iliad*, xiv. 201, with the illustrations from various quarters in my note.

XENOPHANES.

P. 79. Among the fathers of geological science, or at least the far-sighted prophets of the science to be, Xenophanes certainly claims the first place. The passage, which my text follows almost literally, will be found in Hippol. *Refut. haeres.* i. 14.

P. 89. The attitude of hostility towards the popular theology, which I have represented in the conversation between Xenophanes and the priest of Apollo, is distinctive of the philosopher of Colophon, and was the great point to bring out in this dialogue. The fragments of his wisdom which remain are sufficient to give us a clear notion of his theological position ; and the most significant of them are, according to my general plan, embodied in the text.

HERACLITUS.

P. 105. The honourable manner in which Heraclitus is spoken of by Plato in various places may be taken as a sufficient evidence of the high estimation in which he stood among the ancients. Like the German Hamann, however, he seems to have been as obscure as he was profound ; hence his cognomen ὁ σκοτεινός. I gave myself great pains to get hold of his point of view, and hope I have in some measure succeeded. Among recent writers, Professor Bernays, of Bonn, has made the most important contributions to the understanding of this sage. I made a careful study of Lassalle's book (Berlin, 1858). The edition of Bywater (Oxon., 1877) did not come into my hands till after my work was complete. Ritter and Preller, of course, was thoroughly gone through.

P. 107. That a profound philosopher, who despised the shallow thinkers about him, should prefer playing at astragals with a boy, is quite natural, and stands in tradition. Diog. i. 2, 3.

P. 112. The great truth that there is no such thing as absolute rest in the universe, but that what we call rest is either a balance of contrary motions or a rest relatively to our perceptions, and further, as a consequence of this, that there is no individual being or thing that can be looked upon as absolutely fenced off from the great tidal currents of the unsleeping universe, and that through the marks of change there is a fundamental identity at the root of all changeable : This doctrine, the favourite theme of the Buddhists, and familiarly expressed by the short sentence πάντα ῥεῖ, belongs prominently to Heraclitus, and is set forth in the text in correspondence with what Plato says in the *Cratylus*, 402 A, and the *Theætetus*, 152 D.

P. 116. It was mentioned in the Introductory Epistle that there was no such unhappy divorce between piety and philosophy among the wise Greeks, as we have seen so lamentably parade itself under British skies in these latter days. Here the pantheism of the ancients helped them ; for, though they taught as Heraclitus does here, that FIRE was the first principle of all things, they did not thereby exclude λόγος or Reason, that is Divine Wisdom, as it is expressed in the Book of Proverbs, but rather quietly, and by an instinct of sound Greek thinking, assumed it. Heraclitus, therefore, was no materialist, in the vulgar English sense of the word ; but his Fire, as I have expressed it at p. 123, was "instinct with reason and inventive force." This way of viewing the active forces of the universe is no doubt foreign both to the English and the Scotch mind, but may not be the less true for that. The Scotch philosophy is narrow ; and the English, as a people, are rather inclined to make a boast of having no philosophy at all.

P. 126. I have here quoted two well-known sayings of the dark Ephesian. It was impossible for a real philosopher, notwithstanding the ready help of allegorical interpretations, to accept the theological teaching of Homer without considerable recalcitration. Hence his anticipation of the Platonic expulsion of Homer from the schools, ἐκ τῶν ἀγώνων ἐκβάλλεσθαι καὶ ῥαπίζεσθαι, Diog. ix. 1, 2. Archilochus got his dismissal probably on other grounds, somewhat, no doubt, as Lord Byron might be treated by a modern school-board. The other maxim, about learning, or πολυμαθίη, which occurs in the same chapter of *Diogenes*, was worthy of a stout thinker, and recalls to me the well-known saying of Hobbes—"*If I had read as much as other men, I should have been equally stupid!*" What, indeed, is a great part of what is called learning in the schools, but a laborious record of ingenious drivel, blind blundering, and dreaming with open eyes ?

P. 127. The Diana of the Ephesians (Acts xix.), whom the priest here calls on the philosopher to expound, was plainly identical with Cybele or the Earth, an Asiatic goddess, whom the Greeks, from certain points of merely external resemblance, were forward to confound with their own Artemis, the sister of Apollo, or the Moon.

EMPEDOCLES.

P. 133. There seems to be very little in the philosophical doctrine of Empedocles worthy of a poetical treatment. There was no particular merit in the prominence given by him to the doctrine of the four elements, which, no doubt, had been sufficiently recognised by his predecessors, without being formally talked about. He deserves credit, however, for his doctrine of Love and Strife, which he found in Hesiod, and which is only the polytheistic expression for the modern doctrine of Attraction and Repulsion, exhibited in various familiar departments of physical science. What specially claims notice in him is the peculiar combination of the priest and the philosopher which his character exhibits, and his social action both as a physician—or, as we would say, a member of the Board of Health—and a politician. In his devotion to physical science generally, he seems to have prefigured Democritus; and the story about his leaping into the crater of Mount Ætna, is no doubt only a popular exaggeration of his frequent visits to that mysterious mouth of fire in his neighbourhood. A modern Manfred, in the overstrained style of so much of the best English poetry, recently fashionable, might have indulged in a mock-sublime catastrophe of this kind : not so, certainly, an old Hellenic σοφός.

P. 160. The description of the plague here, as every scholar will recognise, is taken from the well-known chapter in Thucydides, ii.

P. 181. The sacrifice of the young Empedocles, in this place, is not historical, but adapted from a well-known passage of Goethe's *Autobiography*, which seemed to me admirably fitted for exhibiting, in a striking manner, the priestly element, so prominent in the character of Empedocles.

ANAXAGORAS.

P. 197. The sentence from Aristotle on the fly-leaf sufficiently indicates the proud position which Anaxagoras occupies among the exponents of ultimate truth. Not that his predecessors, after the manner of certain modern sophists, believed in the possibility of the creation of a reasonable universe from any combination of blind sequences; but that, by enunciating the word MIND, as the principle of principles, the sage of Clazomenæ brought most emphatically into the foreground the essential reasonableness of the universe in all its parts. The world, according to him, is simply a manifestation of the divine intelligence of the supreme Ζεύς, just as the steam-engine is a manifestation of the lower intelligence of James Watt. He thus struck the key-note to the beautiful exposition of the doctrine of teleology, or final causes, given, as we shall see in the next dialogue, by Socrates.

P. 201. The Thucydides here mentioned was not the historian, but a politician, the leader of the opposition party in Athens, who strained every nerve to oust Pericles from the high position, which he maintained so manfully for nearly half a century, as the leader of the Athenian demos. One great handle which the opposition used against him was the fact that he had used the Delian fund, which was federal in its origin, for the selfish purpose of beautifying Athens. He, of course, replied, that if Greece was to be Greece as a corporate body against Persia, that body required a head, and it was right that the head should be worthy of the body.

P. 209. On the explanation of Eclipses by Anaxagoras, see Plutarch, *Nicias*, 23.

P. 211–12. On the sun and the moon literally, from Diog. Laert. ii. 3, 4.

P. 213. The fact of meteoric stones having fallen on the earth was quite familiar to the ancients. They were generally consecrated and worshipped on the spot where they fell.

P. 214. Anaxagoras taught that the γαλαξιάς, *i.e.* the milky way, was ἀνάκλασιν φωτὸς ἡλιακοῦ, μὴ καταλαμπομένων τῶν ἄστρων.—Diog. ii. 3, 4.

Pp. 215-16. Here, in reference to Aspasia's question about chaos, Anaxagoras takes occasion to explain his doctrine of ὁμοιομερῆ στοιχεῖα, *like draws like*, which, when taken along with the Pythagorean doctrine of ἀριθμός, might seem to be an anticipation of the Daltonian doctrine of atoms and atomic proportions. Fundamentally, he explains the process—not the cause—of the creation of the world by elective affinities, with change of form but conservation of force, as we have seen Empedocles do with his love and hatred. It is to be noted, however, that modern chemistry teaches a much more mysterious doctrine, how *like draws unlike*,—as in the case of oxygen and hydrogen—forming a compound possessed of qualities altogether unlike the qualities of its two component parts. No merely mechanical idea can give any adequate explanation of the action of natural forces. There is a divine mystery behind all laws and all phrases, the key to which lies, not in the chemist's laboratory, but in the bosom of the Divine creativeness.

P. 227. Aspasia here prophesies the banishment of Anaxagoras, on a charge of atheism, concerning which, see Diog. Laert. ii. 3, 9. Religion, of course, had something to do with the matter (see Plutarch, *Nicias*, 23); but the important fact was that Anaxagoras and Aspasia were both the objects of attack to the opposition in Athens, as belonging to the party of Pericles. Whether at Athens, in Rome, or in London, "the church in danger," under various forms, has always been a favourite cry with those who were out-flanked in political strategics by men who had attained to a largeness of thought and a range of view beyond the scope of the majority.

ARISTODEMUS.

P. 233. Protagoras, one of the most respectable of the Sophists, gives the title to one of Plato's best known dialogues; and the words with which he commenced one of his famous books are put aptly here into the mouth of a smart young Athenian, full of conceit and void of reverence.

P. 245. The passage on the wonderful framework of the

human body, taken literally here from Xenophon, places Socrates for all ages in the van of natural theologians, as the first great Hellenic assertor of the great doctrine of design in the universe, or, as it has been technically called, teleology, *i.e.* the doctrine of final causes. Dr. Paley's well-known work is little more than a detailed expatiation of the Socratic text here given. In modern times it has become fashionable in certain quarters, where wisdom is affected, to speak contemptuously of Dr. Paley and the argument from design ; but this, I am firmly convinced, will turn out to have been a mere fashion, which will in due season yield to the general healthy human judgment on this matter. " *Opinionum commenta delet dies ; naturae judicia confirmat.*" It is perfectly true, no doubt, that some persons in this mechanical country may have taken Paley's mechanical simile too literally ; but it formed no part of his argument to say that the world is a watch, or any sort of mechanical manufacture. The world manifestly is a growth, not a manufacture ; but a growth full of indwelling plastic Reason, and pervaded all through, — from root to topmost branch — with reasonable calculation and design. What Lord Bacon said, that the search after final causes is a barren virgin, is no doubt true in the sense in which he meant it ; for to assert the object or purpose for which a thing is made, will help a man nothing to the discovery of the how, or by what means the making took place ; and in this sense Goethe also was quite right when he said that *why?* and *what for?* are not *scientific* questions. The scientific interrogation is *how?* Mere science may easily ignore the question *with what object?* but philosophy will still maintain its right to say that an object or purpose did exist in the construction of the universe, and can, on many occasions, be clearly traced. The only difficulty is, that whereas, in the work of a human architect or engineer, the purpose for which the work is made may often be seen at a glance, and in all cases be distinctly enunciated by a competent judge ; in the works of the great demiurge of the cosmos, there is everywhere too wide a range, and too complex a bond of connection, to be exactly measurable by the human faculty, or predicable by human speech. The true philosophical objection to the argument from design, as it has been sometimes handled, therefore, is simply this,—not that there are no manifest signs of design in the vital machinery or organised growth of the universe,—but that men have been, in not a few cases, hasty to interpolate into the divine works and the divine procedure, a meaning and a purpose conceived more from the narrowness, one-sidedness, and inadequacy of the merely human point of view, than from the large range, comprehensive catholicity, and complex relationship of the divine scheme. Our whole theology, in fact, is more or less infected with this vice, which makes many a pretentious doctrinal structure, when closely examined, a mere castle of cards. But, though man is often foolish in his judgment of the divine procedure, God is always wise in His works and ways ; and, after all the captious babblement of the schools against the grand argument of Socrates and Paley shall have passed away, the voice of Nature, everywhere, will be heard in the words of the great Hebrew singer, proclaiming aloud, *" Understand, ye brutish among the people ; and ye fools, when will ye be wise ? He that planted the ear, shall He not hear ? He that formed the eye, shall He not see ? He that chastiseth the nations, shall not He correct ? He that teacheth man knowledge, shall He not know ?* THE LORD KNOWETH THE THOUGHTS OF MAN, THAT THEY ARE VANITY."

Pp. 249-50. Here the reader will note particularly the contrast which the great Father of Moral Philosophy amongst the Greeks presents to our modern doctors of physical science. He brings into the foreground that distinctive function, viz. the reasonable recognition of a divine Reason in the universe, which elevates man above the brute : they rejoice to track out his brotherhood with the baboon, and to reduce every highest thing in creation to the level of the lowest. What effect this doctrine, if it shall take root, will have in the education of the human species, remains to be seen.

P. 250. The lines in quotation are a translation of the famous prayer of Socrates, at the end of the Phædrus.

ARISTIPPUS.

P. 253. In this dialogue, taken from Xenophon, Socrates appears grandly as the true Father of the Aristotelian Ethics, which place happiness in virtue, and virtue in energy. The revival of the opposite doctrine of Aristippus, placing the *summum bonum* in pleasure, was reserved for the amiable dogmatism of Bentham in the last century; but its insufficiency as an ethical watchword was speedily manifested in its abandonment for the cry, to which only the most selfish of oligarchs could object,—*the greatest happiness of the greatest number*. Bentham, in fact, and Mill, owed their influence rather to their being accepted as mouthpieces of the democracy in opposition to the dominant English oligarchy, than to any peculiar subtlety. soundness, or consistency in their speculations. Bentham was great as a judicial reformer; Mill, as a social reformer and a logical teacher: but the philosophy of both was meagre and inadequate; and, wanting the great constructive idea of God, remained like a plant without a root, a planetary system without a sun. Mill was, besides, somewhat of a crotchet-monger, and had fixed his eye so long and so intently on certain blots and blotches of our moderm social system, that he could see no soundness. In opposition to all such,—and their number in recent times is not few,—Socrates stands forth as pre-eminently the cheerful philosopher.

THE DEATH OF SOCRATES.

P. 275. In this dialogue I have imported from well-known dialogues of Plato some views and arguments, which, though put into the mouth of Socrates, may reasonably be suspected of being Platonic rather than Socratic. My manner of dealing with the arguments in the Phædo was to use only such as appeared most broadly human, and were at the same time most capable of poetic treatment. I believe, however, nothing of essential importance in the Platonico-Socratic doctrine of the immortality of the soul has been omitted. Those who wish to contrast the ancient with the modern point of view on this lofty theme will find an excellent statement of them in the Reverend Joseph Cook's *Lecture on Emerson's View of Immortality;* London: Dickinson, Farringdon Street, 1877. Of course, in the concluding pages of the Phædo, where the actual facts of the death of Socrates are detailed, I have not dared to alter a word.

PLATO.

P. 315. The subject of Love is formally treated in two Dialogues of Plato, *The Banquet*, and the *Phædrus*. From both of these I have taken what suited my purpose. The character of Alciphron I have invented, and what belongs to him. The allusions in the opening monologue are to the well-known fact that, like our Hugh Miller, Plato first assayed his plumes as a poet, and was in fact a great poet-philosopher to the very last, though some of his Dialogues, as the *Philebus*, seem conceived rather in the bare analytic style of Aristotle than in the almost Aristophanic play of dramatic humour in the *Banquet*. His attack on the drama, and literature generally, in the last book of the *Republic*, must be looked upon either as the one-sidedness of an octogenarian philosopher, or may find justification in the low standard of moral dignity into which Hellenic literature had fallen since the days of Pindar and Æschylus.

Printed by R. & R. CLARK, *Edinburgh.*